KU-032-460

What Happens at Christmas

Evonne Wareham

Where heroes are like chocolate – irresistible!

Copyright © 2018 Evonne Wareham

Published 2018 by Choc Lit Limited
Penrose House, Crawley Drive, Camberley, Surrey GU15 2AB, UK
www.choc-lit.com

The right of Evonne Wareham to be identified as the Author of this Work
has been asserted by her in accordance with the Copyright, Designs and
Patents Act 1988

All characters and events in this publication, other than those clearly in
the public domain, are fictitious and any resemblance to actual persons,
living or dead, is purely coincidental

All rights reserved. No part of this publication may be reproduced,
stored in a retrieval system, or transmitted in any form or by any means,
electronic, mechanical, photocopying, recording or otherwise, without the
prior permission of the publisher or a licence permitting restricted copying.
In the UK such licences are issued by the Copyright Licensing Agency,
Barnards Inn, 86 Fetter Lane, London EC4A 1EN

A CIP catalogue record for this book is available
from the British Library

ISBN: 978-1-78189-430-9

Printed and bound in Great Britain by Clays Ltd, Elcograf S.p.A.

This one has to be for Kath, Lorraine and Stacey.
And to commemorate Ming – a family legend.

Acknowledgements

Thanks first to Kath, Lorraine and Stacey, my companions
at lunch when the idea for this story first took hold.
To the team at Choc Lit for pulling out all the stops to
get it into this year's Christmas list and to the Tasting
Panel (Melissa C, Jenny M, Jennifer S, Heather P,
Jo L, Lucy M, Rosie F, Joy S, Jo O, Yvonne G, Gill L,
Jane M and Els) for their invaluable feedback. And
to my fellow Choc Lit authors, just because …

Thanks to various people who gave me information to help
the story. Any errors in interpretation are my responsibility.

And finally thanks to everyone who has supported
me in getting back into print after a long gap,
when life threw stuff, in large amounts, and
especially to Evelyn and Jenny. They know why.

Chapter One

28 April

Any minute now all his fingers were going to break.

He'd lunged too soon, or not got the angle right, or both. His hands and arms were taking the whole weight of his body, and he was flailing against the side of the train carriage like a badly landed fish. With a gigantic effort, that almost wrenched his shoulders out of their sockets, Drew pulled himself up and belly-flopped onto the roof of the train, legs still dangling over the side. Clint, the stunt coordinator he was *paying* to choreograph this torture, was standing further down the roof, smirking and curling his fingers in invitation. 'C'mon, Mr Best-Selling Author, let's see what you're made of.'

Right now? Try a hank of wet string. Or over-cooked spaghetti.

Drew sucked in air. He didn't have the brain power to remember or the spare breath to utter the choice collection of insults and curses he ought to be flinging at Clint's fat, grinning, turnip head.

Just get on the damn roof.

With an undignified heave he gathered the rest of his body onto the stable surface, where he crouched on his hands and knees, panting. Clint was ostentatiously looking at his watch. 'You planning on standing up any time soon, Mr Vitruvius?'

Drew mustered just enough breath for a low-pitched 'Bastard.'

He tottered to his feet. Still half crouched against the

light breeze that up here felt like a howling gale, he *knew* he deserved a medal for making it this far.

Clint didn't look impressed. Instead he pointed to the ladder leaning against the side of the carriage. The ladder that led back to safety and solid ground and the ability to walk upright. 'Down you go and do it again.' He flashed Drew an evil smile. Two gold teeth glittered in the pale morning sun. Drew had never had the nerve to ask what had happened to the originals. 'Once you get this right, maybe we can even try it when the train is moving.'

Chapter Two

'No. Definitely not. No way.' Drew shook his head as well, for added emphasis, letting out a long disgruntled breath. Normally he enjoyed the visits to his agent's offices, tucked in a tiny Georgian courtyard off the Strand. Books and good coffee and the occasional bottle of champagne, if he'd cracked another award or best-seller list – what was there not to like?

But today? *Not so much.*

Geraldine Ennis rolled her eyes. 'Come on, Andrew. It'll be fun.'

'You think?' Drew shrugged himself out of Geri's 'visitor's chair' and prowled over to the window, reaching over a row of bright red poinsettia parading along the sill, to tilt the blind and look down into the courtyard. It wasn't an inspiring view – two large dustbins and a pile of cardboard waiting for recycling. A ragged scrap of tinsel had fastened itself to the wheels on the bottom of one of the bins and a column of thin winter sun made patterns on the facade of the building opposite, eye-wateringly bright when it hit the narrow windows. Drew squinted, looking up. A square of blue showed over the roofline. Four weeks to Christmas and the weather was cold but clear, and forecast to stay that way.

No snow again this year.

Not that you really care whether it snows or not.

Drew dropped the blind and turned back to face the woman who had masterminded his career this far with steely efficiency, but who now seemed to have taken a brief detour into crazy. 'What exactly is *fun* about being kidnapped?'

Geri had stopped rolling her eyes. She fixed him with a beady look – the look she used when he launched one of his time-travelling protagonists off on another trek after Mayan temples or Viking gold, when the dude should be spending quality time with the heroine of the book. It wasn't that Drew had any objection to quality time with a heroine. It was just that they'd been a little thin on the ground lately in real life. Writing about bloody battles in the Highlands or break-neck chases through rampant alien jungles on distant planets was a whole lot easier.

Just the basics. Kill or be killed.

He breathed in with a jerk. His mind had been wandering. Not a good idea with Geraldine anywhere in the building. She'd propped herself against the edge of her desk, still giving him that sceptical eye. A steel-smooth fifty-something, with a mind like a hunting leopard.

She looked him up and down. 'Considering that your idea of *fun* is being dumped on an uninhabited island, or in the middle of a desert, or some equally inhospitable place, I'd have thought you'd have jumped at this.'

'*That* is research,' he pointed out, with dignity. '*This* is just nuts.'

'It's for charity.'

'Which one?' *Hell, are you weakening already?*

'Your choice.'

'Huh!' Drew chucked himself back down in the visitor's chair. Geraldine knew about his support for a couple of groups who worked with the street homeless and ex-offenders. *If this damn stunt can make a difference ...*

4

'Of course, if you *really* don't want to do it, I can always offer them Brandon Phipps ...'

Drew raised both his hands to point at her. 'Unfair. You know that *supposed* feud is something a journalist thought up. I've only met the guy twice. We did not come to blows on either occasion. I don't give a shit if his debut novel shoved *The Irish Stone* off the top of the best-seller list. Something had to.'

Geri tilted her head, sizing him up for her next gambit. 'Andrew – it's the *Phil Philmore* Show.'

'It's also a crazy time for something like this.' *Not to mention that I'm on a deadline for the next book. Yes – definitely not to mention* ... 'A few days before Christmas?'

'All the better to touch people's hearts, and their wallets.'

'Assuming you haven't scared them to death! Kidnapping? Yes, that's right up there with tinsel and mince pies for Christmas spirit.'

Geraldine made a noise that in someone else would be classed as a snort. 'I would have thought that alone would have sold it to you.' She reached behind her on the desk to locate a slim folder in a glossy green cover, waving it from side to side. 'You know what Philmore is like. He's only just come up with the idea. This is the brief. It was couriered round an hour ago. Super top secret. "If I tell you I have to kill you stuff". He thought you'd be totally up for it.'

'So if I say no, he puts a contract out on both of us?' Drew flexed his shoulders and sighed. *Definitely weakening, you sucker.*

Phil Philmore was *the* TV host of the moment. By force of personality and an inventive mind, he'd taken a weekly chat show from late-night, low-budget to award-winning, top-billing, prime-time viewing. The man was clever and confident and with his production company had come up with a distinctive and quirky formula. An in-depth interview with a featured author, with insights into their research methods, locations they had used and special plot features, which was then broadened out into an analysis of depictions of their work on stage and screen, head-to-head discussions with actors who had brought their characters to life, musicians who had written scores, special effects departments – anything and everything for a behind the scenes glimpse at a best-selling book, in all its incarnations. Held together by Philmore's unique style, it had managed to catch and hold the attention of the viewing public. Drew had been a featured author twice, once with a camera crew shadowing him on a training exercise in white-water rafting.

Not, thank God, the debacle with the train.

And now Philmore was inviting him to be kidnapped, live, on TV.

'It's different,' he said cautiously.

'It's Philmore.' Geri shrugged. 'He's a genius for putting stuff together, you know that.'

'Who else is involved?'

'That's under wraps, but the PA "suggested" that it would be another author – female, a sports personality, a couple of actors and a singer – probably other people like you, who have done the show in the past. But at this stage, no names, no pack drill.'

'Until they find out whether the people they want are nuts enough.' Drew held out his hand. Geraldine put the folder into it. *You're going to do this, aren't you, you daft bugger?*

'Philmore has hired one of those companies that specialise in extreme experiences. They don't offer designer kidnapping as a general rule, but they've agreed to stage this as a one-off, because it's for charity and because—'

'—it's Philmore.' Drew finished the sentence. 'The guy could charm snakes out of trees.'

Geri indicated the logo on the front of the file. 'Have you heard of them?'

'I've used them.' Drew flicked through the pages. 'They do outward bound stuff, survival courses – they're good.'

'Maybe they'll decide to add this to their repertoire.' Geri gave a small, theatrical shudder. 'I'm told there *are* people out there who pay money to be snatched off the street and held hostage.'

'And now you want me to be one of them.'

'It's your call.'

Drew sat still for a moment, the file resting on his knee. Geraldine nudged his foot with hers. Instead of her usual killer heels, today she was wearing trainers, exactly like the ones he was wearing, he noted with surprise.

All the better for chasing down recalcitrant authors and biting their heads off?

She'd never really sunk her teeth into *him*, but there *were* stories. And he'd once found a junior assistant, sobbing on the stairs. *Not one to cross, our Geraldine.*

She was watching his face.

'Go on. You know you want to. It'll be for a good cause.'

'Run it past me again.' Drew leaned back in the chair, arranging his face into sell-it-to-me mode. He knew from Geri's expression that she wasn't really buying his reluctance, but what the hell? He didn't *have* to roll over straight away.

She sighed heavily and nodded towards the folder. 'These people stage a series of kidnappings. The PA did "let slip" that they were hoping to kick off with the American actor from that West End play that's so big at the moment—' Geri snapped her fingers.

'The Conquistador,' Drew supplied helpfully.

'That's the one.'

'Which probably means that he's already agreed to do it.'

Geri nodded. 'Doubt if the name would have been mentioned, even in confidence, if he wasn't already in the bag. The other kidnappings will follow. Philmore has his usual early evening spot, with spaces for updates throughout the evening and a big finale around midnight. Viewers pledge money to ransom their darlings.' She gave Drew a sly grin. 'Including an internationally best-selling fantasy author?'

Drew kept his face as deadpan as he could. Geraldine pouted and carried on. 'After the first kidnap, everyone is going to cotton on to what's happening. The excitement will be revved up with speculation about who might be next. And then, at the end, there's the grand bidding war, to see how high donors can get the various ransoms.'

'Humiliating for the poor sod who comes bottom of the list.'

'I doubt if you'll have any need to worry,' Geraldine said, looking off, over Drew's shoulder. 'The sexiest beast in the best-seller list.'

'And *that* was a journalist too.' An excitable freelancer whom he'd determinedly avoided ever since. Unfortunately the tag the woman had chosen had stuck. Now it got rolled out practically every time his name was mentioned in print.

'Whatever is raised from the ransom goes to the charities, and Philmore has privately pledged to match the sums out of his own pocket.' Geri shrugged. 'Okay, he's looking to knock all the other Christmas specials out of the park, but he *is* prepared to put his money where his mouth is.'

Drew ran his finger over the glossy cover of the brief. It was pure Philmore. The off-the-wall stuff that he did so well. If anyone could convince the viewing public to add one more gift to the ones they'd already spent too much money on, he was the one to do it.

But even so …

'I don't know …' he paused. *Are you really going to say it? Out loud?* 'It may have slipped your mind, but I have a deadline looming.'

'Which you will be meeting several days before this happens.'

Drew didn't miss the thread of steel in Geri's voice. *Yeah, well …*

'You already have a sold-out speaking date for that night,' Geraldine continued briskly. 'We sweeten the audience with some freebies and TV screens in the room, showing the other kidnappings as they happen. They'll love being part of it.'

'And if they don't, I get lynched with a string of fairy lights, just in time for Christmas?' he enquired dryly. He tapped his finger on the brief. 'The audience does need to be in on it. I don't want to risk anyone trying to have a go and getting hurt.'

Geraldine's eyes glittered. 'You'll do it?'

'Yeah.' Drew made a face. 'You know bloody well you had me at "charity".'

'Darling'. The slight tension in Geri's shoulders dialled down as she leaned forward for an air kiss. 'The money will make such a difference.' She patted his arm. 'Aveline will take care of all the details.' She straightened up with a pussycat smile. 'All you have to do—'

'I know.' Drew was ahead of her. 'All I have to do is lie back and enjoy it.'

Chapter Three

18 December, 4 p.m.

The Christmas lunch for Cardiff Bespoke Home Office
Installations – *we promise you the best service in the
Principality* – had gone really well.

Damn right it did, as you were the one who organised it.

Lori France grinned. *Self-satisfied, much?*

But wasn't she entitled to a little self-congratulation for a
job well done? The last before the firm knocked off for the
Christmas and New Year break. And everyone else had said
how much they'd enjoyed themselves. As always, it had been
fun. Good food, good company and good wine, although, as
she was driving herself home, she'd stuck to one glass.

*And also good that you will not be seeing any of the
people around the table again for two whole weeks.*

Lori surveyed the pile of Secret Santa gifts heaped
precariously on her desk. The company's way of doing
Secret Santa, where everyone bought an anonymous gift
for everyone else, worked really well too. Expensive – Lori
grimaced at the thought of the dent in her credit card – but
a big part of that Christmas fun. Lots of laughter, a few
surprises, and no one got stuck just with the really difficult
person to buy for, like Mike the accountant – which was so
frustrating, when you'd found the perfect gift for someone
else. Even Mike had got a lot easier though, since someone
had discovered his passion for obscure brands of beer. *His*
desk now held a proud row of exotically named products
from local micro brewers.

There were always a few unusual choices too. Samantha,

the receptionist, was going to be trying to find out who gave her the huge stuffed squirrel, and *why*, for months to come. Lori snickered. It had been a complete nightmare to wrap, and Sam was never going to figure out why, *because I don't know myself*. Just that as soon as she'd seen it sitting cosily on the shelf in the gift shop, she'd known exactly who it was meant for.

Lori's own pile was fairly predictable, but very welcome. It had been nice to have so many presents to unwrap. She'd followed her mother's instructions – over a crackling phone line from Greece – to open the parcel from John Lewis as soon as it arrived, 'to make sure that it fits'. And her sister Lark ... Well, she might get a card from L.A., or Mauritius, or the Seychelles or the Bahamas.

Lori picked up one of her two new notebooks – this one had a gorgeous sparkly, multicoloured cover. The other was a posh leather affair that she suspected might have come from Thom, the boss. There was an assortment of pens, one with a fluffy pink bird perched on the top, a dictionary of baby names, which had left a lot of people around the table puzzled, but which was quite an inspired choice and one that was going to be really useful when it came to naming new characters. A large china mug threatened dire things to anyone who interrupted her while she was writing and a slim paperback offered advice on how to write erotic fiction. That one had to be from Dean, one of the fitters, who was convinced she was writing the next red, hot, sexy bonk-buster. *Or ought to be.*

She began to gather the gifts into a carrier bag. Around her other people were packing up, exchanging handshakes and kisses and wishing each other 'Merry Christmas'. The office would be closed until the sixth of January. No one needed an emergency home office at this time of the year, and if they did, Thom would have his phone on and would deal with it. They'd completed their 'in time for Christmas' orders yesterday.

Stowing the last parcel, a pamper pack with 'For that big date' optimistically printed on the label, Lori looked up, to see Sam weaving, slightly unsteadily, through the desks towards her. Lori was pretty sure that the pamper pack had come from her. Happily married, with nine-year-old twin boys, she was tenacious about everyone else having their own slice of domestic bliss.

Yeah, well. One day. Maybe.

'And how are you going to be spending the holiday?' Sam made a scribbling gesture, of someone writing in the air. 'As if I couldn't guess.'

'That,' Lori agreed. 'And this.' She mimed painting a wall, laughing when Sam's brow crinkled in puzzlement. 'I have the builders in – once they've finished, I'll be decorating,' she explained.

'Builders.' Sam shook her head. 'But Lori, it's Christmas!'

'And that's *totally* why I have the builders in – Paulie's done me a special deal because no one else wants them at this time of the year.'

'Mmm.' Sam pouted, before her face lightened. 'Paulie – big shoulders, washboard abs, dimples?' Sam's husband had big shoulders, washboard abs and dimples.

'All of the above,' Lori agreed. 'And a fiancée, and I don't think she's into sharing.'

'Oh well.' Sam shrugged, then another thought occurred to her. 'Builders – are they doing the stuff for the insurance? Lori, are they taking off the roof?'

'Yep.' Lori nodded. 'But it's okay. I'm staying at the B&B in the village until the worst is over. They've agreed to take me and Griff.' *After a bit of persuasion.*

'Griff?' Sam looked puzzled again. 'Oh, your cat.' A frown replaced the puzzlement. 'Will there be other people at the B&B – celebrations and stuff?'

'No, only me. They don't usually open in the winter. But I will be fine, honestly and it will be a relief to get the work done.'

'I suppose.' Sam still wasn't happy. 'You could have come to ours for Christmas Day, at least, but we're going to the in-laws in Northampton.'

'I know, and you will have a *great* time.' Lori picked up her bags, leaning over to kiss Sam's cheek, and preparing to distribute goodbyes and good wishes at the other desks between her and the door.

Then, after a weekend of clearing the house and getting the last of her stuff into storage, she was free. Free to forget about being an office manager and instead to be a would-be author, with nothing to do but write.

Bliss.

'Happy Christmas.'

Chapter Four

Somewhere in the depths of the house, a clock was chiming.

Drew leaned back on his chair and counted. 'Ten … eleven … twelve.' He stretched his arms above his head, working out the kinks in his shoulders. Midnight, and the book was finally, definitely, irrevocably finished.

At last.

He closed his eyes and let out a long breath.

The scene on the roof of the train hadn't turned out the way it was supposed to. *And we all know why* that *was. A dozen attempts, and no cigar.* The ending wasn't the one he'd planned, either, but that happened when you were writing. Things sort of shifted, and the words crept up on you when you weren't watching them. He'd had his doubts about that ending, but it had seemed to work out. *What the hell – it's done.*

He opened his eyes, clicked on his e-mail and typed a covering note, attaching the manuscript. For a second his hand hesitated over the keyboard. Then he pressed send, and it was gone, winging its way to Geri and his editor. *Just in time for Christmas.*

He scrubbed the heels of his hands over his face, blinking blearily at the screensaver on the computer screen – a shot of a high cliff, a strand of pale sand and a whirl of swooping sea birds that he'd taken on a remote island, off the coast of Scotland. He lowered his hands and exhaled. With the book, and the charity thing which was coming up fast, he'd done nothing about his usual holiday get-away. Maybe there was still time to find somewhere suitably isolated – well away from anything festive.

Christmas.

There was a chill gathering in his chest. He pushed away the coldness and the swirling flashes of memory – a wind-swept railway station, the hunched and silent crowd, sick and scared like him, waiting for news.

And then – the bleak-faced official.

And the massive engulfing shock of total loss …

A shiver ran through Drew's body, shaking the dark images lose. He exhaled.

Don't remember. Plan.

If it was too late to organise a get-away he'd hunker down in the London flat with maps and guides and a good single malt, disconnect the phone and plan his next trip.

He leaned back in the chair, aware of the stiffness in his neck and shoulders, turning to stare out of the un-curtained window. The study was at the top of the house and the view in daylight was stunning. In darkness it was just that – darkness. At this time in the morning the unrelieved black of a cloud-filled night was unbroken by even a glimmer of light.

He might be alone on the planet.

The house, on the edge of the Peak District, had been the perfect retreat to finish a book that had got decidedly sticky in the middle. Now it was done he'd have been happy to spend Christmas here. *Alone.* Unfortunately he had to give it back. He squinted at his watch, abandoned on the desk beside the computer.

In about twelve hours' time.

The friends who had lent it to him while they made a trip to the States would be home this afternoon, and he would be gone before then, avoiding any invitations to stay for Christmas. *House returned, with grateful thanks.*

Actually he couldn't have stayed. Tomorrow night he had his date with a gang of kidnappers. *And how crazy is that?* He wasn't regretting it exactly, but it still felt weird. Geraldine's office had handled the arrangements – her latest assistant – a dark-haired girl with intense eyes. Adele? Ada? No, it was *Aveline*. Aveline had done the work with Philmore's people. All he had to do was show up. He'd been out of the media loop for weeks, head buried in the book, with no idea if the details of what was going down had leaked out. Not exactly a surprise if they had, with so many people involved. *Not your problem.*

Geri and her PR people would spin it. That was probably what she'd been thinking, some free publicity for the new hardback, in time for the Christmas trade. She'd been pretty keen for him to be part of it ...

His stomach gave a loud, disconcerting rumble, surprising him into a bark of laughter. Leaning forward, he closed down the computer. He couldn't actually remember when he'd last eaten a proper meal. There was an empty packet that had once held chocolate biscuits on the desk. He shook the wrapper hopefully, but there were only crumbs. Three coffee mugs stood in a group, two empty, one half full and stone-cold. He drank it anyway, grimacing, gathered up the debris and headed down through the dark house, to the kitchen.

Hauling out bread, cheese, a pot of home-made chutney and a celebratory beer, he slumped at the kitchen table to wolf down a doorstep sandwich. He stifled a yawn. Was it late supper, or very early breakfast? Whatever it was, it had hit the spot.

He savoured the beer – brewed locally especially for

Christmas, according to the label, which was liberally illustrated with snowmen and reindeer – and looked idly around the dimly lit kitchen. It was big and warm and homely. And probably very expensive, he concluded, swinging back in his chair. Deceptively simple grey painted units, granite surfaces, carefully placed lighting, most of which he hadn't bothered to turn on, under-floor heating. Tranquil and comfortable.

He really needed to get himself a place like this. Not so big, or so lavish, but somewhere more remote than Chelsea. Even being around the corner from the Physic Garden, it hardly matched the kind of books he wrote. He took a sip of beer, pondering. The flat was convenient. And paid for, thanks to a couple of film deals. And as he was rarely there, it was really all he needed. He didn't see much of his neighbours, but Kaz and Devlin were in the next street, if he wanted company. They'd be at home at Christmas. Kaz had invited him to a drinks party they were giving on Christmas Eve. Drew grinned. It might be worth sticking around for the holiday, just to see how Devlin, the original ice man, coped with the concept of 'party'. *Flawlessly, of course, like everything he does.*

Drew shook his head, and finished the beer. In the New Year, he'd start house hunting. Maybe. *Do you really need anything more than the flat you have now?* A small space to store his books and clothes and occasionally to sleep. For the rest of the time he was on the road for one thing or another – research, promotion or just plain old restlessness.

What are you running from, Drew?

The voice in his head whispered, and the dark memories flickered again, just for a second. Echoes from a long, long way back. A place he really *didn't* visit any more, in his head, or out of it.

He rose abruptly, dropping his plate and knife into the sink and the empty bottle into the recycling bin. After a moment's thought, he fished the bottle out, rinsed it and dropped it in again. Then he headed for his bed.

By lunchtime he'd be on his way back to London.

Chapter Five

20 December, 9.30 p.m.

The air in the hotel conference room hummed with excited anticipation.

The audience had filed in just over two hours ago, to find a tote bag bulging with goodies on each seat – including, Drew noted wryly, a new novella from Brandon Phipps. *Signed, of course.* Aveline from Geri's office had been around earlier, checking that each bag contained one, but she'd disappeared as soon as they'd opened the doors.

The arts journalist who was hosting the event had made a short speech, explaining the change in the running order and the added entertainment for the evening, pointing out the TV screens and cameras, which had already attracted some nudging and whispering from a few of the audience, and offering anyone who did not wish to take part the chance to leave, with a full refund.

And they got to keep the goodie bag.

No one had taken up the offer.

Drew had signed a shedload of books – mostly, it seemed, to be given as Christmas presents – being careful to add the date. Maybe in years to come they'd be classed as collector's items. They'd done an edited version of the question and answer session, in amongst watching celebrity kidnappings going down to order on the big screens. Philmore had scored a coup to kick things off – five members of a boy band who'd topped the charts for six weeks in the summer with the theme tune to a blockbuster thriller. He'd scooped them up at a 'secret' gig in a room behind a pub somewhere in Islington. A well choreographed chase had ended in all five being rounded up and dragged away from screaming, sobbing 'fans'. The American actor had been grabbed leaving the theatre after a 'special' technical rehearsal. They'd set up a creepy Dickensian looking scene, in a narrow passage-way beside the stage door, with dark-cloaked figures materialising out of the shadows. They'd even managed to create an atmospheric fog, swirling at ankle level. The footballer had been intercepted by three men in a fast car when he arrived for a 'Christmas party' at his club's home ground.

Drew checked his watch. Any minute now three heavies would burst in, and after some token resistance would hustle him out to the limo parked in the alley behind the hotel. Then it would be across London for champagne in the green room that had been set up at another very new, very up-market hotel. The bidding war would take place in front of a live audience in the hotel ballroom. Drew shifted in his seat. Everyone who'd lined up to have books signed had promised to bid for him, but that boy band was going to take some beating.

Wow! Afraid you're going to come bottom of the list after all, Mr Best-Selling Author?

The questions from the audience had dwindled to expectant silence, the atmosphere tense with anticipation. Everyone was waiting, just as he was. He glanced around the room. Collection buckets for his chosen charity had been strategically placed in the aisle between the rows of seats, and were gratifyingly full. He heaved a sigh, maybe ...

A shot of a building flashed up on the big screen on the side wall. The building they were in. Inside the room the cameras were rolling. Drew took a deep breath and stood up. 'Ladies and Gentlemen, I'd like to thank you for coming here this evening and for your generous—'

Even though he was expecting it, he still jumped as the door smashed open and three black-clad, hooded figures tumbled into the room, waving realistic looking guns and threatening reprisals to anyone who moved. From his vantage point on the dais Drew could see staff from the hotel crowding the corridor, craning to get a look.

A tall guy at the front of the audience jumped up. Clearly a big fan, he was wearing a well-washed *Stren Rules* T-shirt that had to be five or six years old – the last book that had featured tortured superhero Stren in more than a walk-on part was at least that long ago. Making a play to get in on the action, he was promptly invited to resume his seat with a threatening wave of the nearest gun. Drew caught a glimpse of the images on the TV screen at the end of the room, which was showing a live feed, out of sight of the cameras.

And how surreal is that, watching yourself getting kidnapped on TV?

Drew jerked himself back into the moment. He had a part to act in this. The images on the screen were looking good.

So there's no way you are screwing it up.

Two of the men had stationed themselves on opposite sides of the room, covering the audience. The third was advancing towards him. Drew slid into his role, looking frantically round for a way out, spotting the fire exit and heading for it. Absurdly, his heart was beating fast and his mouth had gone dry. *It's only an act.*

As he dived for the exit he saw himself again on the monitor, diving for the exit.

You and how many thousand TV viewers?

He was less than a foot away from the door when the third guy reached him. They scuffled, as per the script. Two women in the front row squealed and fluttered and Drew's breath hissed out as a misplaced boot caught him on the shin. Several people were filming on their phones.

Well, hey, at least that's *gonna look real.*

Shifting his weight, Drew got his balance, feinting to the right and trying to figure out if he knew the guy under the hood. Had they hung out together in a tree, somewhere in the Welsh mountains, during a survival course? He couldn't tell.

Feinting, and feinting again, he took off to the left, aiming for the door. The assailant barrelled forward. Drew went down, hard, back against the wall.

Shit, and *that. Tomorrow there will be bruises on your ass.*

He was still struggling to regain his breath as his captor hauled him unceremoniously to his feet. His mate sprinted forward to grab Drew's other arm, and together they dragged him through the fire exit and into the bleak concrete walled corridor beyond. The door banged behind them, cutting off a babble of excited voices, as the third man brought up the rear.

Drew ducked, trying to regain a stable footing. They were half dragging him along. 'Hey, fellas—'

'Don't talk, just keep moving.'

Drew swivelled his head to check the walls. Were there cameras still operating here? The grip on his arms wasn't lessening. The guy on the right matched him in height, with massive shoulders and a thick neck. The eyes behind the swathe of fabric, on a level with his, were cold and flat. Drew's heart unexpectedly ratcheted up a notch.

The third man had dodged past them and already had the outer door to the back alley open. A non-descript white van stood waiting, motor idling, sending a plume of white exhaust fumes into the chilly night. The back doors were hooked open.

A shock of confusion laced with alarm speared through Drew's system. *This isn't right. It's supposed to be a car, not a van.* He turned towards the man who had spoken. 'Hey, guys, can we just hold on a minute here—'

The sudden blow to his abdomen from a bunched fist doubled him over, gasping for breath. *Shit, shit, shit.*

There was a brief stinging pain in his neck. *Insect bite? In December?*

His feet scrabbled ineffectually on the tiles of the alley as the three men hoisted him into the van. The doors slammed shut. Drew's head swirled as the engine revved.

Not an insect bite. A needle.

This is for real.

The world swung drunkenly as he struggled to his knees. Reaching for the door handle he caught it, wrenching it down. Nothing happened. His grip fell away.

They were nosing forward, out of the alley and into the late evening traffic, when everything finally went dark.

Chapter Six

He was trapped in the middle of an earthquake.

His head was spinning and he couldn't see, couldn't breathe. Panic spiked. He fought it. *You have to* think.

Even getting that far hurt. Better if he could drift back into the welcome darkness …

Not happening.

Whatever drug he'd been given – and he recognised it for a drug from the pounding in his head and the disgusting chemical taste in his mouth – it was wearing off. Slowly his senses were coming back and his mind was beginning to process. He couldn't see, and breathing was difficult, because there was some sort of bag over his head. The world was moving in a stomach-churning fashion because he was being half dragged, half carried over uneven ground. The persistent buzz from somewhere near his left ear resolved itself into low-pitched rumble.

'Bloody, buggering hell, the bugger weighs a ton!'

Drew's left side dipped a little. Whoever had charge of that side was flagging.

'Shut up and keep moving.' *That* was the right side.

'We should have been out of here hours ago.'

'And whose fucking fault was that?' Heavy breathing and grunting, as they heaved him over some sort of low obstacle. *Where the hell are we?* 'Sodding flat tyre. Your sodding sister and her poxy *sodding* van.' Another heave.

'My sister's *kid*. It's my sister's *kid's* van,' Lefty corrected. 'Kyle – my nephew. He wasn't supposed to know we borrowed it.' A disgruntled huff. 'You should have let that bloke help. At that farm. He wanted to. Dead keen to get us out of the way of his gate.'

'Oh yeah. Thanks very much, mate. Don't mind if I do.' In amongst the laboured breathing Mr Right's voice dripped sarcasm. 'Yeah, I got a tool kit. I'll just open up the back. No worries about the unconscious bloke lying next to it.'

'We could have said he was drunk or something. Christmas – everyone gets drunk at Christmas.'

Mr Right didn't even bother to answer that one.

It sounded as if his captors had had a rough night.

Know the feeling.

Drew took as deep a breath as he could manage inside the constrictions of the hood. They didn't seem to have realised he was coming round. He was more or less awake, but there was still an uncomfortable swimming sensation as they heaved him along. Doggedly he concentrated on keeping his body limp. If they thought he was still unconscious, he might hear something useful.

Spy School 101.

There was a sudden curse from Lefty as he stumbled over something. It was all Drew could do to stop himself bracing for a fall. Mr Right was made of sterner stuff and kept them all more or less upright. 'Mind what you're doing!'

'Can't we just dump him here? It's well off the road.' Then something Drew couldn't make out. A low grumble that sounded like 'bloody trees' and 'leaving the van'.

'Nah.' Mr Right was still dragging them forwards. 'The hut's all ready, so he can't get away.'

'I dunno …' Drew had the impression, head drooping and through the folds of the bag, that Lefty was looking around him. 'We dump him there, and he can't get out, is he gonna get that hypo thing?'

'Hypothermia?' Mr Right filled in. 'Nah. Anyway, it's not our problem.'

Their progress had slowed to a crawl. The ground seemed to be getting even rougher and Mr Right was doing most of the work. He was big.

The second guy, the one with the needle.

'But what if he – you know – if something, like, goes wrong.' Lefty's voice rose on the last word.

'Not. Our. Problem. We're just delivery. What we're getting paid for.' There was a pointed edge to Mr Right's voice.

'Yeah, but—'

'Just doing what we was paid for.' Mr Right repeated. 'None of this is down to us. We was hired to take the bloke and bring him here. All part of the stunt, innit?'

'Yeah – but – the stunt was those other guys.'

'Different stunt.'

'But why—'

'Look it's all for publicity, innit? Them celebs get up to all sorts of weird shit to get themselves noticed. Just shut up and get it done. We're making a thousand apiece for this. Pick up the bloke and deliver him. And *that's it*.' Mr Right was breathing heavily again. 'What happens then is nothing to do with us. For fuck's sake, let's just get it finished and get out of here. I think his head moved just now. If he's coming round we got to get him in that bloody hut before he wakes up proper. So shut up and get a move on.'

Busted.

They set off again at an increased pace.

Hanging limply between his captors Drew digested the price that had been put on his head. Four thousand, assuming the third guy and the driver got the same rate. Someone was prepared to shell out four thousand pounds to make the kidnap real. A slow, cold shudder went through him, bile rising in his throat. *Oh, God, don't throw up. Think! Somehow you've got to get out of this.*

Mr Right and Lefty had been told it was a second stunt. *They probably think you're in on it – weird shit.* Could he admit to being awake, tell them it was all a mistake, offer them more money to take him back? Would that work? If he made a break for it, would they bother to chase after him? *Lefty, possibly not. Mr Right?* He wasn't sure Mr Right entirely believed the story about the stunt, but he was damn sure he'd stick to it.

Where the hell were they? Was it still night, or was it daylight outside the confines of the hood? He focused his senses. The sacking was thick, but not that thick. He had the feeling that what was out there was daylight, not darkness. If he strained hard to listen, over his captors footfalls and heavy breathing, he thought he could hear birdsong. Something soft and papery scuffed against his feet. Fallen leaves? Were they in woodland?

He caught himself up with a jerk that he hoped wasn't distinguishable to the two men hauling him along. He had to concentrate on getting out of this, not falling into the writer's trick of assessing experience as material, for God's sake!

If you get free, can you run for it? He'd mapped out plenty of fights and escapes on paper, then choreographed them with stunt men and martial arts experts, but he'd never done any of that stuff in cold blood and for real.

Trying it out on two men in a wood with a sack over your head is not *a good place to start.*

Owning up that he was awake and striking a bargain was the best bet. *Plus you can get a name. The person who paid for this.*

He was about to straighten up and stand on his own feet when there was a sudden yell, his left arm was yanked hard and then it was free. From the sounds and the cursing, Lefty had gone down. On pure instinct Drew straightened and swung on the balls of his feet, giving Mr Right a hefty shove. Mr Right let go, with another volley of curses.

Both arms free, Drew powered forward, scrabbling at the covering over his head. He raised it enough to get mouth and nose free, wincing as he pulled it higher and the brightness of a low winter sun hit his eyes. Squinting, he could make out shapes and a blur of colour.

The edge of a wood. Straggling trees. Grass. A hillside.

The fallen branch caught his ankles, half swung, half thrown from behind. He pitched sideways, off the rough path, in a tangle of limbs. The sack fell back over his eyes.

The boot hit his ribs before he could roll away.

Mr Right.

Gasping for breath he grabbed Right's leg, pulling himself up, or the other man down, he wasn't sure which. They swayed together for a moment. Right's hand closed on his throat, dragging him upright. Drew hauled in an agonised breath. 'Not stunt …' He sucked in more air. 'Pay you … more.'

'I don't give a shit, you stupid bastard.' Right's voice was soft, low and deadly. 'Getting this *done*.'

The edge of the hood twitched. Drew tried to raise his hand, to block the move. 'No … I …'

The needle stung against his neck. Two sets of hands closed on him. *Lefty's back.* The thought formed woozily. *Will* he *listen?* 'I'll pa …'

Before he could finish the word, everything faded to black.

Chapter Seven

The Christmas hamper, emblazoned with the logo of a famous London department store, was huge. So big that the delivery man staggered a little under the weight as he pulled it loose from the back of his van.

'Where do you want it, Miss?' He threw a dubious glance at the cottage at the end of the row, shrouded in scaffolding, with a pile of rust-stained radiators stacked in the tiny front garden. The builders had already begun to strip the dark grey Welsh slates from the roof.

'Um.' Lori was distracted by the sight of her sister's name on the prominent gift tag. *What's going on?* 'Can you put it in the back of my car?' She gestured to the open boot of her Fiesta. There was just about room. Remembering her manners, she added, 'Please.' It wasn't the poor man's fault that the sight of Lark's name sent her heart somewhere down to her boots. The delivery man grinned. 'Right here, next to the box from Carluccio's?'

'Er, yes, thanks.' Lori bent to shift the other box further into a corner.

Why does your family think you need all this food?

To be fair, the present from her parents and her brother, as well as the edible Italian goodies, included a cashmere sweater in a soft pearly grey. In a spirit of goodwill – it really *was* a lovely sweater – Lori was assuming her mother had chosen it because she remembered that it would echo the colour of her elder daughter's eyes. It was two sizes too big, but that meant she could get plenty of layers on underneath it. Although when the cottage had its new heating system …

'Sign here, please, Miss.' The delivery man was holding out an electronic pad. Lori scrawled something that didn't look anything like her name on the small screen, but the man seemed happy with it. He clambered back into the cab of his van and made off down the little cul-de-sac as Lori leaned into the back of her car to look at the tag again. The hamper was definitely from her sister and with a message she hadn't noticed. 'Hope you both enjoy it.' *Both?* Was Lark assuming she was still with Frazer?

'Not going to starve then?' Lori jumped as Paulie walked past from his truck, with a couple of lengths of copper pipe over his shoulder. He nodded towards the boot with its cardboard boxes.

'No,' Lori agreed. She looked doubtfully at the hampers. 'Not that I'm going to be able to do anything much with them until you've finished and I get my kitchen back. I hope there's nothing perishable in there.'

'Nah. It's all Christmas puddings and fancy jam and tea and stuff, isn't it? My Mam has one every year, pays into it weekly at the club. Not a posh one like that though.' He grinned. 'Think there's any booze in it?'

'Possibly. It seems to be heavy enough.' She was looking for any sign of a list of contents when a yell from the cottage made her turn. Mike, the lanky apprentice, was standing in the doorway, peering out from under the scaffolding.

'You ready to turn the water off, boss?'

'Yeah. I'll be there now, in a minute.' Paulie put the pipes down carefully, so they lay along the edge of the path. He rubbed his hands down his overalls. 'You about set to go?'

'Just need to get Griff in his basket and I'll be out of your hair until the end of the week.'

'No problem.' Paulie grinned. 'Last time I saw Griff he was asleep on the roof of the old privy, down the garden. Will you be okay to get him in the box or should I send Mike along?'

Lori shook her head. 'Thanks, but Griff will be fine. He's the most placid cat I've ever come across.'

Lori was coaxing the boot of the Fiesta to shut over the unexpected gift when a large black car nosed its way into the narrow road in front of the row of cottages and parked behind Paulie's truck. A big black car with a lot of chrome and an expensive looking shine to it. Lori's heart-rate picked up as the back door opened.

'Lori!' Lark was as beautiful as ever. Cascading blonde curls, eyes like a startled doe and the pink and white complexion of a porcelain doll. Lori stifled a small sigh. It wasn't that she envied her younger sister her looks or her lifestyle. She was quite happy with her own life, thank you, but when she was around Skylark ... she had a brief flashback – herself, age fifteen. Their mother, standing in the kitchen looking up at her. 'Your build is more ... athletic, darling.' *If athletic is wide shoulders and small boobs, then athletic is what I am.*

Her sister's cream wool coat had a deep fur collar that was almost the same colour as Lark's platinum hair. Lori knew for a fact that her sister had a little help with that. Her natural colour was closer to Lori's dirty blond. The coat swept dramatically all the way to the floor, a vision straight off the Russian steppes.

Is someone casting for a remake of Anna Karenina?

Automatically Lori checked behind her sister, expecting a small figure to be scrambling out of the back of the car. The implications of the hamper were suddenly becoming clear. *Oh no! Not now.*

'Darling.' Lark flowed forward to engulf Lori in a blast of expensive scent, and then leaned back, holding her at arm's length to survey the worn tracksuit and washed-out fleece, with the broken zip, that Lori was wearing to move furniture. 'Oh sweetie, what are we going to do with you?' She tilted her head up, face turning tragic. 'And you've been cutting your own hair again.'

'My hair is fine.'

Something that felt distressingly like panic was building in Lori's chest. She breathed deep, trying to make it evaporate.

It worked.

Sort of.

'Lark, why are you here?'

'To wish you a happy Christmas, of course.' Strangely the easy response wasn't doing anything for the panic. It was rising again. *Just say no.* Lori stepped back, out of her sister's embrace. *And breathe.*

The doe eyes, which missed nothing, unless they wanted to miss it, had noted the hamper. 'Oh good, my present arrived. I have a few little things—' She waved towards the car that had brought her. 'But we can get them out in a moment. Maybe someone could help my driver ...' She paused, as if expecting a flunky to appear at her elbow – possibly in uniform. Lori stifled a grin as, almost on cue, Glyn, Paulie's plasterer and tiler edged past them, behind Lark. He raised his eyebrows and grinned at Lori before sauntering up the path, heading for the sounds of hammering and Radio One that were coming from the back of the house. Lark, looking put out, turned her attention to the cottage as if she'd only just noticed the scaffolding. 'Darling, what are you *doing*?'

'New roof, new heating, new flooring. After the flood,'

Lori explained, knowing from the blank look that her sister remembered nothing of the storm that had swept through the village, ripping tiles from the roof and sending water down through the back of the house and up from a blocked drainage ditch two fields away. The new kitchen and two new windows were add-ons that Lori could just about afford, as the builders were on site, but she wasn't going into that much detail.

Lark had already lost interest.

'That man ...' She waved her hand to the side of the house, where Glyn had disappeared, perfect eyebrows drawn together in a frown and perfect mouth pouting.

Lori knew immediately what the grievance was. 'He's gay.'

'Ah.' Reassured that her powers to stun were not slipping, Lark smiled. It was like the sun coming out.

Oh no, no, no. Do not *let her talk you into anything.*

Her sister's butterfly attention had returned to the scaffolding swathing the house. She surveyed it doubtfully, the hint of a frown back to disturb the unlined brow. 'I expect it's ... er ... fun. Like camping out,' she suggested brightly, with the tiniest suggestion of concern buried in the depths of the blue eyes. Only a sister would know it was there. *Oh hell.* Lori took another deep breath. The panic subsided abruptly, replaced by dogged determination. Whatever it was her sister wanted, and she had her suspicions, the answer had to be no.

'Lark,' she asked the question again. 'Why are you here?'

Skylark laughed, and it really did sound like the tinkling of fairy bells, as one enraptured theatre critic had declared, after witnessing Lark's portrayal of Titania. She patted Lori's arm. 'To see you, of course. And Misty.' She looked around. 'Where is she? Where's my little girl?'

The edges of Lori's vision seemed to go black. It was much *much* worse than she'd thought. In everything she'd imagined, she'd never imagined *this*. Her voice, when she found it, was hoarse and scratchy. She could barely get the words out. 'Misty isn't here.'

'What do you mean?' For a split second confusion shifted across Lark's perfect face. 'Oh, you mean she's with a little friend? On a play date?' she pronounced the words carefully, and with a shade of triumph, as if they were something in a foreign language, looking down at the slim rose-gold watch adorning the equally slim wrist. 'Look, I don't have too much time. My plane – can we go and fetch her?'

'Lark!' Horror made Lori grab her sister's shoulders. 'Lark, it's not a matter of a play date. Misty isn't here. You didn't leave your daughter with me.'

Chapter Eight

They'd moved inside the cottage. Lark had inspected the narrow hall and stairs suspiciously, apparently still not entirely convinced that her daughter was not somewhere on the premises. Now she was sitting on the window-sill, staring around her with a disgruntled expression. 'Darling, what have you done with the furniture?'

'Storage.' Lori leaned against the wall, arms folded. Both her panic and horror had subsided in the face of practical necessity. Discovering where her sister had left her niece. 'We need to find Misty. Is she with Dan?'

Lark waved a dismissive hand. 'Dan's in L.A. with his latest woman.' Lori sighed. Dan, Lark's ex husband and Misty's father, had been happily married to 'his latest woman' for nearly two years, but Lori let it go. *More important stuff to deal with*.

Lark was fidgeting, looking disconsolately around the room. 'Honestly, I don't know why you didn't stay up at the Court, instead of moving into this pokey little place. There would be so much more room for Misty to run about and play.'

And to live with me on a permanent basis?

Lori had given up explaining to her sister that their parents had used the proceeds of the sale of their former home to set up their holistic retreat in Santorini – unexpectedly giving her the deposit for the 'pokey little place' as part of the deal. Under the urging of the local solicitor, who had known Skylark from childhood, her sister's share was safely tucked up in a savings account for her daughter. Their younger brother, Merlin, would eventually take over the retreat, where he worked as chief yoga instructor. Somehow Lark's selective thought processes hadn't grasped that the family didn't actually *own* the Court any more. But Lori didn't have time for that. Right now the selective thoughts had to be focused on Misty. 'Come on, Lark, when did you last see Misty? Or talk to her?'

Lark thought for a moment. 'On my birthday?' *Oh God, that was in October.* 'Yes.' Lark smiled. 'It was so sweet, she sang Happy Birthday over the phone and Gilly said—' Lark snapped her fingers. '*That's* where she is. I knew it was in Wales, that's why I thought she was with you.'

'Hereford isn't in Wales.' Fleetingly Lori wondered what the mitigating circumstances might be for strangling your sister. Misplacing her four-year-old daughter surely had to come high on the list? But if Misty was with Gilly, Lark's former hairdresser, who had babysat her when she was tiny, that wasn't so bad. Except – 'Wait a minute. I ran into Gilly in Cardiff at the end of the summer. I'm sure she said she was pregnant.'

'How should I know?' Lark pushed out her lower lip, looking more like a discontented four-year-old than Misty ever did. 'I noticed that she'd put on a lot of weight when I dropped Misty off, so maybe that was it.'

Lori covered her eyes with one hand. The thought of a heavily pregnant woman or maybe, even worse, a woman with a newborn, lumbered with a precociously lively little girl who wasn't even a relative … She dropped her hand and held on to her temper. 'Has Gilly tried to contact you, at all?'

Lark looked shifty, if fairy princess hair and doe eyes could look shifty. 'She might have …' She shrugged. 'Bruno has people to take care of fans and those sorts of people.'

Including babysitters, enquiring when your new muse and favourite leading lady might be coming back to retrieve her daughter?

'Ring her.' Lori settled her features into her most scary office manager look. 'Now.'

'Couldn't you …?' Lark took in the set jaw and hard eyes and scrabbled in her bag for her phone.

Lori couldn't fully hear the other side of the conversation, but the tones of relief in the responses from Gilly were distinguishable, even if the words weren't.

Lark ended the call, giving her phone an angry stare, before dropping it back in her bag. 'She tried to ring *you* a couple of times,' she said accusingly.

'My old phone died.' Another casualty of the flood. She'd got a new number with an upgraded phone, conveniently putting paid to irritating calls in the middle of the night from Frazer, when he'd had too many beers and decided he regretted his decision to break up.

And as I had no reason to think that my niece's supposedly former babysitter would (a) have my number or (b) need to contact me on it, I refuse to feel guilty about it.

Quite how Lark had managed to dump Misty on Gilly was something she wasn't going into now. And probably not worth asking what had happened to Misty's latest nanny either. Her sister was unlikely to remember. This whole thing would have to be sorted out with Dan.

After Christmas.

'Gilly wants me to collect Misty.' Lark's voice was perilously close to a whine.

'Off you go then.' Lori made a shooing gesture. 'You said you had a plane to catch.'

'Oh yes.' Skylark brightened. 'The Seychelles. Bruno has bought this wonderful villa—'

'Then the sooner you collect your daughter, the sooner you can be on your way. Misty will love the Seychelles. All those long sandy beaches.' That last part wasn't malicious. *Well, not much*.

'Oh!' Realisation widened the blue eyes. 'Could you—?'

'No,' Lori said firmly. 'I'll be leaving straight after you.' She hardened her heart. She had to, in the circumstances. 'The sooner you get going, the sooner you can be on that plane.' She knew Bruno had his own jet. It would wait for Lark.

'Lori ...' Lark's voice had gone low and husky. *Her wheedling voice*. 'Do you think—?'

'No!' The panic was rising again. Laced with guilt. It wasn't Misty's fault that she had the most self-absorbed mother on the planet. *Do not weaken*.

Lark waved her hand at the bare room, wincing at the sound of hammering from somewhere above. 'Can't you get these people to come back later?'

'I can't, Lark. They're doing me a special deal because no one else wants them just before Christmas. Now you go and fetch your daughter. It would be lovely for you to spend Christmas together.' *And possibly the first Christmas since Misty started to walk*. Her heart tripped a little. Guilt again. But there would be *someone* in Bruno's entourage capable of taking care of a child. And if there wasn't, he'd undoubtedly hire someone. The relationship was fairly new, but from the photos in the gossip magazines the man was besotted. He already had teenage children from a previous relationship who appeared healthy and well-adjusted, so he'd probably make a suitable step-father. *If Skylark manages to put a ring on it*. But that wasn't going to turn Lark into celebrity mother of the year. *Dan will have to sort this out*.

'I really don't want ...' Lark pouted 'She's growing so ... big.'

Clarity hit Lori like a blast from next door's massive array of fairy-lights. It had been fine when Misty was a very cute and pretty baby. There had been a spate of celebrity pregnancies and newborns around that time. Lark had been thrilled to be part of the fashionable trend, posing for photos and showing off her svelte post-baby figure and her charming bundle with the rest. She'd even given interviews on her top ten tips for the new mother. *Wonder who wrote them for her?*

Lori stifled the burst of cynicism. *Not the issue here.* Misty was still pretty, cute and bright as a button, but the older she got the greater the reminder that Lark too was getting older. Lori did some quick mental calculations – just past twenty-eight, with the big three zero looming, ever closer, on the horizon.

Lori took a good look at her younger sister. There were three years between them. Despite the immaculately applied make-up and no doubt phenomenally expensive skincare products, applied with religious zeal, Lark's currency as a fresh-faced beauty *might* be starting to slide, just a fraction. There were tiny expression lines at the corners of her eyes, and slight indentations around the deep pink pout, which were no doubt magnified to monumental proportions in her sister's mind. For Lark, the fact that she was an excellent actress, with an Oscar nomination to her credit, wasn't going to make up for that. In Lark's mind her face was her fortune.

And it's not going to get any better. But you can't fix that today.

Lori detached herself from the wall and crossed the room to kiss her sister's cheek, while pulling her to her feet. 'Go to Gilly's and collect Misty. She'll be thrilled to see you,' she said encouragingly, watching Lark's face brighten.

Admiration always got to her, even from a four-year-old. *Should that be* especially *from a four-year-old, when she was your daughter?* 'Collect her, and catch the plane. Everything will be fine.' Slowly she steered her sister out of the front room and out of the cottage. The driver had emerged from the limo, and was leaning against the bonnet. From the resigned expression on his face, he was Lark's regular chauffeur. Lori shepherded her sister into the car, prompting her to give the driver Gilly's address.

'It's okay Miss France, I remember taking the little one there. I've got the car seat in the boot.'

'Oh good. Thanks.' She turned to Skylark, who had removed her coat and was settling herself in the back of the car.

If we'd just thought to ask the chauffeur.

The driver had slid smoothly behind the wheel.

Lori put a hand on the open back door of the car. 'You'll soon be seeing Misty and off on holiday together. You will have a lovely time, an absolutely super Christmas,' Lori added encouragingly, as she closed the door and stepped away.

The car backed carefully out into the main road.

With a shaky sigh Lori crossed to the cottage. Her own car was packed. All she had to do was put Griff in his basket, and they too could be on their way.

Except that the cat was nowhere to be found.

Chapter Nine

'I don't believe this!' Lori collapsed in a disgusted heap on the stairs. There was no sign of Griff, anywhere. She'd called, banged food bowls and rattled treat bags, and called again. She'd toured the neighbours, those who were in, and peered into the gardens and over fences of those who weren't. 'He's never gone missing before! He's too bloody *lazy* to go missing!'

Mike, Paulie's apprentice, staggered by, clutching a radiator. 'You tried the cupboard under the stairs? My mam's cat always hides in there.'

'Twice.' Lori dropped her head in her hands. She was hot, sweaty and hungry. The weather was unseasonably mild for December and the bowl of cereal she'd eaten, standing up in the kitchen, before the last trip to the storage locker with her dismantled bed, was a very long nine ago. Her handbag, with her emergency chocolate stash, was in the front room. She hauled herself to her feet to go in search of it, half her mind picturing Griff as a cold stiff corpse on the side of a road somewhere, and the other half contemplating a nice pair of fur-backed gloves. Grrr!

She'd eat a few squares of chocolate, then tour the house and garden again. Paulie and his crew hadn't taken up any floorboards yet, but maybe Griff was asleep in some discarded packaging somewhere. The chocolate melted slowly on her tongue. She leaned on the window-sill looking idly out – the house at the other end of the row was empty during the week, and on quite a lot of weekends too. If Griff had chosen to sleep somewhere there …

A car was pulling into the small street of houses and moving slowly along the road, stopping behind her Fiesta. It took Lori a few seconds to register, and then she was out of the door and into the garden, half choking as the last of the chocolate went down the wrong way.

'No. No. No.' The last 'no' was almost a wail. She lurched towards the car, with a vague half-formed thought of making it turn straight back around, but she wasn't fast enough. The door had already opened and a small figure in a sparkly pink jumper, a stiff net skirt and twinkling red shoes, darted out. With a casual wave to her aunt, Misty sped past to greet Griff, who had miraculously emerged, in perfect health, from under next door's hedge.

And her sister was out of the car now, with an elegantly wrapped parcel and an envelope in her hands. 'Darling, I knew you'd wait.' She gave Lori the benefit of one of the most famous smiles in Hollywood as she too slipped past. 'I'll just put this down somewhere safe, inside. Fragile.' She mouthed the last word as she glided into the cottage.

'No ... I ... Lark ... You can't ...' Lori could hear her heart beating in her ears.

Misty staggered over, arms full of cat. 'I *love* Griff.'

'I know you do, sweetheart, look I—'

'Mummy says I'm staying with you for Christmas.' The little girl looked doubtfully at the scaffolding. 'Is that for Father Christmas to climb up?'

'Um, sort of, but I don't think ...' Lori's mind was racing as fast as her heart. *You can't do this. No way.* But how do you have a stand-up fight with your sister with her daughter looking on? Well, she was going to have to try. Seeing Misty was happy cuddling Griff – *You and I, Houdini, will be having words later* – Lori turned to stalk back into her house to find her sister and whatever impractical ornament she'd chosen as a present, and get them both, plus Misty, back in the car, pronto.

In the pocket of her tracksuit her phone began to chirp and vibrate. With a muffled curse she pulled it out 'Yes!' she barked into the phone.

'Ms France? This is Bella Hughes from Small Homes Insurance – about your claim for additional services in relation to your repair work—'

'What about it?' Lori knew she was being brusque, but she really had to find Lark. *And put her, and Misty, back in the car.*

'I'm afraid there's been an error ...'

Lori sat down hard on an upturned bucket that had been left under the scaffolding, listening to the woman at the end of the phone who was turning a bad day one hundred times worse.

'That isn't right.' Cutting in when the woman paused, Lori got up to pace to the other side of the garden. The woman proceeded to tell her how it *was* right. Lori paced to the gate. Misty, with Griff in her arms, had taken possession of the bucket and was whispering into the cat's ear.

'This was all cleared weeks ago. It was negotiated as a special arrangement, with your colleague.' Lori paced back, entirely focused on convincing the woman at the insurers that they *would* be paying her accommodation bill while her home was rebuilt.

Too focused.

At the last minute something alerted her. A fugitive waft of her sister's perfume, a quick click of a car door ...

It was already too late.

Misty was standing by the gate, waving, as the limo backed away from the kerb, leaving a pile of luggage, lavishly wrapped Christmas presents and a child's car seat neatly stacked on the side of the road.

Chapter Ten

'That bastard driver must have been unloading stuff the minute Lark got out of the car!' Lori was pacing again, this time back and forth in her narrow hall. Paulie was leaning placidly against the wall, listening to her rant.

Mike, the apprentice, had taken Misty round to his mam's for something to eat. 'It's Monday, so it's cold meat and bubble and squeak – there'll be enough for a little 'un.'

Lori's stomach rumbled and abruptly her anger evaporated. She flopped onto the stairs, shoving both her hands into her hair. 'It's not just the insurers refusing to meet the cost. I had to sweet talk the guesthouse owner into agreeing to let me have *Griff* in my room – if I turn up with a four-year-old!' She rolled her eyes.

'What did the insurers actually say?'

'Administrative error, resulting in my being given incorrect approval,' Lori recited, making a face. 'I know the woman is wrong. She was just being officious and throwing her weight about, but the person who agreed it is on leave until the New Year.' She looked around her house-cum-building site with a sigh. 'Since strangling my sister isn't an option, I've just got to get on with it. If we bring both the beds back we can put them up in the front room and if I take Misty out every day …' She tailed off, looking up at Paulie. 'It's not going to work is it?'

'Actually, it doesn't have to.' Paulie was grinning. 'I don't know why I didn't think of it before, but you had it all sorted with the insurers.' He pulled a ring of keys off his belt and selected two, taking them off the bundle. A shadow crossed his face as he held them out. 'My gran's place.'

'I thought it was sold?' Lori knew that after a long struggle to cope with his grandmother's worsening dementia, Paulie and his parents had admitted defeat when she had been found wandering on the hills behind the converted barn, in just her dressing gown and slippers. She was safe, and as comfortable as they could make her now, in a care home in Hereford.

'We've done the contracts and stuff, but it's not final until the sixth of January. Until then it's standing empty.' He grimaced. 'The buyers are going to use it for holiday lets, so they won't be waiting outside with a removal van, even then.' He shrugged. 'Not what we wanted, but what can you do? It's still got the furniture, they bought that as well. I was going to take the truck up on Boxing Day and clear out what's left of the personal stuff, but there isn't that much.' He held up the keys. 'It's yours until we have this place sorted.'

'You're sure?' Lori took the keys. 'It'll be okay with your mam?'

'Mam won't mind. She's left sorting out the barn to me. She and Dad are in Tenerife. Staying until the middle of January.' The shadow crossed his face again. 'First holiday they've had since Gran ...' He swallowed, then he grinned. 'Anything to keep you and the nipper out of my building site. Come on.' He jerked his head at the front door. 'Let's go and re-pack your car with Misty's stuff. You know where the barn is. We had the power turned off. But there's a back-up generator and the range in the kitchen is a wood burner. It does the heating and hot water and cooking ...'

Still slightly dazed, Lori followed his retreating back and a deluge of instructions out of the cottage door.

Chapter Eleven

21 December, Afternoon

The return to consciousness was slow and painful. This time he felt *really* sick, but the hood had gone.

Probably because Mr Right and Lefty had gone too.

Drew squinted around. This was the hut. He was sitting, slumped rather, on what seemed to be a low bench against the wall. Light was filtering in from a narrow row of cobweb-covered windows, just under the roof. High over his head. The corners of the structure were deep in shadow. From the faint, lingering odour of motor oil, he guessed the place was normally used to store small machinery and tools. There was no machinery here now.

Perfect for storing an unwanted best-selling author.

Instinctively, Drew shivered. It wasn't particularly cold, just dank and gloomy, but the thin jacket of his suit wasn't going to be much use when night fell and the temperature dropped.

You have to be out of here by then. He pushed himself up from the bench to investigate a thin line of light on the opposite wall, that seemed to indicate a door – and then came to a painful, clanking halt as his left arm pulled, jerking him back. Where his watch should have been was a narrow metal cuff, anchoring him to the wall with a business-like length of chain.

'Fuck!'

He stepped forward, carefully. Sideways on, with his left arm stretched back and his right stretched forward, he was a few inches short of the door. With another curse, he subsided back onto the bench. Something under the bench clanked as his foot hit it. He peered down. Great. They'd left him a metal bucket. *No prizes for guessing what that was for ...*

Carefully he felt along the bench. In the darkest corner his questing hands encountered a large paper bag that rustled as he lifted it. Gingerly he extracted a little of the contents, sniffed, then tried a bite. Some sort of trail mix. Nuts and dried fruit. Tucked right against the wall were a box of energy bars, a carboy of water and what seemed to be a small thermos flask. He unscrewed the top and sniffed again. Coffee. Wondering if it was laced with anything – *from choice, a good slug of whisky* – he took a mouthful. Lukewarm, stewed and bitter. It tasted like heaven. And it was *warm*. The damp chill was getting to him. Gut instinct told him that the coffee was neither doped nor poisoned. *That isn't how this thing is going down.* He drank it, and felt immediately better.

More exploring, to the length of the chain in the other direction, yielded nothing else. He flopped back down on the bench. From the look of the fragile winter light coming through the windows it was at least midday, maybe later. They'd taken his watch and emptied his pockets – no phone, money, keys, Swiss Army knife. He wondered, briefly, if someone was right now riding his customised Harley. Or raiding his Chelsea flat.

But that wasn't how this thing was playing out either, unless Mr Right or Lefty was indulging in a bit of private enterprise.

Someone has been clever, setting this up – especially the coffee.

The necessities of life, and a pot to pee in – plenty for a few hours of hostage experience for a writer known for research on the stupid side of realism.

Except this isn't research, and I don't think it's meant to end in a few hours. Unless I've pissed someone off, big time, and this is a spot of revenge, it only has one end.

When he was found – *God, when* – it was going to look like a crazy accident. A tragic breakdown in communication over the Christmas break that left Andrew Vitruvius trapped in his wooden prison, instead of being picked up by a support crew. There were holes in it, but it was just plausible enough for doubt. His reputation would be enough to swing it.

Hoist with your own petard, you stupid tosser.

No one was coming to the rescue and somehow he didn't think Mr Right and Lefty were going to be raising any alarms and putting their hands up as the ones who'd dumped him here.

He had to find a way out of this bloody hut.

Oh, and figure out who might just possibly want you dead.

Chapter Twelve

21 December, Late Afternoon

The barn was beautiful, with high windows, bright rugs, big squashy sofas in autumn colours, throws of soft Welsh wool and a mountain of cushions.

And fabulous views over the hills of the Brecon Beacons, just dipping into a hazy twilight. Later there would be stars.

It was already getting dark. They explored the house in the fading light. Lori got the wood burner in the kitchen going more easily than she expected, with the logs stacked in a carrier beside it, before dragging what they would need for the night out of the car. Misty was crooning to Griff, still incarcerated in his basket and beginning to get restive. Lori straightened up from hefting a rucksack out of the back of the car, which was parked on the gravelled area in front of the barn. The place looked magical, with lights from the oil lamps that were dotted around twinkling inside it, visible through the uncurtained windows.

Very Christmassy. And that's how it's going to stay. No way am I pushing my luck and tangling with that generator tonight.

They would make do with the lamps and candles and the glow from the wood-burning stove. *And probably a lot of giggling.* She found bedding in a large linen press on the landing and after a few moments thought, made up the twin beds in the larger of the two bedrooms on the mezzanine level over the main room. If Misty woke in the night, disoriented, she would be nearby, and Griff wouldn't have to patrol the corridor, deciding whose bed to sleep on, if they shared the room.

Lori hauled some more bags and boxes inside, before concluding that the rest could wait until morning. It was too dark now to see clearly. She unpacked what they would need for a simple meal. Rolls, cooked ham, some Christmas pickles, a large bag of salt and vinegar crisps, apples and a chunk of Victoria sponge that Mike's mam had sent over with Misty, after feeding her lunch. Lori had grabbed a sausage roll in the village, on route to explain in person to the owners of the B&B why she was cancelling her booking. Thankfully they seemed relieved not to be having Christmas guests. Now she was *starving*.

Released from his basket, Griff had clearly decided his humans were currently a bauble short of a Christmas tree and had retreated to the highest beam he could find, spreading himself out like a basking leopard, only yellow eyes and a vague shape visible in the darkness.

Lori laid out the food and lit a couple of candles, placing them carefully in holders on the table. The stove was already sending warmth stealing into the corners of the barn.

'Come on, sweetheart,' she called to Misty, who was settling her favourite toy rabbit on one of the sofas. 'Let's eat.'

Chapter Thirteen

By the time light began to fade from the windows Drew had given up the faint hope that this *was* all someone's idea of a joke, and that the cavalry would be coming over the hill any moment. He hadn't managed to find a way out of the hut, or figure out who wanted him damaged – perhaps irrevocably.

This is not going well.

The bruises supplied by Mr Right and Lefty were aching, and his muscles were sore and beginning to stiffen. He'd eaten some of the trail mix, although he really wasn't that hungry, and drunk some of the water. He'd explored every part of the hut he could reach and found no weak spots anywhere. He'd tried yelling and then banging on the wall, just for a change of pace. For a heart-stopping moment there had been a noise outside the hut. Drew held his breath until the noise resolved into snuffling and rustling. *Not human.* He'd yelled again, just in case it was a dog, with an owner nearby, but when he paused to listen the noises had stopped completely. He'd probably scared whatever it was away.

He'd gone methodically over the cuff and the chain and the fastening that anchored it to one of the support struts of the building. Without anything to pick or prise at the metal he'd simply scraped and torn his fingertips bloody. Crouching, then lying on the floor of the hut, to the extent of the chain, he'd located a heavy cotton dust sheet piled in a corner and laboriously inched it towards him with his feet, until he could grasp it and pull it in. It felt sticky to the touch and reeked of mildew, but it would keep off some of the night chill.

Now the hut was pitch black.

He fought a flicker of panic, deep in his chest. He had food, he had water and he wasn't out in the elements. His head was throbbing, but he forced himself to concentrate.

Why? Why the hell are you here?

If this was someone's idea of a clever stunt – *that no one thought to tell you about* – he'd surely have been picked up by now, so he could more or less rule that out. If it was revenge, then maybe after one night they'd be satisfied. Whoever *they* were. If someone wanted him dead, it was a chancy way to go about it. *But a damned clever one.* The hut had been prepared. Not very comfortable, but not life-threatening.

Yet.

It was the twenty-first of December – with Christmas just around the corner – when workplaces shut down while the country celebrated. The odds against anyone coming close to his prison were lengthened considerably just by that simple fact. He shifted uneasily on the bench, trying to remember statistics for deaths involving exposure and thirst. He was reasonably young, healthy and fit, with survival skills.

'You can do this. You've spent nights out in worse conditions than this.'

He rolled himself into the dust sheet, resting his aching head on his shoulder, as best he could.

You've done this before, sure. But then you knew when and how it was going to end.

Chapter Fourteen

After visiting the generator in the morning, in its little house behind the kitchen, Lori decided she still wasn't going to tangle with it. The wood-burning stove took care of everything but the lights and the fridge, and they could manage without both. Milk, butter and cheese were keeping cool in the unheated laundry-cum-boot room on the north side of the kitchen, and she would improvise with vegetables and using the stores in the nearest village as a pantry. The envelope with Lark's present – a crystal figurine of a ballerina that was so *not* Lori – had proved to contain a hefty cheque, rather than the expected Christmas card. *Guilt money.*

This time, instead of folding it up to return it later, Lori had cashed it straight away at the bank in Abergavenny and taken her niece on a mini spending spree. A local budget shop had contributed tinsel and streamers, balloons and four large bags of LED fairy lights, which were now twinkling away merrily around the barn. She'd topped up the lighting with a couple more battery lamps and an industrial supply of batteries. They'd found a potted Christmas tree in the corner of the local florist, just a little taller than Misty and, ambling around the stalls in the market, some colourful carved wooden ornaments to decorate it. They'd made a great find in a charity shop – a windup radio – that would also charge Lori's phone. Not that there was much of a signal in this area of the Beacons. Some cosy new Christmas Eve pyjamas, a pair of stripy wellington boots for Misty and three different kinds of hot chocolate, a small iced cake, some mince pies and a box of dates had been added to the haul. They'd had to go back to the car twice to deposit their swag. Lori had sneaked a couple of Bailey's miniatures into her basket in the supermarket. And she'd surreptitiously assembled some small presents to go in a stocking for Misty. She had a pair of oversize bedsocks in her rucksack. One of those would do. They'd ended up in a local child-friendly pub for an early Christmas dinner. Turkey, with all the trimmings.

Now Lori was sipping hot chocolate and watching the sunset from the Cwtch, a reading nook in the gallery at mezzanine level towards the front of the barn, with a fabulous view. Misty was sitting on the floor, leaning on a stool and deeply engrossed in filling in a complicated scene in her Christmas colouring book, lit by one of the new lamps, her face intense, and with the tip of her tongue caught between her teeth.

The sun was going down in a blaze of pink and red, with ribbons of dark purple cloud streaking across the sky. Lori settled herself more comfortably in the low-slung leather seat, her mind on a knotty problem she had hit in the plot of the current work-in-progress. She couldn't help a low-pitched sigh. This week had been set aside as precious writing time, holed up in the guesthouse, away from the day job. She had *not* intended to spend it babysitting her niece. She would probably get a little writing done, once Misty was in bed, but nothing like the amount she'd planned. At this rate she was never going to achieve the dream of getting published.

This afternoon they'd enjoyed a short ramble through the woods on the hill behind the barn and then decorated the tree. Griff had prowled all round it, then graciously condescended to leave it alone, preferring his perch on the beam. Lori was hoping that he'd remain in a tolerant frame of mind.

Lori looked over at her niece, still intent on her colouring. Lark was missing all this. Precious time with her daughter that could never be retrieved; but Lori knew her sister well enough to realise she wouldn't change. After the holidays something would have to be done. They would be at the barn now until after Christmas, rather than returning to the cottage on Christmas Eve, as she'd planned to do when she was staying at the guesthouse. The cleaning up and painting she'd scheduled for Christmas Day would have to wait.

She made a face into the dregs of her hot chocolate. She was going to make it a good Christmas for Misty, even if they were kind of camping out.

They'd drawn up a sign and hung it outside the barn, so Father Christmas would know that they were there. Christmas lunch was probably going to be fancy pasta from her parents' Christmas hamper, with a sauce out of a jar, but she was pretty sure Misty wouldn't care. And they had crackers and a proper Christmas pudding. All in all Misty was an easy-going child, considering the way she'd been brought up so far, but it couldn't go on.

Lori looked down at Misty's bent head. None of this was her niece's fault.

The sun had finished its light show and darkness was setting in. Lori shivered slightly, putting down her mug as Misty looked up with a beaming smile, colouring complete. She held it out to be admired.

'It's lovely.' And it was. Neatly, if imaginatively, coloured and nearly all within the lines. 'And now I think it's time we went down and gave Griff his tea.'

They'd had fun today, and would have more tomorrow.

He'd experienced worse cold than this. When he'd made the trip to the Artic Circle the weather had been biting.

But then you had proper equipment, and the chance of hot food.

He'd managed to sleep for most of the night, huddled in the dust sheet, and spent the day again exploring his prison, wrestling with the cuff and chain and occasionally shouting in the hope of attracting attention. His throat was sore and when he tried it, his voice had turned husky. There had been another heart-stopping moment when he'd heard noises from outside, but again they'd come to nothing. He'd thought, at one point, that he made out the sound of a car engine, very faint and distant, but then that too had died.

Now the light was fading and he was facing another night in captivity.

And no nearer to figuring out who was behind all this.

And even less idea why.

Chapter Fifteen

'I've had a nice day, Auntie Lori.' Misty let out a contented sigh that turned into a yawn halfway through.

'It was a nice day, wasn't it?' Lori snuggled her niece closer to her on the sofa. 'I'm glad you enjoyed yourself, pet.'

One of the local farms had set up a reindeer walk, through a small coppice, complete with elves and live reindeer. After exploring that, they'd spent the afternoon in the village hall, for a screening of Christmas cartoons that had gone down a storm with the audience of tinies and frazzled mums, a few of whom had certainly rested their eyes during the show.

They'd driven home by what had immediately become Misty's favourite route, which they'd found when Lori had turned off too soon the day before. A short cut that would probably be impassable after heavy rain by anything less than a four-wheel drive, it cut through a wooded area with mature trees on one side and a small stand of birches on the other, their trunks and branches pale and ethereal in the winter sun.

Today, fired up by the elves and reindeer, Misty had wanted to get out and hunt for evidence of fairy inhabitants, but Lori had managed to persuade her against it. The road was little used, not much more than a track. To Lori it felt slightly creepy.

And it had been getting dark.

She'd diverted Misty with promises of a slice of chocolate cake with her tea. They'd eaten by the light of the fire, beside the Christmas tree, with carols playing on the radio and Griff stretched out on the rug, purring like a traction engine.

Or a cat full of best tuna.

Now Misty was sleepily watching the flames in the fire, listening as Lori spun a bedtime story full of elves and reindeer and purring cats.

Lori thought again how much her sister was missing.

Another night.

His beard was growing, getting to the itchy stage, which was a small irritation to take his mind off the bigger ones. The dust sheet was doing a good job – he shuddered to think how it would have been if he hadn't located it, folded in the corner. He didn't even notice the mouldy smell now. But it didn't stop the cold settling into his bones and making his fingers and toes ache. He was sick of the taste and texture of the trail mix and the energy bars and the level of water in the carboy was going down. Tomorrow he would have to start rationing himself.

Tomorrow, unless he had miscalculated, was Christmas Eve.

The time of the year when he always avoided people, and celebrations.

Reminders of all that loss.

Now he was desperate for contact with another human being.

Irony?

There'd been more snuffling and grunting outside the hut early this morning, as it was getting light, and later he'd heard a dog bark. He'd shouted then, even though he'd known that the animal was probably too far away for him to be heard. As dusk was falling he'd thought again that he heard a car, but he couldn't be certain. He wasn't sure if his ears were playing tricks on him. He spent a lot of time staring into space, playing counting and word games, anything to stop his mind drifting.

Or returning to the hamster wheel of who and why.

He slumped against the wall of the hut, feeling the rough wood against his back. The wind was getting up. It was rattling the windows and there was a draught blowing through an ill-fitting panel near the door.

Happy Christmas.

Chapter Sixteen

Christmas Eve, Early Morning

Lori stood in the Cwtch, nursing her first mug of tea of the day and watching mist drift around the valley.

Like standing in a cloud.

Maybe not a day for outdoor activities – although she suspected the fog would burn off by lunch-time.

She started a little, slopping tea, as Griff jumped down from some hiding place on one of the beams, and began to strop around her legs.

'Okay, yes, breakfast. But first we go and see if Misty is awake. She was dead to the world when I snuck out about ten minutes ago.'

She was still dead to the world, spread out like a starfish across the bed, with Bunny, her favourite and well-loved toy, clutched in one small hand. Lori smiled and gently brushed a strand of hair away from her niece's face. When she was awake Misty was confident and articulate – so grown–up it was sometimes hard to remember that she was only four years old. Asleep, she looked very sweet and very young.

Lori edged out of the bedroom and padded downstairs to start on breakfast. Smiling, she flipped on the radio at low volume, to hear the news. Misty found the task of winding the handle to power up the radio entirely fascinating, which was fine by Lori. There was probably nothing to smile about in the news, which she'd somehow managed to miss hearing for a few days, but it was Christmas Eve, so there might be *one* cheerful item.

'... Fears are growing for the safety of best-selling author

Andrew Vitruvius. Vitruvius was last seen on Sunday night when he was taking part in a celebrity kidnapping for the Phil Philmore show, but failed to turn up at the rendezvous at the close of the evening.'

Caught by the words 'best-selling author', Lori stopped in the act of pouring cereal into bowls, to listen. She hadn't watched the Philmore show. Her ancient TV had already gone to storage, but in any case she'd been too busy with last-minute packing. Paulie and Mike had been talking about the show and its aftermath on Monday morning, but then she'd been dismantling her bed and hadn't really paid proper attention.

'The fundraising event netted nearly three quarters of a million pounds for a selection of charities, chosen by the participants. Friends of the author, known for his in-depth research for his best-selling action fantasy novels, have expressed concern at his disappearance, which coincides with the eighteenth anniversary of the Brighton rail disaster, in which his wife and baby son were tragically killed. Police are appealing for any information ...Yesterday a weather system over the Atlantic—'

Lori put down the cereal packet and opened a drawer, looking for spoons and listening with half an ear to the rest of the bulletin. Andrew Vitruvius was a mega best-seller. She stifled an ignominious twinge of envy. *I wish*.

She'd never read anything he'd written – not her thing – but there was a whole row of his paperbacks in the bookcase in the Cwtch. She'd been curious enough to investigate and found two of them were signed. Probably when the man had come to the Hay Festival, she thought idly, as she let herself into the laundry room to retrieve the milk from the window-sill. She gave it an exploratory sniff. It was fine, but if they could get out to pick up some fresh milk today, it would be a bonus – otherwise it would be long-life or powdered tomorrow. She carried her trophy back to the kitchen. Griff slurped the last mouthful of his breakfast and gave the plate a hopeful push, making it clatter on the tiles.

Lori shook her head. 'That's your lot, mate. I don't know where you put it all as it is.'

Irritated but not surprised, Griff stalked off to sit in the long French windows to wash, giving her the high tail on the way. Grinning, Lori gave him the finger back.

'Love you too, sweetie.'

She poured apple juice and sliced a banana to add it to the bowls of cereal. The humans' breakfast was now ready. All she needed was someone to eat it.

She loped up the stairs, on impulse diverting to scoop one of Vitruvius' books from the shelf, turning it over to look at the author photo on the back. The picture confirmed that the guy was traditionally tall, dark and handsome, brooding beside a dust-covered jeep in a desert somewhere. It took a second to figure out the reason for the desert shot, and then she made the connection. The man apparently had a taste for stunts, dressed up as research. She remembered Dean, the fitter from work, going on at length about some TV programme he'd watched, where Vitruvius had been shadowed by a camera crew while white-water rafting. Dean was a *big* Vitruvius fan. She wrinkled her nose. *Is that what this is about? Publicity to make people buy more books?*

She turned the book over. A heavily armed and partially clad Celtic type was wielding a fancy looking sword over the red slash of the title.

The Irish Stone.

Maybe she should read it?

She turned the book again. Difficult to believe the author

shot was of a widower of nearly twenty years. It could be an old photo or good Photoshop, or perhaps it was just luck and excellent genes. *Or maybe the guy has a portrait degenerating in the attic?*

She studied the author picture, staring at the eyes, narrowed against the desert sun. There'd been a hint of something dark in the news broadcast, and the loss of his wife and son *was* heart-breaking. Was there still pain there? Hard to tell from a photo. She remembered that crash. She'd still been in school. It had hit all the headlines, so close to Christmas. A lot of people had died. *Leaving families whose Christmases would never be the same.*

She sighed. All her family members were still with her. Maybe they were difficult and distant, but they were still alive. She'd never been in that position, but anniversaries could be hell, she knew that much.

But would a man take on something for charity and then …?

No. She shook her head. According to Dean, the guy was notorious for extreme research – being abandoned on desert islands, climbing mountains, trekking across the tundra. No doubt he'd re-emerge with some story to tell. Probably today, as it was Christmas Eve. Maybe the extra publicity would do the charities some good. *Maybe that was the idea?*

She put the book back on the shelf – *really* not her thing – and went to call her niece.

'Christmas Eve, Christmas Eve, Christmas Eve,' Misty chanted as she arranged a sticker of a fairy on a piece of stiff card. Satisfied with her labours, she propped it gently next to a pine-cone. 'Pine-cone, Holly, Ivy.' She counted along the row. Her morning's work. Each cardboard fairy was arranged in a display with its natural equivalent.

Lori looked up from the pan of risotto she was cooking.

With leaves and cones, some cotton-wool snow, a handful of animal ornaments and miniature pine trees that Lori had found in the back of a cupboard in the kitchen – probably supposed to go on the top of a Christmas cake – Misty had created a creditable woodland scene on a low shelf beside the back door. Some of the proportions were a bit off, the pine-cones towering over the tiny trees, but the effect was still charming.

'Mist-toe.' Misty looked up from her sticker book. 'We need it for the mist-toe fairy.'

'Mistletoe,' Lori corrected. She checked the picture in the book that Misty was holding up for her to see. Her niece was right; she'd correctly identified the white shiny berries in the last fairy picture of the Christmas section. Someone, maybe Gilly, had been teaching her to read. Lori grinned. Misty was precocious enough *now*. Once she could read, there would be no stopping her.

Misty was nodding 'The fairy wood,' she pronounced confidently. 'We'll go and look for some in the fairy wood.'

The fairy wood was the clump of white-barked birch trees on the edge of the woodland track.

Lori stirred the risotto. There was unlikely to be any mistletoe in the wood, but it wouldn't really matter, Misty would be happy just to go and look. Lori glanced over her shoulder, beyond the island of units that separated the kitchen and the main room, to the French doors that gave onto a small terrace beside the barn. As she'd hoped, the fog had lifted and the sun was beginning to shine. It would be good to get out and the lonely track wouldn't be creepy in daylight.

'Lunch first.' She reached for shallow bowls to dish up the risotto. 'Then we'll go and hunt the mistletoe. And when we come back we can look for the best place in the barn to hang up your stocking and put out the mince pie and the carrots for Father Christmas and the reindeer.'

The water was getting low. The bucket, on the other hand, was full. His stomach was growling for some more substantial food, he was sore, stiff and his skin felt itchy all over, not just his beard.

The wind had dropped in the night, as suddenly as it had come, but the light had been a long time coming. Drew suspected a morning fog that had been slow to lift. It was brighter outside now, but the hut felt even more dank and chill. And soon it would be getting dark again.

Christmas Day.

He'd had a few seconds of hope when he heard a dog bark again, this time close to the hut. He'd held his breath as it came sniffing around – probably lifting a leg. He'd called out then, provoking a volley of barking, but nothing had happened. If the dog had an owner, they hadn't come near enough to hear.

He was battling a growing seed of panic. He'd tried again with the cuff and chain, risking splinters of wood in his fingers and under his nails as he grappled to work the fastening off the wall. If they'd attached the chain to the bench, not the hut itself, he could have picked up the whole thing and used it to batter his way out. That was what one of his protagonists would do.

But you didn't arrange this scenario.

He breathed deep, trying to stay calm. He'd gone missing in just about the most public way possible. People would be looking for him. He had friends who were good with that kind of stuff. All he had to do was hang on. People *would* be looking.

But how will they know where to look?

After hours of staring into darkness, chasing his thoughts around, he'd arrived at a short list of people who had sufficient information to sabotage the arrangements, but he hadn't been able to come up with a whisper of motive for any of them.

Which means that there's someone else?

He was looking down the barrel of another night under the dust sheet. And then it was Christmas Day. For exactly half his life, this had been the worst time of his year. And this year looked like it was going to be worse than worst.

Chapter Seventeen

The sun was shining when they reached the turning into the woods. The trees enclosed them, but it was still light under the leafless branches. Lori nosed the car cautiously along an even narrower track that ran off to the side, that they'd learned about at the village shop. In summer the farm workers apparently used it to get to a hut, where they stored tools and chainsaws and other equipment, for use on that side of the wood, but in the winter the building was cleared and empty and the place deserted.

The owner of the small store in the village had explained all this, when they were buying milk, after a long and involved conversation with Misty about the fairy properties of silver birch trees.

'If she wants to visit again, that old track would be shorter for little legs. It gets you right in amongst the trees. There's a clearing where you can turn the car around and we've had no rain lately, so it shouldn't be too muddy. '

'I don't have little legs,' Misty protested indignantly.

The shop owner grinned. 'I was thinking of your auntie, pet.'

Now tall, pale trunks loomed on either side of the car. And there was the clearing, as Misty's new friend had promised.

Lori turned the car carefully, to face the way they had come, and stopped. The ground was dappled by sunlight under the trees, which showed ruts where another vehicle had parked recently in the same spot. Misty was chattering excitedly about mistletoe and fairies.

'In a minute, sweetheart.'

Lori opened her door, leaning out to check the state of the ground. Not soggy enough to cause problems getting the car out and no problem at all for two intrepid mistletoe hunters equipped with stout wellingtons.

She could see that the trail was much narrower leading out of the clearing on the other side, presumably towards the equipment hut, and then up over the hill behind, but someone had made a rough job of pushing back the undergrowth on either side, breaking it and bending it out of the way.

Lori looked up at the fragments of sky she could see though the branches, and then at her watch. They probably had about an hour before it started to get dark.

Plenty of time.

'Come on, trouble.' She helped Misty out of her car seat. 'Let's go and look for those fairies.'

He'd finally lost it. He was hallucinating. There were voices coming towards him and then receding.

Two voices.

Singing.

Christmas carols.

He *was* hallucinating.

Good King Wenceslas and his page were coming for him, through the woods.

Drew jerked upright from the half doze he'd been lost in. The voices were still there. It wasn't a dream. The page was warbling now, in a high treble. The singing was real.

Oh God.

He stumbled to his feet, leaning against the wall of the hut, as close as he could get to the source of the sound. His heart was thumping so hard it took him two attempts to find his voice, and then it came out as a hoarse rasp. Frantic, he tried again.

'Hello! Can you hear me?' That was better. 'I'm here, in the hut. I can't get out. Can you hear me?'

The voices had stopped. The silence stretched, ominously. Was it kids? Had he scared them in to running away?

He tried again. 'Hello?' There was a humiliating catch in the word.

'Hello?' A voice answered him. A grown-up voice, not the page.

'Hello.' Relief was making him dizzy. And repetitive. 'I'm here, in the hut. I can't get out. I need help. It's not a joke. Please. If you can just open the door.' The unhappy thought that the door might be padlocked raised its ugly head. 'If you could try.'

He strained to hear. There seemed to be a muffled conference going on, too low-pitched for him to make out the words.

'Who are you? What are you doing in there?'

The location of the voice had changed. It sounded as if she, he thought it was a she, was standing closer. In front of the hut. *Oh God, a woman and a small child?*

'My name is Andrew Vitruvius,' he said the words carefully. 'I got locked in here ... by accident. If you could just open the door.' He tried to make his voice as reassuring as he could. The dry rasp was no help.

'Andrew Vitruvius?' Now the voice sounded suspicious. 'The writer?'

'Yes. If you could open the door ...'

More muttering. He thought he could hear the words 'stupid joke'. Panic flared. 'It's not a hoax, at least, not on you. *Please.*'

Relief like he'd never experienced before threatened to swamp him at the sound of a hasp being lifted.

No padlock.

The door opened, outwards, very slowly and cautiously, and scraped to a standstill. There was a long beat, and then a silhouette appeared in the opening, with a much smaller figure bouncing around behind it. The child, a girl, if the pink bobble hat and mittens were an indicator, stopped bouncing to sneak closer, peering at him from behind her mother's legs.

He blinked to clear his vision. Two sets of identical grey eyes stared at him, out of two heart-shaped faces.

The little girl spoke first. 'Is it Jesus?'

Chapter Eighteen

Christmas Eve, Afternoon

Lori squinted into the dark interior of the hut, ready to run if necessary. She had a stout branch in her right hand, hidden by the doorframe, and Misty had strict instructions to run to the car the second Lori told her to. She wished they both had footwear suitable for a quick sprint, rather than wellington boots. She balanced on the balls of her feet, as far as she could, ready to slam the door on whoever or whatever was inside.

He was sitting on a bench on the far side of the hut. Dark hair and broad shoulders, which matched the picture of Andrew Vitruvius, as far as it went. He didn't look like the picture on the back of the book. He didn't look too good.

In fact, he looked terrible.

A few days growth of beard, bruises and ... Lori swallowed. Was that dark stain blotching the front of the once-white shirt *blood*?

'What happened to you?'

'Long story.' He tipped his head back to rest against the wall of the hut. 'Thanks for being brave enough to open the door.'

Misty had crept forward and was peering around the doorframe, obviously having forgotten her instructions not to get too close. 'We're *very* brave.'

He clearly saw his mistake. The dark head tipped forward again. 'I'm sure you are, and I'm very grateful.' He hesitated. He seemed uncertain how to go on, which was strange. *Why isn't he standing up and getting out of there?*

71

Automatically she checked out his feet and legs. They seemed to be intact. No visible damage. 'Um … would you like to come outside? To the fresh air?' The air inside the hut was pretty fetid. She was trying not to breathe too much of it. He'd shut his eyes, probably against the light. They blinked open again. Dark pits in a drawn face.

'Nothing I'd like better.' He raised his left hand. Something clinked and jangled. He held it out to her. 'If you could lay a hand on a bolt cutter?'

'Shit!' Lori put her hand up to her mouth, swallowing the exclamation and hoping that Misty hadn't heard it. 'This is real isn't it? Not a publicity thing. Someone did a number on you.'

'Yep.' His mouth was a flat weary line. He chewed his lower lip with a very white, even teeth. It was a completely vulnerable gesture that caught Lori unexpectedly under her heart. He seemed to be debating something with himself. 'Look, on second thoughts, I think you'd better get out of here, with your little girl.' He hesitated, as if making up his mind on something. 'Is there someone local you could send, who wouldn't ask questions? I'll pay … for discretion. And if you could forget about all this too, I'd be very grateful,' he said. The half smile was forced and disjointed. Something new and different shifted under Lori's heart. If the guy really tried … 'It was, er … sort of a joke,' he said awkwardly. 'Not a very good one, and I'd really like to sort it out privately.'

'X for no publicity.'

'Exactly.'

Lori didn't have the heart to tell him he'd been all over the news this morning. It was Christmas Eve and the man had been through some sort of wringer, whatever the circumstances. *If this is a joke, I'm glad I don't know any of his friends.*

She dropped the branch and stepped forward into the hut to examine the chain, with a quick glance behind her, to check that her niece was not following. Misty had sat down in the doorway to wait, watching the show with the same interest as she gave a TV cartoon. Adults were clearly strange and fascinating creatures.

Relaxing on that score, Lori stood to one side of the bench, avoiding a bucket with contents she *didn't* want to investigate, and tracking the chain back to its fastenings. Vitruvius was looking over his shoulder wearily, following her movements. She put out a hand to confirm her thoughts, tracing the metal loop that attached the chain to the wall. *Jackpot!*

'I don't have access to a bolt cutter, Mr Vitruvius.' She couldn't help grinning. 'But I do have a screwdriver.'

Chapter Nineteen

Christmas Eve, Late Afternoon

Drew slumped back against the wall of the hut, staring through the open door. The light was just beginning to fade, but he could see the pale trunks of trees and scrubby undergrowth beneath. The woman and the little girl had hiked back into the wood, to find their car. *There must be some sort of track that the locals use.* The two men who brought him here had known about it, or been told. His tired brain turned the thought over, but it wasn't much help. He knew Mr Right and Lefty were Londoners. The accents gave it away. They weren't from around here, wherever *here* was.

Wearily Drew pushed his hair away from his face. Now that rescue was in sight, he felt floppy and lifeless, like a puppet whose strings had been cut. With an effort he pulled himself upright, wincing as his torn fingers scraped on the bench. The dark was gathering, the outline of the trees becoming less distinct. He couldn't see or hear any sign of the woman. He took a sharp breath, over a tiny spurt of panic. How long did it take to locate a screwdriver? Maybe even now she was getting in the car to drive away. *It's what you told her to do.*

Would she just go and leave him here?

Relief made him light-headed again when he saw the beam of light picking its way through the trees. She'd got a torch as well as the screwdriver. She paused on the threshold, looking in.

"Still here.' He dredged up the feeble attempt at humour, aware of the strain in his voice. 'Where's your sidekick?'

'Misty?' She stepped into the hut. 'Sitting just outside on a tree stump and pretending to be a Christmas elf. Apparently, Christmas elves sing.' She put the torch, a heavy-duty affair, down on the bench. Now Drew could hear the high-pitched treble coming from outside the hut. He couldn't make out words, but the tune sounded vaguely familiar.

'She says you're not Jesus, by the way. And you smell.' There was a hint of amusement in the voice.

'True, on both counts,' he admitted. 'Jesus?'

'*Whistle Down the Wind*. It's an old black and white film.'

Drew nodded, as if he understood. Maybe he *was* hallucinating. Could you hallucinate a woman brandishing a very business-like electric screwdriver? 'Sorry about the smell.'

She smelled rather good, as she leaned over to unscrew the chain. Cinnamon, with some sort of citrus undertone.

'No problem.' She was fiddling with the light. 'You're going to have to hold this, I need to see better.' He held out his hand and she put the torch into it, illuminating the blood on his fingers. There was a small in-drawn breath. 'You tried to free it with your bare hands!'

'Desperation.' No point in hiding it. He pointed the beam and the screwdriver buzzed into action on the fastenings holding the chain to the wall strut. 'Do you always travel with a loaded screwdriver?'

'I've been doing a bit of DIY lately.' The first two screws fell out and the hasp sagged away from the wall. She tilted her head listening, the elf was still singing gustily. 'I don't like Misty being out there when it's beginning to get dark, but she didn't want to come in.'

'I can't say I blame her.'

Straightening up she moved quickly over to the door

of the hut, looking out. Drew could see a light and the outline of a small shape near the trees. The child waved and his rescuer came back, quickly fitting the screwdriver into the next screw head. 'Thank goodness these seem to be coming out easily.' Another screw dropped. 'I'm Lori, by the way.'

'Thank you, Lori.' The hasp clattered onto the bench as the last screw lifted out. 'Thank you.' Drew put down the light and reeled in the chain and fastening, fumbling to wrap it around his wrist. He was stuck with the cuff and chain, but he was free. And without conscious thought, he'd made a decision. He *wasn't* dragging his rescuers into this mess. 'You go now, back to … Misty? If you just point me in the direction of the main road—'

'What?' She was storing the screwdriver in some sort of holster. Her head jerked up to look at him. 'We can't leave you here. You need medical attention—'

'No!' He'd managed to wrap the length of chain around his wrist and wedged the wall fastening in the cuff, to hold it. 'I don't want to involve you and the child in this.'

'And I'm supposed to just drive away and leave you here?' The light from the torch was strong enough for him to see her eyes narrow. 'Do you even know where you are?'

'Um …' *Oh hell.* 'No?'

'Ufff.' The noise was exasperated, low-pitched and rather cute. She'd grabbed the light and his arm and was towing him out of the hut. He didn't have the energy to fight her off, but he was going to have to try. 'Please, Lori, I can't—'

'Yes. You can.' She navigated them over the threshold. He stumbled and almost fell into her, then righted himself. His legs were disturbingly unsteady, now that he was trying to

76

use them. 'It's Christmas Eve, it's getting dark and you're in the middle of the Brecon Beacons.'

'Ahhh!' Heart definitely sinking, he still tried to dig in his heels and free his arm, but she wasn't having any of it.

Wimp.

Misty was dancing around the tree stump now, waving a small torch. She ran up, wide-eyed, when they emerged from the hut. 'Off you go, Madam Elf.' Lori nodded to the path through the trees. 'You can lead the way back to the car. Don't fall over.'

The child turned and headed for the path, still singing, lighting her way with the torch beam.

The ground was uneven, sloping down into the trees. Lori was breathing heavily with the effort of keeping them both upright. Shaking his head to clear it, he concentrated on keeping his feet moving and his weight off her as far as possible. And tried again. 'I don't want—'

'Look.' She flipped her hair out of her eyes. 'I get that there's something going on here that is beyond a joke. Way beyond – and I appreciate that you're trying to keep me and Misty out of it, but you really can't stay here. I'm not leaving you wandering about on the hillside alone. Come home with us now, so we can sort it out. Or if you really don't want to do that, as soon as we get somewhere with a decent phone signal, we can phone the police to come and pick you up.' They'd reached a narrow track through the trees. She kept pulling him forward. 'You know they have an appeal out for information on you?' she added conversationally.

'Shit.' Drew shut his eyes, swaying slightly and breathing heavily. He opened his eyes rapidly again when he tangled with a trailing bramble and nearly fell. *Shades of his journey with Mr Right and Lefty.* Briefly his stomach heaved. He fought the nausea, trying to order his thoughts. He should have been ready for this, but who the hell expected to be rescued by a woman with a kid in tow? A deep instinct to keep them both well away from the whole sordid mess was coagulating in his gut, along with the totally stupid but equally strong impulse to deal with the whole thing himself. *With a little help from a friend.*

A small surge of anger powered him to stand straighter. He wanted answers, and he wanted to look someone in the eye while he got them. The police would have to be involved eventually, but he didn't want to wait meekly while they investigated. He'd done enough helpless waiting, chained in that bloody hut. Now he was free …

His stomach gave another queasy heave and the brief power surge faded. His legs, stumbling over the uneven terrain, had the texture of wet cotton wool. He wasn't sure he had it in him to talk to the police tonight, even if he wanted to. *And after the police, will the press be far behind?*

He swallowed. He needed time to get a handle on this mess. 'This thing …' he said softly. 'I don't really think it was a joke. I think it was … malicious, but I don't want the police … um … I'm not sure I can face them tonight, anyway.'

He heard her inhale. Which was not surprising, as she was more or less carrying him along the path. 'Do you have to? Can it wait until the morning, if you contact your family tonight?'

Ahead of them he could see the bulky shape of the car parked under the trees, with the little girl standing beside it, waiting for them. *Thank you, God.*

He shook his head. 'No family.' She was offering him the chance of warmth, light, food and drink, maybe a shower. *So much for the bad-ass action man.*

Would it matter if this was kept quiet for another twelve

hours or so? Until he could call up his cavalry and start the process of kicking ass and taking names? It wasn't as if there was anyone who *loved* him who would be worrying. And no expensive search parties scouring the hills either, when no one had any idea *which* hills. He caved in. 'Until the morning.'

'Fine,' she acknowledged briskly. 'Things always look better in daylight.'

Chapter Twenty

Christmas Eve, Early Evening

The place looked like fairyland.

Maybe he was hallucinating *now*.

He remembered a book tour through Scandinavia at New Year. The car had turned a corner and in front of them was this whole town, spread out over a hillside, and every house with candles lit in the windows. That's what this looked like – the indoor version. He'd stepped through the front door into a tall space, full of twinkling lights.

And blissful warmth, and the scent of cinnamon.

The child, Misty, scooted past him to wrap her arms around a very large white and ginger cat who jumped down from a chair to greet her. She'd bombarded him with chatter in the car, most of which had simply washed over him, as he struggled to keep focused on his surroundings through a buzzing head. An occasional grunt in response seemed to satisfy her, in between grateful gulps from a water bottle Lori had produced from a bag in the back. He'd demolished a chocolate bar that she'd handed him too, then felt nauseous again from the sugar rush. *At least that, and listening to Misty, kept you from falling asleep. And you found out there was no daddy waiting at home.* He was apparently in America.

Realisation hadn't hit him, until he was crawling into the car. In caving in so pathetically to the promise of a night to get himself together, he hadn't thought that he might be bringing trouble along with him They hadn't seen another car until they were well away from the hut and there was no sign that they'd been followed. Which helped him to breathe a little easier. Now he appeared to have been demoted. Misty had lost interest in him when she could have the cat. Lori shut the door behind them, pulling off her boots.

'Shower?'

'God. Yes, please.'

She was moving around, lighting oil lamps and real candles, not just the L.E.D. ones. That was the source of the scent.

'Bathroom is upstairs.' She nodded to the staircase that ran up to a gallery. 'I think I can find you some clothes.'

'That would be … very kind.'

She tilted her head to look at him, clearly decided that he wasn't firing on all cylinders – *too true* – and began herding him gently towards the staircase. He reached the top by an effort of will. The chain at his wrist came lose as he stepped onto the landing, clanking against the banister. 'I'm sorry.'

'Why should you be?' She was frowning as he gathered it up. 'Maybe we can fix it somehow.' She showed him the bathroom, turning on yet more lamps, then left him, shutting the door with a soft clunk.

The clunk echoed around his brain.

He spun and opened the door again. She was part of the way down the landing, towards what were presumably bedrooms. 'Lori.'

She turned, stepping into the light of a large lamp at the top of the stairs, and he at last got a proper look at her. Nearly as tall as he was, slim, he guessed, under narrow jeans and what appeared to be several sweaters. Her hair was dark blonde, curling loosely around her face. Big eyes, perfect skin. *Lovely.* The word whispered in his head.

'I …' He put up his hands, fingers spread, not quite sure what he was trying to say. *Protect. You have to protect them.*

'Forget the police, I'll just get out of here in the morning.' He shook his head as she opened her mouth to speak. 'I know it's Christmas day – it doesn't matter. It's better this way. I'd be grateful then if you'd keep quiet about all of it. I … I'll sort it out.' He knew exactly who he'd call for help. Not the police. Not yet. *Someone who would do his digging without drawing attention.* He'd have to have a story for all this, but something would come, when his brain was functioning properly again. *Hell, you're a writer. You tell lies and earn money for it.*

He wasn't so out of it that he hadn't figured out a few things. He didn't think it was going to happen, but just in case …

'If by any chance someone comes looking for me tonight, I'll leave with them – just treat the whole thing as a joke. Go along with whatever they say.'

She was looking coolly at him. 'Do you think we are in danger?' Her eyes darkened. 'Misty—'

'No. I don't believe there's any real threat,' he hurried to interrupt. 'I don't think anyone will come looking, but if they do … Just let them take me, okay?'

'Okay.' She looked doubtfully at him. '*Should* we be calling the police tonight?'

Suddenly he felt unbearably tired. 'Maybe. I don't want to … but I really don't know.' He put his hand up to his face. His skin felt strange and stiff. 'I can't think straight, or not straight enough.' He leaned against the door jamb. 'You know about the kidnapping stunt, for charity?' She nodded, without speaking. 'Well, someone made it for real. Someone wanted to … hurt me. I don't know who. It was meant to look like a joke gone wrong. That's what it's going to look like to the police too. Whoever it was … I don't think they'd harm anyone else.'

'But you can't be sure.'

'No. Which is why I'll be gone in the morning. I promise.'

She thought about it. 'That will do.' She hesitated. 'I'm sorry. About all this.'

He huffed out a breath. 'So am I.' They stood for a moment, just looking at each other. With an effort of will he turned back into the bathroom.

'Mr Vitruvius …'

'Drew.' He swung to face her again. 'My friends call me Drew.'

'Right.' She nodded 'Drew.' She gestured over her shoulder. 'When you've finished in the bathroom, you can use the bedroom along there.' She waved her hand. 'I'll go and make up the bed and see about those clothes. I'll leave them here, outside the door.'

When she turned and walked away he stood for a moment, looking after her, not wanting her to leave.

Back view is as good as the front.

He gave a self-disgusted snort, shoved open the bathroom door and came face-to-face with himself in the mirror. Wreck didn't come near it.

Zombie might.

Dirt, bruises, bloodshot eyes, four days of beard growth. His hand half mangled. He looked down at it. As he thought, he'd all but ripped off one of the nails in his attempts to get free.

He stared at his reflection. It didn't matter how lovely Lori was, nothing was going to happen.

The pull of desire he'd experienced on the landing had taken him by surprise. He wouldn't have expected to have the energy.

Which proves something about the human male.

He wasn't sure he wanted to know what.

And she wouldn't be looking twice at you, *mate, even if she wasn't already with someone else.*

He put up his hands, scrubbing the heels into his eyes, and nearly knocked out a tooth with the end of the chain. He was an asshole, thinking what he'd been thinking, when there was a chance he'd brought a threat into this tranquil house.

How bad was it? He tried to order his thoughts as he started to strip off his soiled clothes. He couldn't imagine that anyone was watching the hut to make sure he didn't get away, although there might have been a camera in the woods. The thought sent a cold spike down his spine. He shook his head. *No – if they'd been watching, someone would have been banging on the door by now.*

The thought steadied him.

The whole thing was much more casual than that. From the outside it was meant to look like he'd either organised it himself for more publicity – he shuddered at the thought – or that someone had played a practical joke on him. Either way it was intended to appear that somehow everything had gone disastrously wrong. He'd reached that conclusion during all those hours in the hut. He'd wondered too what sort of spin Philmore had managed to put on it. He'd have found something. The man was a master.

But if anyone else became involved, it would be a whole different ball game.

His gut told him he was meant to die there, despite the debate between Mr Right and Lefty. An 'accident' was one thing. He couldn't see either man going in for wholesale murder. But whoever was behind them ...

His gut twisted again. Had he brought trouble here, to a woman who'd only tried to help him? A woman with a child.

He really should get out now.

He leaned one hand against the wall. Instinct told him that if he attempted to leave, his hostess would hunt him down. *Never argue with a woman who packs a loaded screwdriver.* If he got cleaned up, then maybe he could sneak away later, after Lori and Misty were asleep? He lurched towards the shower, hoping that hot water would make his brain work faster.

Outside the wind was picking up. A soft flake of white spiralled down and settled on the cold ground on the shadowy side of the barn.

Then another.

And another.

Chapter Twenty-One

Christmas Eve, Evening

Lori looked over the banister from the gallery, to check on Misty, relieved to see the little girl had found her colouring book and was totally engrossed, colouring in a picture to leave for Santa, with the mince pie and carrots for the reindeer. Griff sprawled watchfully beside her. Both would be wanting their tea soon, but in the meantime ...

She dithered for a moment. The Cwtch or the bedroom?

She chose the Cwtch, speeding along the corridor. It was unlikely in the extreme that Andrew Vitruvius would come along here before morning, but she wasn't taking any chances. She scooped up the evidence of her writing – a thick pad and a bundle of pens, mostly culled from writing courses and festivals – dumping it in the wicker basket that held the ring binder with her notes, her thesaurus and her dictionary. Her travelling writer's toolkit. She shoved the basket behind the chair and felt better.

She wrinkled her nose at the row of Vitruvius's books on the bottom shelf of the bookcase. She'd like to hide them too, but there wasn't time and she didn't have anywhere to put them. She belted back along the landing, checking on Misty again on the way. Still colouring. She could hear the shower running in the bathroom, so she had a few minutes.

Shaking up pillowcases and wrangling with the duvet gave her some time to think, but she wasn't sure it was such a good idea. She'd brought a complete stranger into the house, with her small niece, *just because he was a best-selling author*. She thumped a pillow to make it lie flat. That was as bad as thinking you knew characters in *Coronation Street* or *EastEnders* as friends. *And what the hell is the man mixed up in?* Had he really brought something dangerous with him?

Involuntarily she glanced over at the curtained window. Without immediate neighbours, Paulie had installed good locks and bolts for his gran, and in a borrowed house Lori was meticulous in making sure they were all engaged and locked before she and Misty went out. They were still locked. No one was going to be breaking in here tonight and Vitruvius would be gone in the morning, taking whatever trouble he was in with him.

She still wasn't one hundred per cent sure he hadn't engineered the whole thing himself, but if he had, someone had messed up, and he had paid for it.

And could you really have left him there? The state he was in?

He hadn't wanted to come with them. *You were the one who insisted.* Unless he was a master double bluffer, she took that as a sign that *he* wasn't a threat to herself or Misty. She didn't have trouble under her roof, although he might bring it to the door. *I really hope you're not being a fool here.*

She smoothed down the surface of the duvet and straightened up, looking her guilt in the face. Remembering. It wasn't just concern for the *man* that had prompted her in those first seconds. She could still feel it. That leap of excitement, avarice – she didn't know what to call it – when she'd recognised *who* he was. A writer, and a famous writer. The kind who might launch careers …

How low can you get?

That she'd discarded the impulse in the next minute, didn't make it go away. Which is why there wasn't going to be any sight nor mention of her own writing. And he would be gone in the morning. *Hold that thought.*

The bed was finished. She trotted over to the chest of drawers. Paulie had left a few clothes here, shirts and a pair of old cargo pants with paint stains on both knees that matched the colour of the kitchen walls. There were a couple of unopened packets of cheap boxer shorts and a new toothbrush too. Left, she guessed, from when Paulie was staying over with his grandmother to help his mother out. In the early days before the dementia got too great a hold, when she'd still recognised her grandson.

Lori rummaged, pulling out a shirt and holding it up. It looked okay. Drew Vitruvius was big, but Paulie still played rugby and had the build to match, so that was no problem. She dropped the clothes on a chair and looked round. Water. He'd demolished a whole bottle in the car. There was an unopened litre bottle in her room. She fetched it, dropping the clothes beside the bathroom door as she passed and returning to put the bottle beside the bed, along with the first aid kit that lived with a fire extinguisher in a small cupboard on the landing. She wasn't planning on playing Florence Nightingale, but there were antiseptic and plasters in there, if they were needed.

She'd got close enough to Vitruvius helping him get here. She could still feel the tingling in her fingers from holding on to that well-muscled arm. Once he was out of the shower, smelling good and looking at her with those deep brown eyes ... It might be Christmas Eve, but she wasn't helping herself to that sort of present. The man was attractive, even bruised and battered. More attractive in the flesh than looking macho on the back of a book jacket. She'd always been a sucker for a wounded hero.

Wounded, not totally screwed up.

With a silent whisper of thanks that they would only be under the same roof for a few hours, she went down to see about food for Misty and Griff. She'd deal with food for her unexpected guest later. The presence of a strange man in the house meant there wouldn't be any cuddling on the sofa tonight in Christmas pyjamas, but she could still break out the mince pies and amaretti biscuits.

They'd eaten cheese on toast and shared a mince pie and now Misty was inspecting the room, inch by inch, deciding on the best place to hang her stocking, with Griff pacing solemnly beside her. Lori sat on the sofa, nibbling on an almond biscuit and wondering what had become of their unexpected guest. She'd heard the bathroom door open, followed by a waft of damp, soap-scented air, which had rolled down the staircase when she'd been cutting up the cheese, but since then, nothing. She swallowed the last delicious crumb of biscuit and stood up. 'I won't be a minute, sweetie.'

She knocked softly on the door. 'Hello?' before cautiously putting her head round it. The bedside light was still on. Drew was flat out on the duvet, face down. He didn't stir as she moved to stand at the foot of the bed. She waited, to see if he'd sit up, but nothing happened. She looked round, taking stock. The level in the water bottle had gone down; he was dressed in Paulie's shirt and one of the pairs of underpants. She kept her eyes away from a sturdy pair of legs, furred with dark hair, walking round to stand at the head of the bed. His hands were splayed out either side of his head. He'd done a workmanlike job with plasters and a bandage to tether the cuff and chain in place.

She rescued the first aid kit, still open and balanced precariously on the edge of the bed. Gingerly she put her fingers on the side of his neck. His skin was warm and his

89

pulse was even. She pulled her hand away quickly as he moved one of his, to rub where she'd touched him. He let out a muted puttering noise and dropped his hand again.

The tension in her shoulders eased away. *Not unconscious, just asleep*. She picked up a heavy knitted throw from the chair and wrapped it around him, leaving the light on, but pressing the base so that the brightness dimmed a little. It might help if he woke up later, disorientated.

Everything was done. The stocking was in place, displaying interesting bulges, the foil container from the mince pie artistically arranged on a plate, next to the empty Bailey's glass. Misty's colouring book, with the completed picture, was propped open beside it. Misty was upstairs, fast asleep, with Bunny on one side and Griff on the other. When Lori peeked in, Drew Vitruvius was still out for the count, although he had turned on his side, burying his face in the pillow.

Lori had hauled the presents out of the cupboard beside the front door and piled them under the tree, wondering what the parcels from her sister contained for her abandoned daughter. There was even one from Dan. She recognised his large blunt handwriting on the card. What sort of convoluted route had *that* taken to get here?

Lori circled the room, extinguishing lights and setting the burglar alarm. She hadn't used it since they'd arrived, but tonight she armed it, just in case. Satisfied with the precautions she had taken, she climbed the stairs, carrying the radio so that she could listen to the midnight carol service, hopefully without disturbing her niece. She checked her phone and found a surprising four bar signal, rather than the usual grudging single. *Something to do with the weather? Or a touch of Christmas magic?*

She stopped on the landing. Vitruvius was fast asleep. With a signal on the phone, should she be ringing the police?

They'd made a deal. No police, no contact.

And no loved ones waiting anxiously for news?

No one he'd felt the need to get in touch with.

Isn't that a little sad?

That wasn't anything do with her. It was reassuring to know that she had a phone signal if they did need to summon help, but she wasn't going to break their agreement.

Around her the barn was quiet and still, although the wind was moaning a little at the outside corners of the building.

Christmas Eve and all was warm and safe.

No one could get into the house without them knowing about it.

Not even Father Christmas.

Chapter Twenty-Two

Christmas Day, Early Morning

It was still dark, but Lori's inner alarm clock told her it was morning. She lay on her back, staring up at the beamed roof of the barn above and wiggling her toes under the duvet. She was thirty-one years old but Christmas morning still had that magical breathless quality. Gratitude to Lark, for the gift of her daughter for the holidays, washed over her. And to Paulie for the gift of the barn.

Cautiously she raised herself on one elbow, looking over to the other twin bed against the wall. Amazingly, considering what morning it was, Misty was still sleeping. A head popped up though, and a pair of pale eyes gave her a long stare. Griff was awake. Lori put her finger to her lips and flopped back onto the pillow, frowning slightly. The first hint of daylight was creeping around the edge of the curtains and there was something about the quality of the light ...

With a muffled exclamation Lori slid out of bed and over to the window, pushing aside the corner of the curtain. It *was* getting light.

And at some time during the night, the whole world had turned white.

'Is it Christmas? Did he come?' The small sleepy voice from behind her made her turn. Misty was sitting up, rubbing her eyes. Griff jumped off the bed, stretched, paws extended, and stalked over.

'We'll have to go downstairs and find out.' Lori pulled the curtain back a bit further. 'But there's another surprise. Look.'

Misty rolled out of bed and scampered to the window. 'It snowed!' She looked up at Lori with wide round eyes.

'It sure did, kiddo.'

Together the three of them stood and watched as light filtered over the pristine alien landscape. Lori let out a long slow breath. She might be mistaken, but she had a feeling that their unexpected guest would not, after all, be leaving today. Misty, having looked for long enough, was pulling on her aunt's hand. 'Can we go down now?'

'Get your dressing gown then. And your slippers.' Lori reached for her own robe, draped at the end of the bed. Her alarm clock said it was just on the hour. On impulse she flipped the button on the radio.

'... overnight a freak weather front left large areas of South and Mid Wales experiencing heavy snow falls and blizzard conditions, with extensive drifting in places. Police are asking people not to travel unless absolutely necessary, as work continues to free motorists trapped in their cars overnight. At the Heads of the Valleys—'

Lori flipped the radio off again. Misty was darting around, flapping her dressing gown like wings. 'Freaky, freaky, freaky!'

Lori shrugged into her own robe, grabbed her niece, got her arms into her sleeves and did her belt up. 'Right, madam. Slippers?'

Grinning, Misty retrieved them from under the bed and put them on. Griff was already standing by the door, waiting to go. Lori wriggled her shoulders – normally the barn felt slightly chilly in the morning, but today it was warm. And there was a familiar scent in the air ...

They processed down the stairs, Griff in the lead and Lori bringing up the rear. Drew was standing at the window nursing a mug of coffee. The snow seemed to be several feet up the glass. He turned at the sound of the footsteps, raising the mug. 'I hope you don't mind.'

Lori was unsure whether she did or not, but Misty had spotted her stocking and the presents under the tree and was tripping excitedly down the stairs and Griff was making his morning 'going out' and 'breakfast' noises and the room was *warm*.

'I sorted out the wood burner too.' Drew was looking up at her doubtfully.

It's Christmas. Go with it.

'Thank you.' She nodded. 'Happy Christmas.'

'And to you,' he responded solemnly. They stood for a moment, a little awkwardly, she on the stairs, Drew beside the window.

Misty broke the spell, reaching the bottom stair and skittering across the floor, homing in on the empty plate and glass and the bulging stocking.

'He came. He came. Father Christmas came!' Misty bounced up and down with excitement, reaching for the stocking. She'd just got it into a firm grip when Griff let out a demanding yowl. The stocking was immediately discarded to meet the needs of her darling. 'He wants to go *out*.'

Lori completed her descent of the stairs. 'I'm not sure he's going to be too impressed with what's out there.' She cast a doubtful look at the height of the snow outside the French doors.

'I think that's drifted,' Drew suggested quietly.

Lori nodded. 'Let's go and see what the back door is like. Don't open it, Misty,' she warned as her niece darted ahead. 'The alarm's on.' She met Drew's dark look of acknowledgement as Griff stalked past them to mew plaintively beside the door. 'How do you feel this morning?'

'Much better.' He half turned to take in the snow piled against the windows behind them. 'Wasn't expecting *this*.'

'Neither was the weatherman. We'll talk about it later.'

From Griff's point of view, at least, the situation at the back of the barn, once they got the door open, was better. The vagaries of the wind and the protection of the outbuildings had left only a powdering of snow closest to the house, with patches of dark earth showing. Beyond that, the whole world seemed to be unbroken white.

And from the look of the low and lowering sky, there was more to come. Leaving a disgruntled Griff to his privacy they trooped back into the main room. Lori fell on the coffee pot and poured Misty some juice and they set to unwrapping presents.

Once Misty had extracted the contents of the overstuffed stocking, down to the tangerine, shiny pennies and sugar mouse in the toe – Lori had been rather pleased at finding the mouse on a sweet stall in the market at Abergavenny – and had been dissuaded from starting straight away on the peppermint candy canes, Lori decreed a pause for a proper breakfast before they tackled the presents under the tree.

'You must be starving.' Drew had followed her over to the breakfast island, leaving Misty to show off a new pair of novelty socks to Griff, who had returned from the snow and was contently full of *his* breakfast. Lori cracked eggs to scramble and slid a tray of rolls in the oven to warm.

'Just a bit.' He caught her eye and laughed. It sounded rusty, but it was a good sound. His voice had a husky edge. *Is it always like that, or is it the effect of a few days shut in a hut in a Welsh wood?* She flipped the eggs into the pan and stirred, taking stock of him. Clean, dressed in Paulie's clothes and with a night's sleep, he looked a great deal better, even if the heavy stubble, which she suspected may be hiding a few bruises, did make him look like an off-duty buccaneer. A sexy buccaneer.

The shock of the thought jolted her back to the job in hand, shaking the eggs so that they wouldn't stick. 'I should have said, there's cereal in the cupboard and the milk is through there. On the windowsill.'

'It's cool. I can wait.' He nodded to the eggs. 'They smell exceptionally good.' He was looking around the kitchen. 'You don't have power …'

'Generator.' She shrugged, bending to check the rolls weren't scorching.

'You want me to take a look?'

'No.' She shook her head. 'It's not a problem.'

'You're not cooking a turkey, or anything?'

'Nope. Christmas dinner is wicked witch's pasta.' She grinned at his confused expression. 'I hope you're not allergic to shellfish.'

'I don't think so.' He was looking past her to the kitchen window. 'It's started to snow again. Looks like I'll be staying a little while longer. And breaking a promise.'

'That's not a problem either.' Surprisingly it wasn't. 'Can't leave in this. The radio had weather warnings.' She looked over her shoulder at the swirling white outside the window. 'Apparently some freak weather system.' She turned to reach for a plate to dish up the eggs. 'These are ready.'

They devoured eggs and warm rolls, with Paulie's grandmother's hedgerow jam, and satsumas from the large bag Lori had found marked down in the local shop on Christmas Eve morning. Was that only yesterday?

Drew had a bowl of cereal for dessert.

Then it was time for the serious big box presents. Lori sat on the floor, at Misty's level, not sure if she was surprised when Drew slid down to join them, but at a slight distance. A watcher, not a participant. Misty seemed to have accepted his presence without question. *Well, she lives a life peopled with strangers* ...

It took nearly an hour to disgorge the content of various boxes and parcels, with pauses to allow Griff to kill his share of the wrappings. He was suitably pleased with a gift of a catnip mouse and a bag of his favourite feline treats. Lori was suitably surprised with the unexpectedly well-wrapped present Misty proffered, which proved to contain a pair of sparkly earrings that Lori had loudly admired at a pop-up jewellery stall in the market, before being conveniently engrossed with a display of local cheeses on the next stall.

'The lady put it in pretty paper for me,' Misty confided. 'And counted up the right money.'

Lori stuck the silver hooks into her ears and tossed her head, making the jewelled stars flash and glitter. 'Just the thing for Christmas morning.'

'What all the best-dressed people wear to accessorise their dressing gowns,' Drew offered, admiring the sparkle.

Lori pulled the belt of the robe a little tighter, hoping her face wasn't going pink

'Of course they do.'

She was perfectly respectable in warm brushed cotton and stout terry towelling, but she *was* sitting cross-legged on the floor opposite a virtual stranger. *A very attractive virtual stranger.* To give Drew credit, his consternation was visible on his face. He shot her an alarmed glance. Relaxing, she shook her head at him. 'Now, what's in that big box over there?'

The wrapping paper pile had reached mountainous proportions and all the boxes were empty, their contents strewn on the floor and furniture. Lark's presents for her daughter had been a selection of new clothes, with conspicuous designer labels, in tastefully sludgy colours, that barely got a glance from Misty, and a complicated looking fairy castle, which Misty greeted with delight, then pushed aside when she found it had to be assembled. The presents that were the biggest hits proved to be Lori's own and the one from Misty's father – a very grown-up looking box of paints and a handful of colouring books featuring animals, which showed that Dan was in touch with his small daughter's world, even if he was rarely able to see her. Lori had been a little worried that her own present was too young for a mega sophisticated four-year-old, but Misty had been delighted with the battery operated puppy; a furry bundle with a selection of coloured collars and leads and his own brush, food and water bowls. Lori had made sure that the dog was ready to go straight out of the box and Misty was delightedly towing it around the floor as it yapped realistically.

'She loves animals.' Drew was watching Misty's antics as she tried to introduce the so-far unnamed puppy to a wary Griff.

'Crazy about them. I know she'd love a real puppy.'

Drew slanted her a questioning look. 'Wouldn't Griff approve ... or her father?'

'Not an issue for either of them, but her mother would throw a fit.'

Now he was staring at her, clearly confused. Abruptly the penny dropped. 'Misty isn't mine. She's my niece, not my daughter. I'm just ... looking after her for the holidays.'

'Ahh.' He frowned, clearly putting information together. 'So ... Mummy and Daddy ...' He nodded towards the paint box. 'Not together any more?'

'Divorced. And my sister travels a lot ... for work.' Lori

began to gather and fold discarded wrapping paper. She didn't talk about Lark or Dan, if she could help it. Drew was sitting on the floor, leaning back against the sofa, knees drawn up in front of him. He seemed to be studying the paint stains on Paulie's cargo pants. 'And your ... partner?'

'There isn't one. The clothes belonged to a friend,' Lori explained, then bit her lip. *Hmmm – Might have been a better move to let him think there was a brawny rugby player in the frame, seeing as you appear to be snowed in with a man you know virtually nothing about. Except that he seems to have at least one potentially homicidal enemy?*

He wasn't looking at her. His eyes were glazed over, turned inwards to something inside his head. She stopped smoothing down a piece of paper covered with red-nosed reindeer. *It must be weird to be violently dropped into someone else's Christmas. And I haven't even asked ...*

'I know you said last night that you didn't want to contact anyone, but is there someone you should be phoning? The landline is off, but my mobile was working late last night.' She made a face. 'Possibly down to the weather, there's not usually a signal out here.'

He shook his head. 'No-one. I've been finishing a book, so Christmas kind of crept up on me. I usually go away, somewhere remote. With no phone.' Suddenly he grinned. Lori's stomach did a loop de loop that she was totally unprepared for.

'Err ...' She scrabbled to regain her cool. 'Like the Brecon Beacons, in a snowstorm?'

He nodded slowly. 'Somewhere like that.' He hitched himself to his feet and she noticed a slight wince. 'More coffee?' He put out a hand for her mug. 'I'll get it, if you want.'

'Er ... no. I'm fine ...but ... um ... do you do washing-up?'

'I can be trusted with the plates, yes.'

She looked out at the swirling snow. 'In that case, you can stay.'

He laughed. Low and deep and with that hint of huskiness. It trickled over her skin like warm chocolate.

What?

Chapter Twenty-Three

Christmas Day, Mid-Morning

Lori shepherded Misty and the mechanical pup upstairs, presumably to wash and dress, leaving him with the breakfast dishes and her phone. 'Just in case.'

He tried it, but as predicted, there was no usable signal. He replaced it carefully on the kitchen counter, running water into the sink and squirting in lemon-scented washing up liquid. There wasn't anyone he really *needed* to call.

Not on Christmas Day in a snowstorm.

He looked out at the curtain of white swirling past the windows. If he'd still been chained in that hut ... Whoever had set this up would hardly be able to believe their luck. He almost couldn't believe *his*.

What was the plan? Send someone in to make a 'discovery' or simply to wait? Much safer simply to wait. *How impatient are you, you bastard? How soon would you want to know if I'm dead?*

The sink was full. He turned off the taps, glancing uneasily at the phone. There was a handful of people who *might* be worrying about him, his agent and editor, a few close friends. Depressingly few.

Any of those so-called friends could ultimately be behind this, although he still had no idea who. And then there were the police. Lori said they were involved – probably called in by the TV people. Would he be tying up precious resources?

He looked at the phone again. Still no signal.

The sense of relief was strong enough to surprise him. It

was out of his hands. Nothing he could do. By the time he could get out of here, he would have a plan.

There was a jokey pair of rubber gloves lying beside the sink – they looked like hairy paws, and surely much too big for Lori? Carefully he eased them on, over his plastered fingers and the cuff. They fitted.

Washing up?

No problem.

A burst of laughter and the sound of running feet from above made him look up. He wasn't sure what was going on up there, but it was a happy sound.

Finishing the dishes he left them in the drainer. Filling another mug, this time with water, he ambled back into the main area of the barn, where Christmas had exploded over most of the available surfaces. A tent of shiny paper was moving around the floor in a disconcerting fashion. From the guttural noises coming from inside it, he suspected Griff and the catnip mouse. He began to gather wrappings into a pile, looking round. The tree, the lights, the gifts. The setup puzzled him. Lori was here alone with her niece. Misty wasn't with her family. The child's clothes, heaped in a chair, were all designer labels, but the contents of the Christmas stocking were cheap and garish. The barn was a beautiful conversion worth thousands, yet the power and phone line seemed to be off.

He'd gathered all the paper into a heap. He lowered himself onto the sofa and sipped the water. The muscles of his back were stiff from days of restricted movement, and there was a large bruise on his thigh that he couldn't explain.

Probably came from a boot.

He stretched, cautiously. He was used to living rough, but somehow the simple luxury of clean skin and clean clothes was getting to him this time.

Because this time you didn't chose to put yourself into that state?

He looked down at the plaid shirt and faded cargoes. How close and how recent a 'friend' was the guy whose clothes he was wearing? He hadn't missed the fact that the paint stains on the knees of the cargo pants matched the paint on the kitchen walls. *And none of this has anything to do with you.*

Just a writer's irresistible curiosity.

He cleared a space to put his feet up, still looking around. His breathing slowed, as something inside him stilled.

This was Christmas.

Something he'd been missing for nearly two decades. Not that he really knew what Christmas was, not Christmas with a family. The years in care, and then – *with your wife. With Kimberly. And Tyler. Your son.*

The Christmas that never was.

The strength of his grip on the mug was sending spasms of pain through his injured hand. He loosened his hold.

And now here he was, in the middle of ... something. It wasn't a traditional family Christmas, but it was still ... something.

Something you've never had.

Chapter Twenty-Four

Christmas Day, Late Morning

Smelling of Lori's expensive, special occasion shampoo, Misty was engaged in the important task of choosing an appropriate ensemble for the day. The red sweater with snowflakes was a given, considering the weather, and the white canvas boots with red sequins were suitably festive. Now it was a matter of deciding between the pink net skirt, or the purple. Lori, bundled into jeans and a red sweater with glitter in the wool, was sat on the end of the bed, towelling her hair dry. The labels in her niece's sartorial choices – the cheaper end of the high-street chains – suggested that Gilly had been responsible for buying them. The contrast with the tasteful neutrals and pastels of Lark's gifts couldn't have been any greater. Misty had made a decision. She would wear both. Wriggling into them, her eye was caught by the snow, piling up on the outside window ledge. 'Can I make a snowman? Will Mr Drew help me?'

'You'll have to ask him.' Clearly aunts were not considered to be good snowman technicians. 'It will have to stop snowing first. If you go out in this, *you* will turn into a snowman.'

Tickled by the idea, Misty laughed, running over to the window to peer out. 'Lots and lots of snow.'

Lori considered her niece's back view, the glitter and the clashing colours. It was all very Misty. And her sister was missing this. Although, if her daughter had gone with her to the Seychelles, she probably would be wearing pastels. Lori bent to pick up the clothes Misty had pulled from the wardrobe and rejected. She'd wondered again about her niece's reaction to Drew's unexpected intrusion into their Christmas, but Misty seemed to have accepted it without question. Lori inserted a hanger under the straps of a pale blue tutu and carried it back to the wardrobe. From the label and the quality of the fabric, soft and slippery under her fingers, it was one of Lark's choices, so she did have some handle on her daughter's preferences. *Or someone in the entourage does.*

Lori shook her head slowly. Misty was a sunny, outgoing and tolerant child, mature for her years, but was it really the way for a four-year-old to live? Once the holiday was over she had to try to do something about it.

She held out her hand to her niece. 'Come on, snowflake. Let's go and check that Griff hasn't eaten Mr Drew.' Misty put a small paw into Lori's, giggling. 'That's silly. Griff isn't big enough. 'sides, he's had his breakfast.' She tilted her head on one side, looking up at her aunt, suddenly solemn. 'Mr Drew didn't have any presents.'

Lori took a sharp breath. Dangerous ground. In several directions. 'That's because we weren't expecting him to be here,' she said carefully.

Misty was frowning. 'But didn't Father Christmas know?'

'Father Christmas doesn't work the same way for grown-ups. All Mr Drew's presents will be waiting for him at home, where he's meant to be, with his friends.' She held her breath. After a second, Misty nodded, but she still had a question. 'Father Christmas won't be looking in the place we found him?'

'No, pet. That was … a joke. A silly joke that someone played on him.' She knelt down to Misty's level. 'But we found him, so that is as good as a Christmas present.'

Misty preened. 'We were clever. And the fairies in the wood must have helped.'

'I'm sure they did. Are you ready to go down now?'

When they got downstairs Drew had cleared a space on the floor and laid out the pieces of the fairy castle, watched closely by Griff, who was sitting on the arm of the sofa, supervising.

'Ahah!' He looked up with a smile. Lori's insides did the loopy thing again. 'I need an assistant who knows about fairies. You look like a good prospect.' Misty didn't need to be invited twice. Two heads, one dark and one fair, bent over the pieces of the castle. Lori flipped on the radio, to a station playing Christmas tunes, grabbed a bin bag from under the sink and began to collect wrapping paper.

His damaged hand was making construction of the castle painfully slow, but Misty was proving an able castle-builder's mate, knowing exactly where and how to hold the pieces so he could fit them together.

'Tea break.'

'Oh, thanks.' He nodded as Lori put a cup of tea down beside him. There was a chocolate biscuit in the saucer.

'Eat it before it melts.'

Misty was already two mouthfuls into her biscuit. Lori perched on the arm of the sofa that Griff had just vacated, holding her tea. 'I think she's going to be an engineer, when she grows up.'

'No.' Misty denied it through a spray of crumbs. 'I'm going to look after animals and paint pictures.'

'That's good too.' Carefully Drew leaned back, lying on the floor, propped on one elbow. He'd just caught a breath of the same scent on Lori, when she bent to give him the cup, as was on the child's hair. Shampoo, he guessed. That was family. Sharing things. Inside him something twisted. Warmth. Light. People. Close to you and you close to them.

You could have been alone in that hut, slowly freezing …

Lori nudged him with her toe. 'Don't think about it.'

He looked up, and got a shock at the understanding in her eyes. *She knew where your mind was.* And then a double shock when he realised abruptly how much he wanted to hold on to that understanding. *That, and maybe kiss the woman senseless.*

He swallowed the rest of his tea in one mouthful. 'Ready to go back to work, castle builder's mate?'

By the time lunch was ready – Christmas was a never-ending stream of food – he and Misty had the castle put together. Carefully, he lifted it on to a side table. Lori was called over to admire it. 'It looks awesome,' she agreed. 'Wait a minute, I've got an idea.' She scooted off, collecting things from around the room. Misty looked at him with a question in her eyes.

'Dunno mate, your guess is as good as mine.'

'Wait and see,' Lori admonished when she came back. Opening the front of the castle she popped a couple of the Christmas tree lights inside, shut it up and scattered some wisps of artificial snow around the base. The lights blinked in the windows and the snow shone. 'There, now it's a *winter* fairy castle.'

'It's beautiful.' Misty hugged her aunt's legs 'Thank you Auntie Lori.'

Lori gave her a mock bow, laughing. 'Now wash your hands and let's eat.'

Christmas lunch was cuttlefish ink spaghetti paired with a jar of clam and tomato sauce. The pasta was as black as a witch's hat. There was a vegetable casserole too, that had been cooking slowly in the oven all morning, filling the barn with scent – a spicy mix of tomato, peppers and aubergines, topped with cheese, and a plate of warm garlic bread. It looked totally un-festive and tasted delicious. After that, and a helping of Christmas pudding, Drew was too full to move. Lori waved him off from more washing-up. 'I've got this, you can do teatime.'

'Teatime!' He groaned and subsided on the nearest sofa, pulling a cushion over his face. 'Never.'

Lori turned up the radio for the Queen's speech and came to sit on a chair opposite him. Misty was lying on the rug, nursing Griff and the toy dog, still without a name. Drew eased himself into a more comfortable position on the sofa, careful to avoid the various bruises. His hand was throbbing a little, but not enough to worry about. He'd been using it too much. If he rested it, the pain would stop.

If he wanted something to worry about, the sudden surge of feeling towards the woman sitting opposite him could come high on the list. Where had that surge of desire ... lust ... come from?

Proximity, it had to be proximity.

And gratitude.

And circumstances of the day. The child. The decorated barn ...

He dropped his head on to the cushion, listening as the National Anthem played. He'd always avoided all this – the traditional stuff. But today it had wrapped around him. In fact ...

He hadn't finished the thought when he fell headlong into sleep.

Chapter Twenty-Five

Christmas Day, Late Afternoon

When he woke again Misty was seated at the table, carefully painting a picture. Lori had pulled a chair close to the window and was writing in a small notebook. She dropped it down beside her in the chair when he moved, and looked over at him.

He stretched, yawning. 'How long did I sleep?'

'About an hour. It's stopped snowing.'

He shook his head to clear it, then rolled off the sofa to go and stand beside her. Outside was a strange alien world, full of humps and mysterious hummocks and flat plains of unbroken white. There was a brief flash of colour as a robin flitted from a small bird-bath towards a bush that was plastered with snow on one side, but had clear branches on the other. The bird stood on a branch for a second, then disappeared further into the bush.

'He was singing earlier,' Lori said. 'Apparently they're very territorial. They sing to ward off intruders. We got that door open.' Lori nodded to the one sheltered by the bush. 'Just enough to clear the bird-bath and put out some fresh drinking water. On the other door the snow is over Misty's head. It said on the radio that they're still digging people out of cars who were trapped last night.' She paused. 'You've dropped out of the news, by the way ... at least for now.'

'Good.'

Drew stood for a long, silent moment, looking out and thinking about the hut. Depending on the direction of the wind, it could have been nearly buried. With a man inside, hungry and thirsty and already chilled to the bone ...

'Don't.' Lori tapped him on the leg.

He turned, and for another long moment they just looked at each other. 'If you and Misty hadn't come along—'

'Don't,' she repeated, shaking her head. There seemed to be colour high up on her cheekbones, but the light was fading and he couldn't be sure.

'I'm just grateful you were there. When I heard you singing ...' He tilted his head. 'I was a bit groggy. I can't remember whether you said. Why were you in the woods?'

'Why else?' Suddenly she grinned. Something in his chest vibrated. 'Looking for fairies.'

'Of course.' He digested that for a beat. 'And you got me instead. Thank you. Again.'

'There's no need.' She stood up quickly. If he hadn't stepped back, she could have been in his arms.

He let her move past him to fuss with lamps and candles, creating warm scented pools of light around the barn. They had tea – he found he could manage a sandwich and a piece of Christmas cake after all.

Once he'd done his thing with the dishes, they played snakes and ladders, on a board that looked like a museum piece. For some reason he and Misty seemed to find all the snakes. Lori, with some weird alchemy, ascended smoothly by a series of ladders.

'You weren't kidding when you said that was witch's pasta,' he complained as he slithered all the way back down the board for the third time.

Misty was jumping in her seat and crowing when she finally made it up the last ladder and won a game.

'That's it.' Lori ruffled her niece's hair. 'Enough

excitement before bedtime.' She gathered up the dice and counters. Misty wriggled in her chair. 'Can I have a story?'

'Of course you can.' Having stashed the board in a cupboard, Lori flopped onto the sofa and patted her lap. Misty crawled into it. Griff appeared from somewhere and jumped up on Lori's other side. She stroked his head, and the cat butted her hand, purring, before sitting up to wash.

Drew stayed where he was, at the table. 'Do you need a story book?'

'Noooo!' Misty shook her head so that her curls bounced. 'Auntie Lori tells stories out of her head.'

'Good trick.' Drew grinned and moved to settle himself in the armchair by the window. Lori had pulled over the curtains but left a sliver of glass free between them. The moon had risen, casting a cold, clear shimmer over a breathless white world.

Shifting the chair at an angle, so he couldn't be seen silhouetted by the lamp and candlelight, he stared out. The scent of cinnamon and incense curled around the room. Lori's voice rose and fell with the rhythm of the story. Nothing moved on the other side of the window.

He could use the time to figure out the moves he had to make in the game he had unwittingly been drawn into. He'd been manoeuvred like a pawn, and it didn't sit well. *Not to mention the small matter of attempted murder.*

He lifted his arm to rest it on the arm of the chair, and the chain clinked. He'd cleaned the skin and padded around the cuff, but the metal ring had chafed deep into his wrist. It was going to take a while to heal. It might even leave a scar.

He leaned his head against the back of the chair. If he could get to the outbuildings tomorrow, maybe he could find something to get the bloody thing off, or at least clip the chain, although the links looked as if they'd been soldered. And if he could dig out Lori's car from the carport behind the house ... They weren't too far from the main road. Would the gritters and ploughs have been out on Christmas Day?

With a sharp indrawn breath he backtracked smartly. If they used the car they needed to be careful. He didn't want Lori delivering him *anywhere* if there was a chance they might be seen together, or caught on a camera. He didn't want anything to connect them. There *was* no connection and that's how it had to stay. He didn't want Lori or, God forbid, Misty, drawn into this. He'd leave as soon as he could. If he could get to the main road on foot, he could probably hitch a ride.

The thought left an unexpectedly cold feeling, low in his stomach. *Well, yes who wants to stand by the side of the road, thumbing.*

But if that was how it had to be ...

'And then the Princess with the silver dress and the long black hair, climbed to the top of the tower, to the room at the very very top, with the old wooden door, that no one had opened for a hundred years ...'

Lori's voice had been twining itself into his consciousness for some time. Now he leaned forward, attention caught by the story. The little group on the sofa was illuminated by a battery lamp and a candelabra, soft flickering light setting highlights into blonde curls. Misty was sitting up, eyes wide, thumb in her mouth, entranced. Even the cat had stopped washing himself and seemed to be listening. And the battery dog on the floor by Lori's feet. *And me.*

And the story unfolded, drawing them all in. Like magic.

'Then the Prince gave the Princess his mother's ring, and the finest hawk from the palace mews, and the Princess gave the Prince her father's sword, and the boldest stallion from her royal stable, and they rode out of the castle together, into the dawn, and a whole new adventure.'

There was a long pregnant pause. Misty drew in a deep shuddering breath. 'Oh, Auntie Lori, that was lovely.'

Drew's body jerked, dropped back unceremoniously into reality. For a moment, no – a bit longer than a moment, he'd *been* in that castle, travelled that dusty white road …

'You have a gift.' His voice sounded raw and husky. Lori's head turned slowly towards him, as if she'd forgotten he was there. He would almost have said there was alarm on her face. She *had* forgotten he was there.

And isn't that good for a guy's ego?

'I didn't realise you were listening.' She seemed flustered, not meeting his eyes. 'I like to tell stories, and this one's a good audience.' She tousled Misty's hair. 'And now it's time for bed, young lady.'

Misty made a token protest, but her eyelids were drooping. Lori hefted her up onto her hip, along with the fluffy dog, to carry her upstairs. Drew looked at the clock. It was half past eight. He and Lori would be alone for the rest of the evening.

Lori got Misty into her pyjamas and into bed, thinking about the man downstairs. When he'd been standing beside her at the window, without thinking, she'd touched him. Felt the hardness of muscle under the cotton of the cargo pants. And had wanted to …

She shook her head, drawing the duvet up to Misty's chin.

'One more story?' Misty made her eyes big and beseeching. 'Just a little, little story?'

'All right.' Lori sat on the bed and picked up the white fluffy dog from the floor. 'There was once a little white dog

who didn't have a name yet, and on Christmas morning ...'
She let her voice fall to a monotone as she talked nonsense
and watched Misty nuzzle Bunny and fall asleep. She sat
for a while, just watching the rise and fall of the small
chest under the mound of the duvet. She looked over at the
bedside clock. It was just gone nine. Unless she could think
of a convincing reason for heading straight to bed, she was
going to have to go downstairs.

Come on, what are you afraid of? He's just a man.

She smoothed the duvet and stood up, gathering together
Misty's discarded clothes. Just a man whom she might, just
might, find rather attractive. Maybe a bit more than 'rather'.

Oh! Wow!

Shock.

Horror.

She shook out Misty's net skirts and carried them over
to the wardrobe. *What's wrong with spending a few hours
with the man, when you've just spent the whole day with
him?*

Because it was dark outside and there were stars and
snow and a full moon ...

She stopped by the window. The curtains weren't quite
closed. The scene outside might be straight out of a calendar
or off a Christmas card. In the distance she could see
pinpricks of light – the nearest house – but otherwise they
could be alone in the world.

She shivered suddenly, rubbing her arms. Drew Vitruvius
was an attractive man, but that didn't mean anything was
going to happen. It did take two for that particular tango.
Although she'd wondered a couple of times, when he looked
at her ... Would he be thinking ... expecting ...?

He didn't have a reputation as a womaniser, as far as she
could remember. No exposés in the gossip magazines or

'tell all' interviews. She remembered an old *GQ* cover and something in one of the Sunday papers where he seemed to have ducked talking about the personal stuff. One of those 'the work says everything for me' types.

Pompous prick. That's what you thought at the time.

She stood still, then gave a guilty laugh. That *wasn't* fair. Whatever Drew Vitruvius was, it wasn't pompous or a prick. A sudden image of his dark head, with Misty's, bent over the fairy castle, rose in her mind. He was clearly shattered from his experience and still in pain from various injuries, but he'd mucked in with a four-year-old, eaten strange meals, done the washing up ... a perfect guest and a perfect gentleman.

So – he wasn't one of those successful types who thought they were entitled – and who expected to fall into bed with every stray woman they came across. He was probably too busy jumping out of planes and climbing up mountains. *He really isn't your type, at all.* She'd never read any of his books, never wanted to.

And another thing – he'd listened to her story, downstairs. *Oh, terrible, mega-crime, alert the story-listening police.*

Lori bit her lip, trying not to laugh at the conversation that seemed to be going on in her head. That was the problem with being a writer, or trying to be, there were very often conversations going on in your head.

She couldn't deny that praise for her story from someone who knew what they were talking about was a huge ego boost. She hoped she'd hidden it well. She frowned. A lot of the would-be writers she knew, having Andrew Vitruvius almost literally their captive and in their debt, would be all over him, demanding introductions.

She stood still, hit by the thought. That was it. She'd put her finger on it. It wasn't so much that she was frightened of an attraction to the man. She just didn't want to be one of *them*. The same stubborn wish to succeed on her own terms that stopped her from attempting to capitalise on her famous sister and ex-brother-in-law applied in equal measure to Drew.

But he doesn't know you're a writer.

She lifted her chin. Whether he knew or not didn't matter. He was still a celebrity and she was nobody. Even if she gave in to a passing impulse for a quick flirtation, and it would be no more than that, with Misty in the house, he would soon be gone. Back to his real life as fast as he could. And the trouble he seemed to be in, she didn't want any part of that.

Best keep him at arm's length.

Nodding to herself she finished picking up and stowing away the debris a four-year-old could create in the space of a day. She was strong. She was not going to throw herself into Andrew Vitruvius's arms.

Even if a little part of her wanted to.

Chapter Twenty-Six

Christmas Day, Late Evening

Drew pressed his hands down on the arms of the chair. Pain from the right one sprinted all the way up to his neck, reminding him that moves like that were a bad idea. *The same as it is a bad idea to be thinking what you're thinking about the woman upstairs. Good God man, you're a guest under her roof! She saved your life!*

Relaxing his hands, he focused on the flame of the nearest candle. Maybe that was it – the root of his growing ... awareness ... of Lori. A variation of Stockholm Syndrome. Fixing not on captor but on rescuer. He wasn't in a good place right now – vulnerable, needy, reaching out for contact – which didn't mean Lori wasn't a gorgeous, desirable woman who would stir any man's senses.

He shifted his head again to stare out at the snow. *God, you're mixed up. Mixed up and messed up.* He wasn't a monk, but since Kimberly he'd been ... careful about his relationships. It had been a long time since the curve of a woman's mouth had made his skin vibrate. If it ever had. He really couldn't remember.

He wanted to kiss Lori. More than a kiss, if he was admitting the truth, but neither one was happening. She was attractive and apparently free and he got the impression that a kiss – he was torturing himself with a repetition of the word – wouldn't be entirely unwelcome. But he had to get out of here as soon as he could, and if he started something—

The belated recollection of why he had to get out hit him

like a shower of cold snow down the neck. Someone wanted him harmed. Dead. No way was he getting Lori involved in all this. If there had been a husband or partner on the scene he'd have steered well clear, so it could be done. He got up slowly and stood beside the window. A movement on the hillside had his heart jumping straight to his mouth. He froze, then relaxed, smiling. Nothing to worry about. Turning, he padded off to the back door to investigate further.

Lori swung breezily down the stairs. 'Would you like a – oh!'

The big room was empty. Following a breath of cold, snow-scented air, she hurried to the back door, shoving her feet into her boots and dragging her coat over her shoulders. Surely whoever had snatched him couldn't have found him again? Could they have taken him silently, without leaving any sign of disturbance …?

She found him standing beside a large greenhouse at the back of the barn. He was wearing what must be Paulie's wellingtons and an ancient water-proof that probably belonged to Paulie's gran. Cross and relieved she thumped his back. 'I thought you'd been carried off again.'

Wincing, he turned, consternation in the dark eyes. 'Oh shit, I'm sorry.'

'What are you doing out here?'

'Look.' He pointed up the hillside. Lori looked. Her hand was tingling. *Shouldn't have touched him. Shouldn't have touched him.*

The wind had sculpted the snow into uneven patterns. Around the back of the barn and on part of the slope behind, the covering was patchy, with areas of grass showing. The covering on the rest of the slope was thicker. Against the hedges and on one side of the barn, the snow was feet high, in drifts.

Up on the hill where the snow was thinnest, dark shapes were running and hopping in the fragile moonlight. 'Rabbits.'

'I think they're hares,' Drew said softly. 'Look at their ears.'

'I think you're right.' Lori watched, fascinated, as the animals loped about in the snow, hunting something edible in the revealed grass. 'Some of them seem quite small.'

'Maybe a litter born late in the season?'

Suddenly and without warning, a pale shape swooped silently across the field, scattering the picnic party in all directions.

'What was that?' Lori squeaked.

'It was an owl. Didn't get any of them.'

'Good.'

'Softie. Now the poor owl will go hungry to bed,' Drew said, slyly.

'I expect he'll try somewhere else.' She took in a deep breath of cold night air. 'Look at the stars. They're amazing.'

'The Beacons are a Dark Skies Reserve. Very little light pollution. Bloody freezing out here though.' They turned to go back to the house.

Lori breathed again. 'Sorry I thumped you.'

'I frightened you.'

Inside and minus the outdoor clothing, Drew went to the window. 'The view of the sky isn't so good from here.'

'Hold on. I've got an idea.' Without thinking Lori put out her hand as she would to Misty. After a tiny pause Drew put his into it. Lori tried not to gulp. Even with the plasters casing the tips of his fingers there was a lot of warm skin pressed against her palm. *Is taking him up to the Cwtch a good idea?*

119

Lori dithered, but only for a second. It was done now, and he was standing holding her hand and looking curiously at her. Picking up one of the lamps, she piloted him up the stairs and along the landing to the book-lined gallery at the apex of the building.

'Wow!' The valley stretched away below – a long drift of white. Above them the sky was blue-black and full of stars. Lori held the lamp long enough for them to settle in the old leather campaign chairs, then set it down and turned it off. Plunged into darkness, the Cwtch was just a mass of shapes. No way was Drew going to see the contents of any of the bookshelves.

'Is that Venus?' Lori pointed to a particularly bright point of light. 'I can just about put a name to Orion and that's all.'

'You need to wait for a while, let your eyes get used to the dark. It would be better for star-gazing if there wasn't a moon.'

'It looks good enough to me.'

For over an hour Lori sat, enchanted, as the stars became clearer and clearer and Drew explained the constellations. His voice was soft and mesmerising and the Cwtch seemed to float between earth and sky and they were dark shadows, the only people left alive in an otherwise silent landscape. Eventually Drew's voice died away and they simply sat and watched.

Together.

Something that was almost painful stirred in Lori's chest. Drew's presence beside her in the darkness felt as intimate as a kiss.

'Earch!' The unearthly noise came out of the darkness. Lori jumped and the campaign chair rattled as she dropped back into it. 'Griff!'

The cat prowled into view, stretched, then butted his head against Lori's feet.

'I think he wants to go out.'

'Come on then.' Lori switched on the lamp and they both blinked, turning away from the light. Having got his way, Griff ambled off, pausing on the landing to make sure she was following. Lori rose, to stumble after him.

'Here.' Drew got up quickly to follow her with the light. 'Be careful. Don't fall on the stairs.'

Lori turned back as Drew moved forward. For an instant their bodies were so close she could feel his heat, and his breath on her cheek. Then he stepped past her to turn on more lights, Griff yowled again, and the moment was gone.

Lori dragged her thoughts together and followed Griff down the stairs.

Chapter Twenty-Seven

Christmas Day, Night

Drew rubbed his hands through his hair and down over his face. The stubble – which was fast becoming a beard – was itching again. Weariness was pressing on his shoulders. He sat on the edge of the bed, yawning. They'd settled the house for the night and Lori had gone to her room with her head down, barely looking at him.

His skin felt raw in a way that had nothing to do with the beard and the bloody fingernails. Exposed. They'd sat in the dark and watched the stars like lovers. He'd felt closer to Lori, there in the darkness, than he had to women who had shared his bed. It had felt wonderfully scarily *right*.

He rubbed harder. Felt, felt, felt. God, he was losing it, big time. He'd known the woman for twenty-four hours. He pulled himself further onto the bed, breathing deeply and evenly. He had to focus, to centre himself. He was a loner. He travelled. He didn't *do* long-term domesticity and commitment. So why were frightening words like that tumbling through his head? Stress. It was simply stress. He would sleep and in the morning everything would look different. With a groan he dragged himself upright and began to unbutton his shirt.

An hour later, Drew lay on his back, looking up at the beams of the barn, where they disappeared into the dark shadows of the roof. He'd thought he was too tired to *think*, but now here he was, awake and staring at the ceiling. After sleeping all night and then napping for a chunk of the afternoon, maybe it wasn't so surprising that he was wide awake now, his mind relentlessly ticking over.

He was still hollowed out from his episode in the hut – he knew that.

Normally he took time to decompress after one of what Clint called his 'experiences'. Rest, eat, make notes.

You want to make notes now, about being chained up for three days with a bag of seeds and a bucket?

No ... well ... okay, maybe. But not *right* now.

He'd spent the day celebrating Christmas. Something he'd run a mile from for years. And it hadn't been what he'd expected. *You did it.* Christmas.

And playing with a child.

He could cope around kids. Lots of his friends had families and their kids seemed to like him. And Misty was awesome – four, going on forty. There was a story there. It was clear from her chatter as they'd assembled the castle that she'd seen Disney – Paris and the US. Lori had taken pictures of opening parcels and painting pictures, but those seemed to have been for Daddy, not Mummy.

A well-travelled four-year-old, who wasn't spending Christmas with her mother or her father.

And then there was her aunt. Her gorgeous, mysterious aunt.

His breath hitched. He couldn't remember when he'd last had such a powerful attraction to a woman. *A woman you know nothing about – except that she's a great cook and good with kids.*

Kids and cooking? My, my, what a male chauvinist pig you are, Mr Vitruvius.

He grimaced – yeah, well. He couldn't deny that the idea of Lori cooking in his kitchen and then afterwards, being in his bed ...

Groaning, Drew resisted the impulse to bury his head in the pillow. *Do not go there.*

It had to be mixed up with his depleted state, and the fact that she was the one to get him out of that hell-hole. Obligingly the chain on his arm clinked a reminder as he moved. Back to the new version of Stockholm Syndrome. Falling in love with your rescuer.

Hell, wait a minute, who's mentioning the L word!

Whatever it was, he had to keep control of it. He couldn't abuse her hospitality and generosity by coming on to her. Although a couple of times he'd thought ... When she'd taken his hand ... And then on the landing ...

Do not go there.

Lori seemed to be a private person. Although they'd spent the day together, he'd learned very little about her. And he'd respect that. Respect her. Once he was out of here ...

He looked over at the window. He'd pulled the curtain back, so he could see out. He could still see the stars. The freak snow-storm had passed.

Tomorrow he might have a chance to hike out of here. Next day for sure.

A shiver went down his spine. He had to get out, in case someone went to the hut. Although it was sufficiently isolated to keep a prisoner, the hut wasn't that far away, as the crow flew. If they found him gone, would they check the local properties?

Mr Right and Lefty, posing as carol singers?

Well maybe not that, but stranded motorists? That would work.

It was safe for the moment. Nothing much was moving in the snow. He couldn't envisage pursuers tramping here through the drifts, acting casual.

But once the world started to turn again ...

He had to leave. If there was a Christmas gift he could give Lori and Misty it was that.

Lori lay on her side, listening to Misty's soft breathing. The day had gone quite well, considering. Drew Vitruvius had been an easy guest. A surprising one. *Not the man you thought he would be.*

Quieter and more subdued. *What would you expect after being chained up for a few days in the dark and damp?*

Lori chewed her lip for a moment, wondering if he should have had medical attention. He'd seemed okay. Just exhausted. They'd had a good day. And she was proud of herself. She'd kept information about herself and Misty to a minimum. Nothing about writing ambitions and famous relatives.

And the time they'd spent in the Cwtch, looking at the stars ...

He'd be gone soon. Back to his real life. And they could go on with theirs.

A Christmas interlude with an attractive man.

Attractive? Is that the best you can do?

Alright, drop dead gorgeous, sex on a stick.

With a grunt Lori thumped her pillow into a more comfortable shape.

Drew Vitruvius was famous, sought after, poles apart from her world. *And someone in* his *world* really *doesn't like him.*

Stay well away from Drew Vitruvius.

Chapter Twenty-Eight

Boxing Day

Misty was awake with the dawn chorus next morning.

'Wasamatter?' Lori rolled over as her niece poked her hopefully in the ribs. 'Sweetie, it's still dark.'

'But it is *morning*, it's getting *light*,' Misty said persuasively. 'I want to go out and make a snowman. And Griff needs go to pee pee.'

'Oh, all right.' Lori grabbed the clock and squinted at it. Ten to seven, which probably did count as morning? She crawled out of bed and found her dressing gown.

If Misty was early, Drew was earlier. He'd done his thing with the stove again, and there was coffee brewed. Lori fell on it with a moan of relief. Normally she was quite lively in the morning. She didn't know why she was so tired. Well actually she did. She had been dreaming and she wasn't sure, but she thought that Drew may have featured in some of the dreams.

Hoping that any pinkness in her face would be put down to the heat of the coffee, she started to mix up batter for breakfast pancakes. While they ate, Misty and Drew were in deep discussion over the name of the toy dog.

'Rex, Sniffer, Shep, Spot.' That was Drew.

Misty gurgled with laughter and spread more chocolate sauce on her pancake. 'He can't be Spot, he doesn't have spots.'

'Fluffy, Woofie, Snowy.'

'Snowy is good.' Misty put her head on one side to consider.

Lori reached to wipe a smear of chocolate off her face, before it spread itself any further. Drew was giving all his attention to her niece and had barely said ten words to her. Were they both avoiding each other? Suddenly the idea made her laugh. She looked out at the garden, becoming visible as the sun rose, and then at the toy dog, standing at the end of the kitchen island. 'I think he looks like a Snowball,' she decided.

Misty clapped her hands. 'I like Snowball.' She grabbed the dog, with mercifully chocolate-free fingers, and cuddled him to her chest, crooning, 'Snowball, Snowball, Snowball.' She looked up over the dog's furry head. 'Can we go outside and build a snowman now?'

'I think you'd better get dressed first.'

The radio was still giving travel warnings for their corner of Wales. While Misty was rummaging optimistically around the mud room, hoping to unearth a bucket and spade for snowman making, Lori found Drew standing at the open front door, looking over the valley.

Still white, as far as the eye could see.

'I don't think you'll be leaving today, either,' she said softly.

He turned towards her, frustration flaring in his eyes and the tense lines of his body. 'We know that some traffic is moving. If I could just make it to a main road, hitch a ride—'

'There would be no guarantee that you could find a lift. Not one to take you any distance, anyway. In this weather most motorists are probably not going very far. And it's Boxing Day – no public transport.'

He huffed. 'You're probably right.' The frustration was still there.

'So stay.'

'Looks like I will have to.' He was silent for a moment, mind obviously elsewhere. 'Sorry.' His attention came back. 'That sounded ungrateful. And I am grateful, but I said I would go as soon as I could.'

'But that was before the blizzard. The forecast said it would be warmer today and there will be a thaw. Tomorrow things will be getting back to normal. Everything will be easier. Stay and help Misty with her snowman.'

The grin was reluctant. It still did strange things to her abdomen. 'How can I resist an invitation like that?'

Drew was as good at constructing snowmen as he was at putting together fairy castles. Recognising her limitations, Lori found a carrot for a nose and some sprouts for eyes, and an old hat and scarf in one of the sheds to dress him in. Then they threw snowballs and made snow angels. The sun had come up and the temperature of the air was much warmer. Lori shaded her eyes with a hand to look up at the roof of the barn. Water was dripping off the eaves. 'It's thawing.'

Shooing Misty inside to dry them both off, Lori left Drew digging away the snow that had piled up around her car. Tomorrow he probably would be able to leave.

They spent an energetic afternoon, rampaging down the hill behind the house on a vintage toboggan Drew had found hanging on the side wall of the carport. By early evening Misty, overexcited and overtired, was hovering on the edge of a tantrum, mouth and chin stubborn, eyes narrow in a flushed face. Feeling partly responsible and therefore guilty, Drew faded over to the chair beside the window. He knew enough about kids to stay out of the exchange he realised would be coming. *Coward.*

Lori was giving her niece cool stare. 'Time to go upstairs, I think.'

'Don't want to go upstairs. Want to play some more.'

'You can play, but quietly. *Upstairs*. Pick out what you want to take with you.'

Drew sat still and kept quiet as Misty trailed around the room collecting her treasures, before dragging herself up the stairs, one reluctant step at a time.

Lori gave him a distracted smile and followed her.

Drew settled himself more comfortably, watching the night gather over the garden and the hill beyond. The steady drip of water and the occasional thump of dislodging snow confirmed the thaw. Clouds were rolling in, obscuring the sky.

No star-gazing tonight.

Tomorrow the holiday would be over and the world would be coming back to life. And he *would* be leaving. Reality check.

You think?

He looked around the barn, at the twinkling tree, at a fluffy pink cardigan abandoned on a chair, at Griff conducting some sort of stalking game with the catnip mouse in a shady corner. He'd slid into this so easily. Stuff he'd been running from for as long as he could remember.

A different reality.

New, with disturbing knowledge.

Yeah – like you don't have to be risking your neck in order to feel alive?

He looked down at his hands. At the damaged fingers and the chain, still wrapped around his wrist. He'd spent nearly twenty years throwing himself into things that might kill him and now someone else was giving it a try. Irony. Capital I.

He'd not done too bad a job in pushing that fact away, but now he had to face it. Once he stepped outside this ... cocoon ... whoever it was would be waiting. Awareness settled, like a cold lump, in his abdomen.

You don't know that they intended to kill you.

Yeah?

He had a plan now, of sorts, and he knew who he could go to for help, but that didn't come anywhere near the churn of emotion gnawing at him. He hadn't cared enough and now someone – a stranger, a friend, had called his bluff. In spades. *Life is precious when someone else wants it.*

He took in a deep shuddering breath. He'd done crazy things and been in some tough places, but it had always been his choice. Now the dark pit of someone else's will was drawing him in. *You have no control over this.*

His heart was thumping hard, a surge of useless adrenaline.

Fear. It's called fear.

Slowly he opened and closed his hands, watching the motion until his heart fell back to its normal rhythm. A potential murderer was out there, staking out the shadows. But there were things he could still control, and the highest on the list was protecting Lori and Misty. There must be no connection for anyone to find.

These two days never existed.

He'd walk out of here tomorrow, leaving no trace. After that, if he survived ... He shook his head against the bleakness of the prospect. Tomorrow was for leaving. Tonight ...

'Drew? Where are you?' Lori was coming down the stairs.

'Over here.' Darkness had fallen around him, enveloping him so softly that he hadn't noticed.

She came towards him, turning on lights as she passed. 'Were you asleep?'

'No, just thinking.' He looked up at the gallery. 'Everything all right up there?'

'Yes, eventually. She's out like a light.' Lori held up crossed fingers. 'Hope it lasts. Are you hungry?'

He thought about it. Tea with Misty had been a while ago. 'Yes.'

'I put a couple of potatoes in the oven. I can warm some beans. And there's cheese.' She hesitated. 'We could open a bottle of wine?'

He stood up, stepping back into the light and the moment, into the evening and the barn and the woman in front of him. Now he could smell the savoury scent of cooking. 'It sounds like a plan.'

The meal was simple but the wine was something else. An Australian Chardonnay. He'd tasted a few similar in a winery in Australia and said so.

'It was a Christmas present. From Misty's mother, actually.' Lori was absently fingering the label on the bottle. 'You travel a lot for your books. Australia, was that research?'

Which is how he came to be telling her about Australia and Indonesia, and the Rockies and the Isle of Mull. He was still talking when they'd finished the washing up and taken coffee and Christmas cake to the chairs in front of the small wood burner in the main room. Somehow he found himself telling her the real stuff. Not the carefully chosen quotes from press releases, or the interview sound bites, or the polished and edited after-dinner speeches, but the real experiences, like waking up in a tent to find a scorpion on his chest – bowel loosening – or falling from a boulder on a Swiss mountain – bone breaking. He even told her about the debacle of the train. 'I must be boring you rigid.'

She looked up from staring into the fire, watching the flames. 'No, it's interesting. What did you do – about the train?'

'When I found out that there was no way I was going to be able to stand up on the roof of the thing when it was stationary, let alone when it was moving?' The grin was shame-faced. 'Used my imagination – I relocated that section of the book from a steam train in the Wild West to a cog railway on an undiscovered moon of Mars, messed about with gravity and gave my hero superhuman upper body strength.' He flexed his shoulders in memory of a week in post-train agony. 'I think I fixed it.'

She looked startled. 'You do that, just make it up – I thought I read somewhere you research everything?'

'I try, but in this case the reality showed that I couldn't do it, and if I couldn't do it, then the ordinary Joe who was supposed to be my hero couldn't do it either, so I created somewhere and someone that could.'

'Oh.' She was looking at the fire again, thoughtful. The flicker of the flame played over her face. *Her mouth.* Something in his gut, and not just his gut, tightened as he imagined the taste. He wanted to kiss her. 'Lori—'

'Where—' Their voices clashed. 'Sorry what were you going to say?'

'It doesn't matter.' *It was a very bad idea, anyway.* 'You go ahead.'

'I was just going to ask where you were going next?'

'I don't know. I just handed in one book – the one with the train.' He stopped. Normally there was another idea already circling, waiting for its landing slot, but this time there was nothing. He'd even been wondering about taking a holiday. 'Maybe the next one will be set in the Brecon Beacons.'

'In a snowstorm?' She was laughing. 'I suppose your hero would have to build himself an igloo or something.'

'Probably.'

She was curled up in her chair, chin on hand, lit by the warm light of the fire. A log crumbled and fell, in a shower of sparks. Drew leaned into his chair, steepling his fingers, watching the flames. Watching her. They really didn't need to talk, but some imp kept his tongue moving. 'Are you planning another of your stories?'

'What?' Her head came up, eyes startled.

'Misty's fairytales?'

'Oh, yes. No. Really, I'm just looking at the fire. Ideas drift in and out.'

He remembered yesterday that she'd been writing in a notebook. 'It was a good story,' he offered encouragingly.

'Thank you.' The words were clipped and formal. Somehow he had put a foot wrong somewhere. He waited in silence and saw her relax. The tension in his own shoulders eased too.

They sat quietly, looking into the firelight. It felt strange, even a little disorientating. The after-effects of what the papers would probably call 'his ordeal'? Not that any papers were going to get hold of the details, if he could help it.

A wave of cold washed over him, despite the warmth of the fire. The hut had been all *too* real. Somehow it made the research trips, however dangerous and risky in themselves, seem kind of shallow. Playing around with big boys' toys, big boys' adventures. *Yes, but it does put food on the table.*

He looked up, away from the flames, as Lori uncurled herself from her chair and walked over to the kitchen. 'I just remembered.' She came back holding a box. 'Chocolates.' She put the box down on the low table between the chairs and they rummaged happily amongst the wrappings. 'Now *this* is Christmas.' Lori's eyes glittered as she popped the cherry liqueur into her mouth.

No, this is Christmas. A warm quiet house, a child sleeping upstairs, a beautiful woman with eyes dancing in the firelight.

And none of it is yours.

Chapter Twenty-Nine

Boxing Day, Night

They'd finished the wine and half the chocolates and Lori had made more coffee and Drew wanted, quite desperately, to kiss her. *Not going to happen.* He couldn't start something. Not now. *Not when you don't know how any of this is going to play out.*

Didn't stop the wanting though.

The drip of water off the roof had become a steady rush. Drew opened one of the French doors as Lori turned off lights and checked the other doors behind him. He leaned out, careful to avoid falling water. The air was much warmer and scented with wet vegetation. Tomorrow, roads would be clear. He pulled the door shut and fastened the security bolts.

'All done.' Lori set the alarm, then moved towards the lighted stairs. Drew followed her.

'Lori.' What made him say her name, at that exact moment, he didn't know. He had a half impression that she was already turning, before he'd said it. She was a stair higher than he was, which brought her face on a level with his. Her mouth. For a second he hesitated, then he leaned forward very gently, giving her space if she wanted to take it.

Her mouth was sweet, tasting of chocolate and wine and coffee and a spark of heat, against his tongue, that wasn't sweet at all.

She was *there*, coming to meet him, not pushing him away.

He slid his hand up under her hair, holding her head steady to deepen the kiss. Her palms flattened against his chest, not entirely surrendering herself to him.

But she was still kissing him.

Heat and sweetness and desire thrummed through him.

When he finally let go, sealing the kiss with a swift brush of his lips across hers, he drew his head back, looking into her eyes. This close he could see the flecks in the grey, dark striations radiating from the wide dark pupils. 'Lori …' He barely recognised his own voice.

'No.' She moved her hand and put it to his mouth. 'No more.' For a second she tipped her head close, resting her forehead against his. Then she pulled back and was gone, the muffled 'goodnight' floating behind her.

Drew stood still, looking up until she disappeared into the bathroom. His body was tingling, every sense on full alert. He'd just kissed Lori France and he wanted urgently to do it again.

And there is no way in hell that is going to happen.

What part of 'Not My Type' don't you understand?

Lori lay in bed, in the darkness, listening to the night, the silence broken only by the melting snow dripping from the roof and feline snores from somewhere at her feet, where Griff had settled to sleep.

She'd just kissed Drew Vitruvius. And she'd enjoyed it. And she rather wanted to do it again.

And the whole thing was pretty much a mess, because he was *so* not the type of man she was attracted to, except that it seemed that she was, and he was leaving in the morning anyway, and if Misty hadn't been in the house she had a lowering feeling that she might have ended up in his bed, or he in hers, and she really didn't do casual hook-ups.

She turned over, restlessly, to lie on her side. Griff put his head up and grumbled at the disturbance. 'This is *my* bed,' she reminded him in a pointed whisper. Griff gave her the death stare and put his head down again.

Wanting Drew Vitruvius was wrong. She had to convince herself of that. But she'd figured *him* all wrong. On the basis of the scraps she'd read, she'd assumed he was one kind of man, and he'd turned out to be quite another. Even tonight, the tales of his adventures hadn't been the macho boasting she would have expected. They'd been told, often against himself, with a sense of wonder and an understated, self-deprecating humour. He was an intelligent, healthy, well-built male with a nice body and a lovely mouth. It was perfectly reasonable to want him in her bed.

She was attracted to the *man*, not the celebrity, and they had spent two days together, with Misty, somehow making a sort of unit. *Like a family*.

But he was going back to his life and she was going back to hers and in his world someone appeared to be trying to kill him. The sharp pain sliced into her with a force that made her heart stutter. The thought of him hurt … Dead …

She gritted her teeth and dragged her mind away from the images that were projecting inside her head. That was another downside of being a writer – too easy to imagine the 'what ifs' and catastrophise about them.

And if anything told her that she shouldn't get involved with Drew Vitruvius, that was it. She had a normal ordinary life – no killers, scorpions or dangerous mountains in it, and she didn't need a man who had them in his. *Enough*. She rolled over, shook up her pillow, and settled down to sleep.

Things might look different in the morning.

Chapter Thirty

27 December, Morning

Misty was a welcome barrier between them the next morning, chatting to both of them indiscriminately, with her usual bright-eyed bounce, tantrum forgotten. There was a moment of sadness when she looked out of the window at the forlorn stump of snow that had yesterday been the snowman, but the task of choosing the correct collar for Snowball to wear for the day soon diverted her.

Drew seemed distracted, buried in his own thoughts as he inhaled a mug of coffee.

Lori put her phone down beside him on the kitchen counter. 'If you go up the hill you can probably get a signal – to ring wherever you need to ring,' she offered quietly. 'Someone to fetch you? Better than hitching.'

'No.' The unexpected refusal had her heart skipping for a moment, but his frown didn't suggest that he'd decided to stay for some reason. 'I don't want to risk any connection to you and Misty. There's someone who will help me, but apart from him, once I'm away from here, I won't be telling anyone about any of this.' He looked around the barn, then focused on her face again. 'Not even the police.' He grasped her hand. 'You won't be telling anyone either.' It was halfway between a question and confirmation.

'If that's what you want.' She saw the movement of his shoulders as some of the tension relaxed.

'Please.' He gave a clipped nod of acknowledgement. 'I don't want either of you to be caught up in this. It's my problem, not yours.'

She could see from the look in his eyes that his mind was made up. No point in arguing. *And really, why would you want to? This is an interlude. Once he's gone, it's over. Back to real life. Where you belong.*

She looked over at Misty, playing on the rug with Griff and Snowball. 'I can't promise that Misty won't chatter.'

'Once I'm gone she'll probably forget.' He was very still, with something that she couldn't read in his expression. There was a long beat before he spoke. 'Is there a phone box between here and the hut that I can reach on foot? Somewhere not too public?'

'There's a box at the crossroads, about a mile down the road.'

'That will do.' He gave her a strained smile. 'If you can let me have some change for the phone?'

'Of course.' She picked up her mobile and slipped it back into her pocket. 'After breakfast.'

The road was clear and the low winter sun shone fitfully. Drew hiked along the grass verge, avoiding patches close to the hedge, where the snow was still banked up. He had the hood of the old waterproof pulled down to cover his face. It was very quiet. Not even a passing car. He dug his hands into the pockets of the coat, and kept walking.

He could just *keep* walking. Walk until he hit a main road and traffic, where he could hitch a ride. As he'd intended before the snow intervened. But that was when his one idea was to get away as fast as possible. To put as much distance as he could between him and his rescuers, in case the threat was still out there. It might still be out there. That was a consideration. But now he had another objective. Things had shifted, over those two snow-bound days.

You kissed Lori France.

He ground his teeth. His mind had to be focused on the job in hand, not on regrets and hopes inside his head.

He didn't need the involvement of passing strangers, offering lifts, for what he was about to do.

A few days ago Lori was a stranger.

His plan now, such as it was, hinged on the phone call he was about to make. He was going straight to the help he knew would be offered. This call, from a public box, was the first part of the plan.

No connection to Lori or the barn.

The need to protect Lori and Misty had begun on Christmas Eve, when he hadn't known if he was bringing danger into their lives. And it hadn't stopped. He didn't quite know where this urgent need to keep them away from the mess he was in was coming from …

Or maybe you do? Because you couldn't help them …

He pushed the chilling whisper aside and concentrated on where he was putting his feet whilst keeping an eye on his surroundings. Once he got away from here there was no reason for any physical threat to Lori. She would simply be a woman who had helped him. That passing stranger. Of no interest to anyone who wished *him* harm. But that simple act would put her in the spotlight from the press and probably from the police too. At best there would be questions and interviews … and if investigations dragged on, maybe for months …

So no one was going to know. He'd managed to get free this morning, and made his way to this phone box to call on a friend for help. That was his story.

You tell lies for a living.

A shudder ran through him. The secret of an effective lie was to keep as close to the truth as possible, which was why he was using this call box. It was a deception he'd rather not be practising, and a risk, but he was going to do it, even if he didn't really know why. He pushed the whisper away, before it could draw breath in his head. The time at the barn had been precious. He wasn't going to taint it.

He was reaching the crossroads. He could see the call box, alongside a bus stop sign that leaned drunkenly over a wooden seat. Both the seat and the box were empty. He checked the timetable fastened to the sagging post. The next bus wasn't due for over an hour.

Turning slowly he scanned the surroundings. No one in sight. Just sheep in a field and a pair of magpies quarrelling in the hedge.

Abruptly there was the sound of a car approaching. Drew moved quickly back to the bus stop as if he was studying the timetable, the hood shading his face and his heart thumping against his ribs.

Was the car slowing? In country areas good neighbours sometimes offered lifts. *No. Not now.* Not when he'd made up his mind on another plan entirely.

Or … the spike of fear made him dizzy. Had he walked back into the world and straight into the arms of …?

The car sped past.

When the noise of the engine had died away completely, Drew took a deep breath and ducked into the booth.

He shoved the hood of the coat back a little, running his eyes down the instructions for making a call that were printed on the wall. Stacking the coins Lori had dug out from her purse in a neat column, he lifted the receiver. There was a dial tone.

He took a deep breath, with a disjointed prayer under it. 'Please let him be there.'

He'd first met Devlin out running. They'd become friends pounding over Albert Bridge and round Battersea

Park together, when they were both in London – as far as Devlin – no first name – *had* friends. Awesomely cool, the man was ice, except around his wife Kaz and small step-daughter Jamie. When one of Drew's dedicated fans had begun to wander into stalker territory, Devlin had provided some appropriate security. The fan/stalker had drifted away, with no harm done. If Devlin was at home now, he'd help. If he wasn't at home – Drew had no idea who he'd call. At Devlin's insistence he'd memorised his phone number at the time of the stalker incident – Devlin had some sort of an issue with phone numbers going back to the time of a former business partner.

He dialled it now, with hands that shook slightly.

'Devlin?' *Thank you, God.* 'Yes, it's me. I know … Trouble, as you might have guessed. Bad. Look, I'm in Wales. Yeah, the kidnapping was rigged, someone made it real … Thought you might … Can you square it with your police contacts so that they ease back on the search? … not straight away … No, I need to find out for myself who engineered this. Will you – thanks. I owe you. Yeah, I know.'

Heart a lot lighter, Drew cupped the receiver to his ear with both hands, looking at the roads around the call box.

There was no one in sight, in cars or on foot.

'Just dumped. With attitude … Money, phone, watch, keys – everything. I had some help, but I don't want them involved any more. Not until this is sorted. Can you arrange to pick me up?' He explained the location of the barn carefully. 'Terrain? Yes – there are flat fields right next to it … I *definitely* owe you one. No – at least – can you get into my place and get me a coat? There's a parka hanging on the door in the bedroom. And my boots?' Drew looked down at his leather lace-ups, distinctly sorry for themselves after days of hard wear in trying conditions. 'Under the radar, yes.' He moved his hand and the chain at his wrist clanked against the phone. 'And if you've got a bolt cutter handy, you might bring that too.'

Misty lifted her head from her painting. 'Aeroplane.' She slipped off her chair and darted over to the window.

'It's too loud.' Lori followed her over. 'It's a helicopter. Police, or the air ambulance?'

Drew met her eyes, over Misty's head. 'I think it's my ride.'

By the time Lori and Misty had scrambled out of the back door, the helicopter was hovering over the open field beside the barn. Lori grabbed her niece by the shoulders, holding her against her legs, afraid that she might run towards the machine as it settled gently onto the ground. She couldn't see much of the man at the controls – a headset and dark glasses obscured some of his face, but the chin looked determined and capable.

'Your friend?' For a second a thrill of fear spilled through her. Drew had been ambushed once …

'Yes.' Drew was standing beside her. 'Well … I … Thank you.'

'There's no need for that.' Lori ducked her head, pulling at one of Misty's tangled curls. She was proud of how firm her voice sounded. 'Goodbye.'

'Goodbye,' he echoed. As he started to walk across the field towards the helicopter, she took a last lingering look. Surprise put a small hitch in her breath. He was wearing the clothes he'd had on in the hut, and carrying the suit jacket. He must have changed quickly, while she and Misty were watching the landing. His silhouette was tall and dark against the low winter sun and there was an uncomfortable lump constricting Lori's throat. Just short of the waiting machine, he stopped. Her heart gave a strange, uneven bounce. He turned, running back across the field.

His mouth was cool and brief against hers. 'I have to go.' He ruffled Misty's hair and then he was running again, back to his ride, pulling himself aboard. Lori saw the pilot lean towards him, as if asking a question. Drew shook his head, dragging the door closed.

After a pause while the rotors gathered speed, the ungainly looking bird rose smoothly into the air. Misty raised her arm to wave. The wind from the blades washed over them as it lifted away.

When the helicopter was only a dot in the sky, and not even that, they went back inside.

'Well, that was exciting wasn't it?'

Misty rushed back to her paints. 'I'm going to put a helicopter in my picture.'

'That sounds like a good idea.'

Lori was looking at the neatly folded cargo pants and shirt on the arm of one of the chairs. She picked them up. *Go on. Even though you know it's a cliché.* She buried her face and inhaled the scent. Lemon soap and Drew. She laid the clothes down again. He'd cut all ties to protect them. She realised that. But she wouldn't know now if he was safe. He'd just be a figure on the news and in the papers again.

How convenient. A voice in her head jeered. *No messy loose ends left lying around. By the end of the week he won't remember your name.*

Lori looked around the barn. The tree, the lights, the swags of greenery they'd brought back from the woods. Did she really want to stay here any longer? 'Get your coat, pet.' Misty raised her head from her picture, curious. 'We're going up the hill. I want to phone your daddy.'

They trudged to the top of the slope that was mostly

green grass again, with an odd few patches of persistent snow in areas that had been in shade. *Yesterday you were tobogganing down here.* Misty skipped ahead of her to a flat space at the top. Lori looked down at her phone, satisfied with the strength of the signal, and pressed the number.

'Dan? It's Lori ...Yes, lovely thanks, and you? ... Look – I have Misty with me.' She beckoned her niece, who was inspecting one of those remaining patches of snow. 'Talk to your daddy.'

Misty took the phone, excited words tumbling out. Griff, and Snowball, and snowmen, and Drew.

'No, no, not exactly a boyfriend,' Lori answered the laughing question when Misty handed back the phone. 'It's a long story. Look, where are you? ... Oh, that's great. Only we really need to talk ...'

As soon as they were back in the barn she went straight over to strip the Christmas tree. Misty watched, big-eyed. Lori crouched down in front of her. 'Will you start getting your toys together, sweetie? Auntie Lori's house will be ready now. We're going home.'

Dan's black BMW was parked outside the house when they pulled up. The way Misty ran into her father's arms when released from her car seat told Lori she had made the right choice. She followed her niece more sedately, to greet her former brother-in-law. Dan shifted Misty to one hip and Lori leaned in for a kiss. Not for the first time she marvelled that this man, who was a top ten box office star in Hollywood and regularly featured in the world's sexiest men lists, didn't affect her in any way.

But Andrew Vitruvius ...

She shut down hard on that train of thought. Dan was looking at the house. The scaffolding was still in place but the newly tiled roof gleamed in the fast fading light and the front door had received a fresh coat of paint. Which was not, as far as she remembered, in the original plan. 'The place looks good.'

Lori nodded. 'Inside too, I hope.'

Dan set Misty on her feet. 'Now, I have something here you need to see.' He opened the passenger door of the car and stood to one side to let Misty get close and Lori look over her shoulder. What appeared to be a heap of brown and white fur on the seat raised its head at Misty's surprised squeak, revealing the long floppy ears and excited brown eyes of a spaniel puppy. 'Doggie!'

In seconds the pup was on its feet, wagging all over, delighted to find a human on a level easy for licking. The human was equally delighted to have her face washed by an eager tongue.

'Her name is Polly.' Dan reached over his daughter to snap on a lead. 'Now, do you think you could take her for a little walk, just to the top of the road and back, while I talk to your auntie?'

Misty, eyes as excited as the puppy's, agreed with a breathless nod. They set off together, Misty holding on tight and Polly dancing happily beside her.

'You bought the pup for her.'

'With her in mind, though Nevada is just as besotted.' Dan turned towards Lori, leaning against the car while still keeping an eye on his daughter. 'What's this about, Lori?'

'It's time, Dan. You have to take her.'

'There's nothing I'd like—' She heard him sigh. 'Lark has custody, you know that.'

'You have to contest it. And—' Lori swallowed. 'I'll support you.' She put out her hand to stop him interrupting. 'I know you stepped aside and let Lark have her way, because she made such a fuss, but things have changed.

Misty is getting older. She needs school, stability. She's not going to get that from my sister.' They both turned to follow Misty's progress along the pavement, chatting to the puppy as she walked. The little dog had settled down and was walking sedately, eyes turned up adoringly to her new human's face. Lori sighed. 'It was okay when Misty was a baby. She was a cute fashion accessory, easily handed off to a nanny.' Lori could hear the harsh note slipping into her voice. She couldn't help it, it was the truth. 'Why do you think she was with me at Christmas? Lark is staying in a villa somewhere in the Seychelles. She's dumping Misty on anyone who will take her. The poor kid is sofa surfing, at the age of four. But that's not the worst thing.' Lori took a deep breath. 'When she came here, before Christmas, Lark thought Misty was already with me. *She didn't remember where she'd left her daughter.*'

Dan's soft 'oh God' didn't divert her. She had to get this out. 'Once we'd tracked Misty down to Lark's former hairdresser, Lark went to collect her. She brought her back, and then just drove away, without saying a word, knowing that my house was being gutted. If a friend hadn't let me have a place – well, it would have been a pretty poor Christmas.'

Dan gave her a strained smile. 'A friend – this guy, Mr Drew?'

'No. Someone else.' Lori winced slightly. 'Look, I can't say much now, but can you forget about Drew? It's complicated. Misty might have stories …' She glanced towards her niece, still trotting along the pavement with the puppy. 'Can you just treat them as stories? I'll explain it when I can.' She looked up at her former brother-in-law. 'Would you take her? She needs you, Dan. And she adores Nevada.'

'And Nevada adores her.' Dan shoved his hand through

his hair, in a gesture that would have had thousands of movie fans swooning in the aisles. 'It's going to be messy, isn't it?'

'I don't know. Lark is getting agitated because Misty is growing up. And I think maybe Bruno might help. He's enthralled by my sister, but he's not blinkered. He knows what Lark is like. I'm sure if he marries Lark, he'd step up to the plate as a step-father, but he'd probably prefer it if he didn't have to.' Lori paused a moment, hand to her mouth. 'And maybe I'm just as bad as my sister. I haven't asked you whether it's okay, have I?'

An indignant 'of course it is,' from Dan relieved a lingering doubt. 'We're in the UK for the foreseeable future. We've rented a place in the Forest of Dean. That's how I was able to get over here so fast. Nevada is signed on for a short run at the Old Vic in February, and I've got two films back to back at Pinewood, so we're looking to rent a place closer to London.' He looked suddenly bashful, like an embarrassed teenager. 'We just found out. Misty is going to have a brother or sister at the end of next summer.'

'That's great. Misty will love it.' Lori hugged him, then bit her lip. 'Will Nevada want—?'

'Nev will be fine,' Dan interrupted. 'We'll have to have help with the baby. Taking Misty won't be a problem. And you're right, she'll love being a big sister.' The million-dollar mouth hardened. 'At least we'll always know where she is.' He shifted away from the car, drawing a mobile phone out of his pocket. 'Better get Misty's stuff out of your car.' He raised the phone. 'I'll let Nev know we'll both be coming back.'

Relief coursing through her, Lori walked up the street to rescue the puppy, who had got her lead tangled round her feet, and explain to Misty that she and Polly would be going home together.

Chapter Thirty-One

'Thanks for doing this.' Drew buckled himself into the passenger seat of the battered Land Rover, parked next to the administration building of the private helipad. 'I want a bill.'

Devlin shrugged. 'Handcuff keys in the case down there.' He indicated the well between the seats. 'Better than a bolt cutter.'

Drew found the box, wondering how he came to have friends – Clint was another – who carried handcuff keys as a matter of course. The second key he tried fitted. With a sigh he eased the metal apart and the whole thing fell to the floor. He returned the key, leaning back in his seat.

Devlin was navigating them onto the main road. In an hour, maybe less, he'd be in his flat. 'My people checked your place over. Discreetly. Nothing has been disturbed, and the cars and the bike are okay. They're changing the locks and there's a new phone charged and waiting for you.'

'Thanks.' Muscles relaxed that Drew hadn't realised he'd been holding tense. 'I didn't know whether the place would be ransacked.'

Devlin shot him a sideways look. 'Not part of the plan.'

'No.' It was getting dark. Drew blinked through the windscreen at the street-lights and the house decorations as they passed.

What would Lori and Misty ... He shrugged himself out of the thought. 'I need to find out what's going on.'

Devlin grinned. It wasn't a pleasant grin. 'Already started – but do you want to tell me your side of the story?'

Drew did, swallowing down the shadow of nausea as he recollected and relayed as much detail as he could remember of the kidnapping, the trip through the woods and the time in the hut.

Occasionally Devlin prompted him with a question. Drew ended with the rescue on Christmas Eve. 'The woman helped … She's definitely not involved. And there's a child … I don't want any of this getting back at them. I don't intend to talk about it. To *anyone*.'

'Understood.'

Drew took a deep breath. If anyone understood the need to protect, it was Devlin. He was nodding. 'Everything you've said fits with what I've got so far. As soon as it was clear you were missing, Kaz insisted I do some digging around.'

'How is Kaz? I should have asked.'

'Complaining that she can't see her feet. She's still got over a month to go. It's another girl, did you know? I have a house full of women,' Devlin said gloomily. Drew let that one ride. Devlin was fairly new to the family thing, but he was doing okay.

Family, now that's a word. 'What did you find?' he asked instead.

'The outfit that was hired by the TV people, they were paid off. A new lot took their place. Clint Edgerton Associates.'

'Clint. Shit!' Drew bunched his hand into a fist.

'The guy you pay to throw you out of planes and all that stuff.'

'Yes.' Drew was distracted, mind racing. 'Clint would never be involved in something like this – apart from

150

anything else, Mr Right and Lefty, the men from the wood … I wouldn't say they were amateurs, but they weren't of the calibre of Clint's people, not organised the way anything Clint ran would be organised.' He turned to look at Devlin. 'It was done to make it look as if *I'd* set it up – to raise doubts, if the police were involved.'

'They were involved and there were doubts,' Devlin confirmed. 'The TV people called them in. They talked to Edgerton and he denied it, but then, he would.'

'You talked to him too,' Drew guessed.

'Yep. And I'm with you.' Devlin made a turn. They were getting close to home. 'It wasn't him. He was pretty sick about you being snatched, and mad as hell that someone put him in the frame.'

'I put money his way,' Drew observed, dryly. 'But he's a good bloke.' He paused. 'Will you keep digging, but quietly? I need to know, Devlin. Who and *why*. I thought if we didn't let anyone know that I was free, you could keep looking … I had time to think, in that hut.' *All the time in the bloody world.* 'I realised—' unexpectedly his voice hitched.

'Whoever arranged this, is someone close to the action.' Devlin completed the sentence. 'Someone who knew the arrangements in detail, and was able to circumvent them.'

'Yeah.' Drew tried not to grit his teeth. 'But it could have been done on behalf of another person. The "why" might lie somewhere else entirely, and we need to know that. As far as fixing the arrangements is concerned … assuming it wasn't anyone from the TV, and I can't see why it would be, although we'd better look at them too.' He raised his head. 'If it's not them and it's not Clint, then it comes down to one of three people.'

Chapter Thirty-Two

New Year's Day

Lori slurped her cup of hot chocolate. Her last indulgence from the festive season. She'd just set up her desk and laptop next to the window in her tiny third bedroom. Her study! Hah!

The house smelled of new paint. She'd thrown herself into the decorating while the furniture was still in store. Now everything was done and it was back. Mostly still in boxes, but back.

The computer burst into life. Putting down the cup, and trying not to disturb Griff, who was sprawled across her lap like a small fur blanket, she opened her e-mails. And was tempted to shut them down again, when she saw how many had accumulated while she was offline. The very top one caught her eye. It was from Dan. She smiled as she opened the attached photos – Misty and Nevada romping around the garden, with the puppy. Dan had already consulted a solicitor over custody. The power of money, even in the holiday season. The woman was hopeful.

Lori wondered how long it would have been before Lark came looking for her daughter. It might have been months. Now she'd find out that things had changed, when Dan challenged for custody. Seeing the photographs, Lori knew she'd done the right thing.

With a sigh she finished the hot chocolate and scrolled down to the bottom of the long list, to wade through the unopened Christmas wishes and Happy New Year messages. *And it's no good wondering if there just might be a message from Drew. How would he know your e-mail address?*

There'd been nothing on the news bulletins about him being found, so presumably he was still lying low. She damped down the flutter of worry.

No longer your concern.

She'd been reading and zapping for half an hour when she came to it.

Her heart thumped when she read the name of the agent to whom she'd submitted three chapters and a synopsis, back in July.

Don't get excited. Don't *get excited.* Look at the date. Christmas Eve. The woman was probably clearing her inbox before the holiday. 'Thanks but no thanks.'

With her lip caught between her teeth, Lori clicked to open the e-mail. There were two paragraphs, but one line leapt straight out.

'I would love to see the whole of your manuscript.'

Drew waited in the corridor to be called into the conference room. He hunched his shoulders and had to remind himself to let them relax. The corridor was a perfectly serviceable space, with a well-kept if bland décor, as was the room on the other side of the pale grey door. Serviced offices, rented by the day. It was knowing who and what was waiting in the room that was making the space feel gloomy.

In the end it hadn't been difficult to settle on a name. Aveline, the assistant in his agent's office, who'd been responsible for liaising with the TV people over the arrangements. But they couldn't be certain, which was why he was here.

Devlin had set this up. The man had contacts from way back. The kind it was better not to inquire too deeply about.

He pushed himself away from the wall when the door to the room opened. Joe, one of Devlin's staff, gestured for him to enter. He knew Devlin wouldn't be there. He was in a room on another floor, monitoring events on a CCTV connection.

The police inspector was sitting quietly in one corner, flicking through a magazine. Two women in a room, waiting. Drew hadn't asked what excuse they'd used to draw Aveline here. He was just grateful that it had worked. His stomach churned. They'd positioned everything in the room carefully.

Aveline was sitting with her back to him as he walked in, but she could see the door, reflected in the mirror in front of her.

It was all over in an instant.

When she saw his face, she started to scream.

The police officer was on her feet, tossing aside the magazine, as Aveline swung round, toppling the chair, to launch herself at Drew, nails slashing at his eyes.

'Bastard. Bastard. You were supposed to *die*. I wanted you dead.' Her face was contorted, tears of rage and frustration pouring down her cheeks. As the inspector caught at the hem of her jacket, pulling her away, Aveline reared back and spat. 'I wanted to take your *heart*.'

Horrified, Drew stumbled back, towards the door. The gob of spittle landed harmlessly at his feet. Tangling in the chair, Aveline nearly fell. The police inspector grabbed her arms to hold her as Devlin's man helped Drew to regain his balance. The girl squirmed between them, eyes huge and dark and set on him.

'Why?' He got the word out, over the hoarseness in his throat. 'What did I do?' He couldn't think of anything. He'd barely noticed the girl, one in a long line of uniformly pretty assistants and interns with shiny hair and floaty dresses, an interchangeable procession running through Geraldine's office. Was that the problem? He *should* have paid more attention.

'You didn't *do* anything.' The girl's face was twisted and vicious. Alive with hate. 'You just *are*. The great Andrew Vitruvius. You get it all, the publicity, the tours, the TV appearances and for what? Writing stupid *adventure* fantasies. Brandon Phipps.' Her face softened at the name. 'He's worth a thousand of you. He can *write*.' She began to thrash again in the inspector's hold. 'I wanted to take your *heart*.'

'That's enough now.' The inspector shifted her grip on Aveline, who had crumpled against her, sobbing. 'If you'd step out now, Mr Vitruvius.' The inspector nodded towards the door. 'You too, sir.' She looked over at Joe. 'I will take it from here.' She was piloting the weeping girl to a chair.

Drew backed out. Joe followed. The door shut firmly behind them.

Stunned, Drew leaned against the wall for support.

No complex plot, no twisted joke, no revenge, no mastermind.

Just a girl he hardly knew, with an overpowering obsession.

'Fucking hell!' Joe wiped his hand across his mouth. 'What was that about? This Brandon Phipps. He's another writer?'

'Yes.' Drew found he was shaking. It was embarrassing, but he couldn't seem to stop it. 'Apparently a better one than me.'

Chapter Thirty-Three

New Year's Day, Evening

A dark headache was thumping at the back of his head. He probably shouldn't be drinking whisky, but he accepted it anyway. Devlin took his own glass to sit in the chair opposite him. Drew looked around. He'd got over the shakes, but the events of the afternoon were still way too close to the surface. After the confrontation in the office he'd given his statement and completed the formalities. A fresh wave of unease shivered through him. *But you really need to let it go now.*

The room was soothing. The sitting room of Devlin's house. Devlin's wife's house. She'd lived here before they were married. Warm colours and well-used furniture, a jumble of children's books and toys, thriving plants and cut flowers. It reminded Drew of the barn. Kaz, Jamie and Suzanne, Jamie's grandmother, were in the kitchen at the back of the house. He could hear music and occasional laughter and there was a delicious scent of something cooking. He dragged his attention back to the man sitting opposite him. 'The police have charged her?'

'They have.' Devlin took a sip from his glass. 'But she's stopped talking. And she has a lawyer.'

'This afternoon ... What she said?' He'd been running and re-running the words in his head. Couldn't turn them off. 'She wanted me dead, but she never actually confessed to having me locked in the hut.'

Devlin shrugged. 'Aveline was the one making all the arrangements in your agent's office. It was perfectly simple for her to substitute her own.'

'And make it look like it might be me, using Clint's name.'

Devlin nodded. 'If you were out of the way she thought this guy Phipps would get more attention and a better share of the PR budget.' Devlin looked at his whisky. 'There's usually money involved somewhere.'

Drew brooded into his glass. Shoving away an image of hate-filled eyes. *More than money.* 'Was Phipps a part of it?'

'Apparently not. He's been in Iceland since mid-November. Got back two days ago. The police will talk to him, but it doesn't look as if he was involved. They've picked up the two men. Your Mr Right and Lefty. One of them is some sort of a relation, cousin, I think. They're still looking for the others.'

Drew shook his head. 'The stupid thing is that Phipps is a good writer. Already successful. In a few years he'll be really big.' Drew shut his eyes. 'The whole thing was messy and amateur, with a core of something very clever inside it.' He opened his eyes again, staring bleakly ahead of him.

I wanted to take your heart. The words echoed in his brain. That, and her eyes. *Up close, and personal.*

If it hadn't been for the snow, might Aveline ...

He jerked away from the thought. *It was meant to look like an accident.*

He looked up. The shadows in the room were lengthening. 'It could easily have worked. It almost did. Bloody hell.' He finished the whisky in one gulp.

Devlin sipped his more slowly. 'Let it go, Drew. It's done.'

Drew exhaled. 'I never want to go through anything like that again.' He put his empty glass down carefully on a side table. 'I've got another favour to ask.'

'Which is?' Devlin asked warily, but he was smiling.

'I need some lessons in self-defence.'

His headache was gone. Drew walked slowly along the

street, pausing at the corner to look up. He could see the stars, but they were faint in the London sky. Kaz had invited him to stay to dinner, and the evening had helped him to wind down, which Kaz had undoubtedly realised. She was also an excellent cook, and Suzanne, her mother, was entertaining, if risqué company. It was strange watching Devlin relaxed with his family, knowing the other side, the professional face. There was something there maybe, for a book …

Drew hunched into the collar of his coat. The weather had got cold again with the New Year, but it was only a few more yards to his apartment block. He'd be glad to get this day over. He crossed the road. There was a man sitting in a car, parked at the kerb. The car door opened in front of him and the man got out. 'Mr Vitruvius?'

Drew's stomach lurched. Should he run? *Oh hell it might just be a fan. Famous author runs screaming into the night when asked for autograph …*

'Yes?' *At least your voice doesn't have a quiver in it.*

The man stepped into the light of a street-lamp and Drew got a good look at his face. His stomach lurched again. A face he knew – Brandon Phipps.

'I just wanted to say … The police came to see me … that girl …' His words were falling over each other in his effort to get them out. Drew watched his chest heave in a deep breath. 'Aveline. That girl. I barely knew her … We had coffee a couple of times. She seemed pleasant, if a bit too intense. I had no idea what she was going to do. I'm most sincerely sorry.' He held out his hand. Drew found himself shaking it. 'I had to come and see you,' Phipps went on, earnestly. 'I couldn't let you think that I had any part of it.'

'Um. No.' Drew shook his head, bombarded by the flow of words. The headache was coming back. 'That's fine. I'm glad. Er …' He indicated the lighted hallway of his building. 'Do you want to come in?'

'Oh. No.' Phipps was backing away, towards his car. 'I just wanted to let you know. It's all right now. Goodnight.'

Drew stood, slightly dazed, as Phipps got into his car and drove away. A crazy end to a crazy day.

Not quite.

When he reached his flat, the phone was ringing. He recognised the clipped brisk tones of Geraldine, his agent, without needing to look at the caller ID. She was already talking. 'We're putting out a press release. You've been located safe and well, police have made an arrest, blah blah. No further comment. You're now looking forward to your forthcoming American tour. The lawyers want to vet the damn thing.'

With another tide of words washing over him, Drew latched onto the part that mattered. 'American tour?'

Geri laughed. 'Darling, you said that just as if you'd forgotten it! Three months, coast-to-coast. And that thing you asked to go to – where everyone dresses up.'

'It's a fantasy convention,' he supplied dully, stomach churning.

'That's it. It's all arranged. Bloody nuisance though. That girl, Aveline, made all the arrangements. I've had to get someone to check everything, make sure she hadn't messed that up too.'

Oh yeah. Messed up. Like trying to kill me? Drew was beginning to understand the definition of surreal, on a personal basis. 'Er … had she?'

'No, thank God. Everything is fine.' There was a noise in the background. 'Look, I've got another call coming in. I'll e-mail a copy of the press release. Oh, and the new book is awesome, darling. The publishers are simply wetting themselves over it.'

'Ah … good to know.' Drew found himself talking to the dialling tone. He replaced the receiver, staring blankly over at the corner of the room that constituted his home office. Holed up in the flat after Devlin dropped him off, under cover of darkness, he'd broached none of his electronic equipment, not even the lights. Which was a bittersweet reminder of the barn. While Devlin was putting the sting together he'd laid low until it was ready. He'd eaten food from the freezer, slept and read … and thought of Lori.

He padded over to the desk, prodding the computer into life. There it was, on his organiser. Three months. New York to L.A. and all points in between, leaving the day after tomorrow, and he'd forgotten all about it.

Well, you did kind of have other things on your mind.

Normally he loved touring, meeting fans, talking about the books. And the States was his favourite place to do it, but now … Lori.

He stood by the desk, staring at the schedule, then shut the machine off and headed for the whisky.

He really needed another drink.

Chapter Thirty-Four

2 January

He should have been packing. Instead he was surfing the Internet, looking for a way to contact Lori. Nothing was working. Lori France had no Internet presence that he could find. He'd been so focused on protecting her, and Misty, he'd left himself with no way of getting in touch.

At least that way you were sure they'd be safe.

It had been the right thing to do – but now …

Lori might not be anywhere on the Internet, but he was. His reappearance had hit the headlines. He'd put the phone on divert to route all his calls to the virtual assistance company he used when he needed them. The involvement of the police and a potential court case made 'no comment' an acceptable response to everything and also effortlessly upped the level of interest. There were reporters camped outside, waiting for him to emerge.

Not going to happen, ladies and gentlemen.

Public opinion seemed to be divided about his disappearance – most were concerned and intrigued, a few still thought it had all been a publicity stunt.

If you only knew.

He'd found a lot of stuff on the Internet that he didn't want, but he hadn't found Lori. *But you do know where she lives.*

The temptation to get in the car and simply drive back to Wales, and the quiet simplicity of the barn, was so strong, he almost gave in to it.

But why would you go back to Wales? Officially those days in the barn never happened. You can't make a connection now.

Also the street is full of reporters and you have a plane to catch at stupid o'clock tomorrow morning.

Frustrated, he glared around the room.

A letter?

He dug in the drawer in his desk. He had a stamp, but no envelopes. He rummaged some more, unearthing a dog-eared postcard from a stately home he'd visited six months ago for an event.

It was better than nothing – but a brief message that anyone could read wasn't really enough for what he wanted to say.

Come on, you're supposed to be a writer.

After a moment he scribbled 'Thanks again for everything', underlining the 'for everything' and adding his initials. Underneath he printed an e-mail address that he'd had for years, that only a handful of people still knew, completed the address of the barn and added the stamp. If he hurried he could catch the post and get started on the damn packing.

Once you get past the reporters.

When he arrived downstairs, there were two large men in the entrance hall. He might have been worried about this, but one of them was Joe. He introduced his colleague, Tom. 'Boss said you wanted to learn a few moves, self-defence, like.'

'I do, but I'm going to America at some God-awful time in the morning.' He explained about the tour.

'No problem. We're global.' Joe grinned at Tom. 'What you think? Ray in New York and Chris in L.A.?'

Tom nodded. Drew looked from one grinning face to the

other. 'Why am I getting the feeling that this is suddenly not such a good idea?'

The grins just got wider.

Oh, well, he had asked ...

Beyond the narrow glass doors to the block, Drew could see a couple of reporters on the steps, huddling against the cold. He pulled the postcard from his pocket. 'While you're here, can you do me a favour?'

3 January

Lori stared at her computer screen. Displacement activity. Anything rather than sending her completed manuscript to the agent who wanted to see it.

It's as finished as it will ever be. Let it go!

Instead of doing what she'd logged on to do, Lori was surfing the web. There was no reason for it. She was just surfing. Quizzes to check her knowledge of Shakespeare, adverts for writers' retreats in remote locations, videos of cute kittens to make Griff jealous – when she wasn't looking at news reports about Andrew Vitruvius.

At least you know now that he's safe.

She'd seen the proof, excited selfies from two fans, unable to believe their luck, when they found themselves on the same flight to New York. Three months on tour and then what? He'd have to come back for the trial. Two men and a woman had been charged with abduction and a string of other offences. Lori wondered about the woman. *Slighted girlfriend?* It would all come out eventually.

Now that she'd started to dig, she couldn't seem to stop. It hadn't taken long to find out everything she ever wanted to know about Andrew Vitruvius. The books, the reviews, the public appearances, the awards, the six-figure contracts, the film options, the hair-raising research trips, the girlfriends – models and actresses mostly – the fans – girlfriends in waiting?

And at the end, or maybe the beginning … the wife.

She'd read that with a lump in her throat. He'd been just eighteen, *eighteen*, when his wife and three week old son died, along with fifteen other people, in a tangle of wreckage outside Brighton station, three days before Christmas. Two kids who had met while in care, fallen in love and had a child.

And then he lost them.

There was an old and grainy picture of relatives waiting at the station for news. If you knew, you could pick out the painfully young Drew, standing at the back of the group, shoulders stiff with tension, flat cow lick of dark hair stark against pale skin, face trapped in anguish.

Pain coiled around Lori's heart. To bear that sort of loss, so young. But somehow he'd resurrected himself. His first book had been published four years later.

And yours will never be published if you don't send it.

Quickly, before she could think any more, she tapped out a covering e-mail. With a fast beating heart, she attached the manuscript and launched them both into cyber space.

For a moment more she dithered, hands over the keyboard. Should she send Drew a quick jolly message on Twitter or e-mail – glad you survived Christmas? And what would she get in response? A casual, 'Oh yeah, must meet up again sometime'? A standard response from whoever handled his e-mail? Nothing at all?

He said he would forget the time you spent together. And asked you to do the same.

Actually, he said he wouldn't talk about it.

164

Does that amount to the same thing?

It was just a kiss. She ran her tongue over her lips, as if she could still taste …

The man is out of your league. He's already moving on.

Forget the manuscript and Drew Vitruvius.

Write the next book.

Chapter Thirty-Five

15 April

Drew lugged two suitcases full of dirty washing and a slew of small bags – what the hell was in half of them he had no idea – up to his apartment. Once he got them all inside, he collapsed on the floor beside them. Travelling, talking and editing the next book on the road, and he was just about knackered.

The publishers wanted to have the new Andrew Vitruvius in the stores on both sides of the Atlantic *and* Australia to hit the Christmas trade. Someone had mentioned a 'Down Under' tour in September and the usual noises were being made about the next book.

And there is no next book.

A flutter of disquiet shivered through him. There was the usual soup of ideas floating about in his head, but nothing had reached out and demanded to be written. Frighteningly, he wasn't sure how much he cared.

You're just tired. And if you could stop thinking about her ...

He rolled over and dragged the bag with his laptop towards him. With some jetlagged stabbing and cursing, he got his e-mails open.

Still nothing from Lori.

Did you really think being back in the UK would make an e-mail magically appear?

He'd sent three more cards from the States.

Face it, mate, if she wanted to get in touch ...

With a grimace, he shut down the machine. Cards could

go astray, e-mails got caught in spam filters, people got tied up with work, had accidents, got ill …

The last two had his head spinning. No, not that, *please*.

If she'd felt the same way you did …

Hell! He scrubbed his hands over his eyes. One more try. Do what he should have done in January.

It took him a few seconds of disoriented exhaustion to figure out that the vibration against his thigh wasn't weird muscle spasms but his phone. He fished it out and pressed talk.

Clint. 'How d'you fancy Paris, like? I got a mate there, does a bit of Parkour.'

Parkour.

Running and jumping off high buildings without a safety net. Maybe that would trigger the new book?

'You're on. But there's something I need to do first and I'm not functioning tonight. Ring me tomorrow with the arrangements?'

He ended the call and turned again to the computer. The virtual assistant who never slept. He tapped out an e-mail. I need a large bouquet of flowers delivered to my address by 10 a.m. tomorrow.

Arrangements made, he looked at the bags. Nothing there he needed. With an effort he hauled himself to his feet and staggered towards the bedroom.

16 April

It was a *very* big bouquet. He stood in the doorway looking at it, after the guy handed it over. Kaz would have told him what all the flowers were. He recognised roses and tulips, but the rest? He didn't have a clue. All tied up with what looked like a piece of sacking and what seemed to be string. But it was big, and pretty, and that was all that counted. He closed the door and stepped over the pile of bags.

There was a stuffed giraffe for the baby and a pair of mouse ears and an 'I'm the big sister' T-shirt for Jamie somewhere in his baggage, that he needed to find and take round to the Devlin household. He'd sent a good wishes telegram when Lily Olivia had been born, but now he was home he needed to visit.

But first the bouquet.

This time he was taking advice from Elvis.

He was delivering it himself.

He made good time to the barn. Parking the car in a lay-by further up the road, he walked back to the building. There was an unfamiliar Peugeot parked on the forecourt. Had Lori changed her car? Was it a visitor, a boyfriend? His chest tightened. At least it suggested that someone was at home.

Ignoring the sudden heavy thump of his heart, Drew edged past the car to the door, and rang the bell. There was an immediate sound of scuffling footsteps and the door was flung open.

The woman was petite, dark-haired and a complete stranger.

'Oh, how lovely. Mum,' she yelled over her shoulder. 'Flowers for you. They must be from Eldon.' She already had a hand on the bouquet, riffling through for the card.

'No!' Drew didn't quite snatch it away, but it was close. 'You've made a mistake.' She was looking up at him now doubtfully, delight faltering as she began to register that he wasn't a delivery man from a florist. He tried a placatory smile. Maybe this was Lori's sister? Misty's mum? 'They're not for your mother. They're for Lori.' Now the woman looked totally confused. An older woman, a carbon copy but with greying hair, appeared behind her. 'Lori?'

'She lives here?'

'Oh.' The younger woman's face sagged into disappointment. 'Sorry Mum. They're not for us.' She shook her head. 'You must have come to the wrong place.'

'No. It's the right place.' Something cold was clawing around Drew's chest. 'Lori lives here. Or she did ... in December.' Just in time he remembered not to mention Christmas.

The woman was shaking her head again. 'I don't know about December, but no one lives here now. It's a holiday let.' She brightened a bit. 'We've rented it for a week to celebrate Mum's sixtieth birthday. Room for a party, you know.'

'Holiday let.' Drew could hear the hollowness in his voice. 'Rented by the week.'

'Yeah.' The girl was staring at him narrowly. 'Hey, aren't you that writer – the one that was just in the news?'

'No, not me.' The denial was automatic. No way could he start explaining *that*.

'You look like him.'

'Yeah. I get that a lot.' He forced a laugh. It sounded like gravel shaking in a tin.

She was looking at the flowers. 'Sorry and all that, about your friend. The one you were going to give them to. Lauren?' she prompted. He must have been looking blank. 'Perhaps you can find out from the letting people?' She pulled the door open wide. Her mother had disappeared back inside. 'You want to come in, while I look for their card?'

Drew stepped into the barn. Memory hit him like a punch to the gut. It was the same and not the same. The furniture was still there, though the chairs were arranged at a different angle and the rug looked unfamiliar and there were net curtains at the French windows that he didn't remember. It looked less ... personal. Would taking down the Christmas decorations be enough to make that change? He didn't think so. Maybe it was the cushions and the blankets – throws, Lori had called them throws – most of them were gone. And there was a large-screen TV sitting in one corner.

His eyes fixed on the stairs. On that stair ...

'Here you are.' The woman was back, holding out a card. 'I hope they'll be able to help.' Her voice sounded hearty and over-bright. He realised he must be looking around, bewildered, and she was wondering about the wisdom of letting a stranger in.

'Thank you.' He dredged up another smile. 'Look.' He held out the bouquet. 'I think you'd better have these, after all. Tell your mother, happy birthday. And enjoy your party.'

Back in the car, he looked at the card. The name meant nothing, and he had a pretty shrewd idea that a holiday rental company wouldn't be giving up the details of clients to random enquirers, even if he used his own name as a lever. *Which you will certainly not be doing.*

He tapped the cardboard square on the steering wheel. What now? He needed someone ... He needed a private investigator. He sighed. Looked like he would be phoning Devlin for another favour. And he still had the bruises on his butt from the last one. Chris in L.A – who'd turned out to be Christina – a diminutive blonde, who'd been able to throw him across the room with embarrassing ease.

The knowledge that he had a passable ability to defend himself against attack helped him sleep a bit better at night. *Memories of Lori – not so much.*

At least he knew now why there had been no response to his postcards. They had probably already been dumped in the recycling. Or they were lying in a dusty heap of junk mail in an office somewhere. That thought sent a shiver down his spine.

Connections.

He looked back at the barn. The woman had recognised him. He could see now how stupid it had been to come in person.

But the urge to reach out ... to find Lori again ...

He looked again at the card. Could she have been renting the barn for the holiday? It hadn't felt like a rental. It had felt like a home. *Or was that rose-coloured thinking, the state you were in?* No – he answered himself immediately, the place he had just seen had been different, things added and things taken away.

Abruptly he recalled the lack of power, landline phone, television, at Christmas. Had Lori been squatting in an empty property? *No, she had keys. She knew the security system.* He frowned, trying to remember. Could it belong to that friend? Owner of the paint-stained cargoes?

He exhaled deeply. He wasn't going to solve it sitting here. He'd get that private eye.

And in the meantime ...

He found his phone. 'Clint? I'm on, for Paris.'

Chapter Thirty-Six

17 May

Drew stared down at the street from the window of his flat. After a late start, spring was coming in at last. There were flowers in window boxes and in the street the trees were green. He was trying to avoid the depressing pile of letters and documents scattered across the desk behind him. Some of them related to the trial, which was provisionally set for September. He'd engaged a legal advisor, and was given to understand that everything was proceeding as would be expected. The police were apparently still assembling evidence.

Unease fed the depression. As far as the police were concerned, Drew had managed to get free and had contacted Devlin to bring him back to London. Christmas at the barn with Lori had not been mentioned. In a corner of his mind, Drew was almost beginning to wonder if he'd hallucinated the whole thing.

And if you'd told the police the whole truth, maybe they'd *have been able to find her.*

The investigator's report, which was one of those depressing papers, had arrived three days ago. Arranged by Devlin through a third party for 'Mr Williams'. It was sitting now on top of the pile, contributing to the feeling of a lead weight lying in his stomach.

Spiral-bound, with a tasteful matt cover and plenty of fancy platitudes, the report came down to two words. *No trace.* They couldn't find Lori. The barn *had* belonged to a woman – but she was in her seventies and was now living in a home in Hereford that cared for people with dementia. The property had been sold to the holiday company before Christmas, and had been unoccupied until they moved in to prepare the place for letting in the New Year, confirmed by the previous owner's daughter. *So Lori* had *been a squatter?* Discreet enquiries had been made in the vicinity of the property, and while some local traders recalled a young woman and a child, matching the descriptions given, nothing useful had been forthcoming. The usual social media and background checks had not turned up any relevant information. *To paraphrase – a big fat zero.*

Enquiries had been halted at this point, pending fresh instructions. There were further avenues which might be explored. Did Mr Williams wish to pursue the matter?

Drew wasn't sure what the other avenues might be, but he didn't think he would go down them. He'd already been treading too far on dangerous ground.

He'd lost Lori. Just like he'd lost Kimberly. The pain of the similarity and the difference was something else for the cold weight in his stomach.

He had to face it, if she'd wanted to get in touch with him, there were ways. The seventy-two hours they'd spent together had meant more to him than it did to Lori. To her it had clearly been an … interlude.

He'd tried to rationalise, to tell himself his weakened and needy state had made him vulnerable. Susceptible. *You know that's not true, you berk. In those few days you came perilously close to falling in love with Lori France.*

He'd wondered, in the first few hectic weeks of the American tour, when she hadn't been in touch, whether he'd read everything wrong. Whether a 'tell all' story was going to suddenly appear. Lori had never made any attempt to include him in pictures she took of her niece, but there'd been times when his attention had been diverted, or when he'd virtually passed out in a chair, from exhaustion. As the weeks passed the tiny imp of doubt had faded.

Could still happen, mate.

And won't that drop you in it, up to your neck, with the police?

Trying to protect a lady when she's just been waiting for her moment to take you to the cleaners?

And dragging Devlin in alongside you?

Shit!

But was Lori really that woman? He couldn't believe it.

Or don't want to?

Somehow he didn't think it *would* happen. If she'd been using the place illegally, they both had something to hide. The thought left an acrid taste in his mouth.

He wasn't sure he knew what to think, any more.

His heart wasn't broken, but it wasn't in the shape it had been before they met. And now it really was as if that meeting had never taken place. Like something from the Fae, Lori had vanished into the mists on the Black Mountains.

He gathered up all the papers and tossed them into a drawer.

Since agreeing to sign up for that stupid kidnapping stunt, too many parts of his life were disintegrating. The trial, the nausea when he thought of the police investigation, the woman he couldn't find, the haunting doubts.

Aveline's venom was working like slow poison through the future he'd built, warping and tarnishing as it touched, then slowly spread.

He needed to work. Two weeks of throwing himself off buildings in Paris had convinced him that he was still alive, but hadn't given him a book. He'd put a pallid and scrappy outline in to his editor – some stuff set in the French Revolution and a partial subplot about Celtic circles in the Welsh hills. He'd taken out a disturbing reference to a scene of the hero in chains in a dungeon that had drifted up from somewhere and was definitely *not* making it into a script any time soon.

He'd told himself that it was the thought of the upcoming trial that was sapping his energy, which could be true. He needed to get away. Shut himself up somewhere, with only his laptop for company. Maybe then the ideas would come.

Sitting down at the desk, he googled the name of the letting company that had handled the barn. He wasn't going *there*, but maybe….

He frowned. He shouldn't really be looking at these people, but he didn't have the energy to start trawling for holiday lets. If the barn was an example of the properties they offered …

If he found something, the virtual assistant would make the arrangements.

The properties *were* attractive and well presented in the pictures on the screen. Typing in a few details brought up a selection – he scrolled down – too big, too remote, not remote enough.

He stopped scrolling at a slightly sinister looking vicarage on the Norfolk coast, with amazing views of the sea. It was available for longer lets.

Chapter Thirty-Seven

25 May

Misty had shown off her new school uniform and was now demonstrating Polly's ball chasing skills in the garden of what seemed to Lori to be a small mansion, on the outskirts of Gerard's Cross. Nevada, her baby bump in evidence even under a loose-fitting dress, came to stand beside Lori on the terrace.

'She's happy.' Impulsively Lori reached out to hug her ex-brother-in-law's second wife. *Families!*

'I know.' Nevada shaded her eyes to look down the garden. 'And thrilled to bits about Horace here.' She patted her stomach. 'And no, that's not what he's really going to be called. Dan and I are still negotiating.' She grinned. 'Misty may end up having the casting vote.'

'That will please her.' Lori let out a relieved sigh. Something from Christmas had turned out well. The ongoing ache when she thought about Drew showed no signs of abating and somehow he always seemed to be in the news – teasers for the new book, speculation about the trial.

And it's not like you deliberately go looking – like reading the arts pages right down to the small print or anything – is it?

And now, she didn't quite know what to do. Things around *her* were moving. She'd come to see Misty, but the attraction of a base near London for a few days couldn't be ignored. She'd wondered, just wondered, about going to one of the literary festivals that Drew was scheduled to appear at – just an oh-so-casual meeting – but when she'd almost got her nerve up to do it, his advertised appearances seemed to have dried up.

She couldn't help a feeling of relief, mixed with disappointment.

Would he really want to be reminded about those days at Christmas? Not exactly the Andrew Vitruvius of the action man fantasies?

She'd read a few of those fantasies now.

Liar. You've read them all. You even tracked down the volume that had a short story in it, and that's been out of print for years.

They still weren't her thing, but they *were* Drew. She'd heard his voice on every page. She'd enjoyed the first one he wrote the most. It had a wild, uncertain edge that appealed to her.

'Would you like to talk about it?' Nevada's question was soft, breaking into Lori's thoughts. 'It's the man who stayed with you at Christmas isn't it?' She looked slightly apologetic. 'Misty chatters. Not all of it makes sense, but I did understand that you and this man – Drew? You got on very well.'

Lori sighed again. 'We did. But I can't talk about it, for various reasons.' A sudden shot of alarm made her turn urgently towards Nevada. 'We didn't – nothing happened. Not with Misty in the house—'

'I didn't imagine that it did. Knowing you.' Nevada's smile was wry. 'I think that you may have more willpower than I would have. Is that the problem – that nothing *did* happen?'

'Maybe,' Lori admitted. 'I don't know. We're not in touch.' She shrugged. 'So nothing is going to happen now.' She looked down the garden at Misty, cavorting with the puppy. 'Is all the legal stuff finished?'

'Not yet, but Lark didn't make any objection to relinquishing custody. There are details to work out.' Nevada screwed her mouth up in a very un-screen goddess like way. 'You know how it is when lawyers are involved. Crossing every I and dotting every T.' Nevada crossed her eyes, to go with the gurning mouth.

Lori burst out laughing. 'Don't let the wind catch you.'

Nevada relaxed, laughing too.

Lori sobered first. 'It probably helped that Bruno saw in the New Year with a diamond the size of a quail's egg and the villa in the Seychelles where they were staying as an engagement present. Nothing like planning a Hollywood style wedding to put your four-year-old daughter even further out of your mind.' Lori hunched her shoulders. 'That sounds bitchy.' She looked sideways at Nevada with a guilty expression.

'Well – only a bit. Lark is what she is.'

Lori sighed. 'By the time they had her, Mum and Dad were starting on their alternative lifestyle. She and Merlin ran wild most of the time. I was lucky to be born first. Granny Pugh was still alive then too. She didn't stand for what she called "nonsense".'

Nevada shook her head. 'I suspect that your different personalities had something to do with it. Lark is spoiled and self-absorbed. You're not. But as long as Misty is safe and happy, that's all that matters.' Nevada put out a hand to draw Lori towards a table where a pitcher of lemonade and glasses were set out. 'I must admit, I hoped you were visiting London because of this guy. I'm sorry that it didn't work out.'

'Stuff happens.' Lori pulled out a chair for her not quite sister-in-law. 'But there is a reason I'm in London. There's something I need to tell you ...'

Chapter Thirty-Eight

28 May

Drew stood at the window, staring at the sea. A small hurricane was raging outside. Waves hurled themselves at the beach. The ominous sound of falling objects was loud, even over the noise of the waves and the wind, which was howling eerily around the house, like a choir of banshees.

If a pack of wolves had loped along the narrow road between the house and the beach, Drew would not have been surprised.

Inside the room he'd chosen for his study everything was quiet. Nothing was happening at all. No writing, no thoughts, no book. He'd been here a week. He'd hiked for miles on the beach, he'd listened to music, he'd played word games with himself, he'd gone to the pub and played darts with the locals and got mildly drunk.

There wasn't any book, but the pain of losing Lori was getting worse. Filling the void where work should have been. And slowly and uneasily he was re-visiting his opinion about a broken heart. He'd tried to analyse why it was happening *now* and decided that before, he'd assumed that he'd find her.

When you were ready, you arrogant bastard.

In the back of his mind he was haunted by the spectre that if he'd done something straight away, she might still have been at the barn. There were plenty of valid reasons why he hadn't, but beating himself up felt better than prodding at the lonely ache under his breastbone. The vicarage was nothing like the barn, yet he seemed to see Lori everywhere.

See her, feel her, *smell* her in the scented candle that he'd found half burned on one of the bookshelves and made the mistake of lighting. *Yeah, like every night.*

He prowled restlessly around the room. He was being gas-lighted by a ghost. *A ghost in your own head.* He didn't know what to do to exorcise her. Call in the P.I. again, get them to pursue those other avenues?

He'd been on the verge of doing that so many times.

But it all came back to one thing.

If she'd wanted to see him, he wasn't hard to find.

He went back to the window, leaning in, arms braced against the side of the frame. Wild weather, craziness, ghosts.

Something was stirring at the back of his mind. Stren. The edgiest, most bad ass of his bad asses, who flitted through all the books like another ghost. The one whose story the fans clamoured for, the one whose story he'd always withheld.

Because he'd never really known what made Stren who he was.

Come on, you knew, but you were afraid to look it in the face. Afraid you didn't have the depth and the guts to write it. To string yourself out there and hunt it down. That black pit of love, betrayal, guilt and anguish.

Easier just to go and jump off a few more buildings.

Shoving himself away from the window frame he padded back into the room. His hands, when he looked down at them, were shaking. Shit, his whole body was shaking. He really didn't know if he could do this. Yet even amongst the shaking and the fear, he felt it – the cold exultant whisper of 'why not?'

He reached out a still trembling hand for a pad and pen, throwing himself into a chair. If he could just try to rough out an outline …

Chapter Thirty-Nine

17 August, Early Afternoon

'I say, are you okay?' Drew looked up from the pile of books he was signing for readers who couldn't make the afternoon talk. He always enjoyed doing this small but well-attended festival in one of London's larger garden squares.

'I'm fine, why?' He reached for another book.

Brandon Phipps raised one shoulder in shrug. 'You look a bit haggard, that's all. Probably the trial coming up,' he speculated. Drew answered with his own shrug, signing yet another book. Phipps didn't look that good himself. He seemed to have lost weight, the lines around his mouth were more pronounced and there was something sharp and bitter lurking in the back of his eyes.

'The trial ... Do you ever think about her ... you know ... Aveline?' Phipps had his head down, looking at the table piled high with books. He'd already finished his pre-talk signing pile – not Drew's full table, but still a respectable amount.

'No,' Drew replied, slightly puzzled. 'Been working.'

Phipps straightened up, shaking his head, as if to clear it. 'The next book.' He nodded, knowingly. 'Coming along is it?'

'Uhuh.' Actually it was finished, but Drew wasn't sharing that with anyone yet. It was all too raw. Once he'd begun to write, the thing had inhabited him relentlessly, but he was still a little startled at Phipps's suggestion that he looked haggard. But maybe he was right?

After a week of bleeding out on the page, he'd raised a

spectre in the shaving mirror that wasn't him, but might be Stren. After that, he'd taken himself in hand, commissioning the pub to supply regular meals and pots of coffee and setting an alarm to make sure he walked on the beach and that he slept.

And now he had it. Stren's story. Possibly the best thing he'd ever written. The thought gave him a mixture of pain and satisfaction he'd never experienced before. Other people would ultimately judge.

But not yet.

He cast a jaundiced eye over the pile of books that still had to be signed. The publishers had changed their minds about waiting for Christmas and hustled the new hardback out for the summer festival circuit.

Oh shit! He suppressed a groan. One of the festival gofers, a cheerful soul with a well-kept goatee, a tweed tie and a droopy cardigan, was bearing down on him with yet another armful for signing. *Pity you can't get Phipps to scribble on a few.* He bit down on the idea before it made it out of his mouth as a joke. *That would definitely be taken the wrong way.*

This was the third time in two weeks that he'd shared a platform with Brandon Phipps. He guessed that Geraldine might have been behind that, to distance Phipps, in advance, from any mud that might be slung during the trial. Really the guy wasn't too bad – a good speaker, if a little conscious of his dignity. His new book, a saga of soul-searching and shattered relationships amongst the bombs and ruins of World War Two, that apparently contained a surprising level of sex and violence, was getting good reviews and award nominations, even if it hadn't yet achieved the higher echelons of the best-seller lists.

Must get round to reading it sometime.

'Are you going to the thing at seven o'clock? The Festival reception?'

Phipps had picked up one of Drew's books, and was examining the cover. It had turned out to be a fraction racier than Drew would have liked; the blonde on the cover a little too busty. Phipps replaced it on the table with something that might have been a curl of the lip. Drew didn't exactly blame him. Maybe they could change it for the paperback? *You must remember to ask.* 'What is it, drinks and things on sticks?'

'Something like that. There's one every evening, all different. Tonight it's for aspiring writers – in other words, wet behind the ears wannabees. All with the world's next piece of great fiction in their backpack, ready to hand to anyone who shows any speck of interest.' The curl was *definitely* there now. 'But I suppose we have to fly the flag and all that.' Phipps leaned against the signing table. 'That woman that all the fuss was about, back in May, is going to be there. Celebrity guest.'

'Fuss?' Drew had reached the top of the last pile. Once this was done, he was fleeing to the safety of the Green Room, before anyone else wanted him to write his name on anything. Conserving the strength of his writing hand, for signing after the talk.

'You know, the debut book that went to auction. Four bidders.' The pitch of Phipps's voice dropped – awe, mixed with a good dose of envy. Drew could get behind that. Auctions were a pipedream for most. Back in the day, he'd have given his eye teeth for his debut to go to auction. 'It's one of those crossover things,' Phipps was explaining. 'You know, a kids' book that can be read by adults – fairy stories with a message. She signed a three book deal in the end with Klonberger for an "undisclosed sum".' His tone put the quotation marks around it. 'Bet it had a good few noughts at the end of it.'

'Bet it did.' Drew signed the last book with a relieved flourish. 'I've been in Norfolk, must have missed it.'

'We'll be seeing plenty of her, for sure. Mallory Francis – she'll be all over the tube stations and the bus stops this time next year. All done?' Phipps pushed away from the table. 'Green Room? I'm told they at least have decent coffee.'

Chapter Forty

Lori stood at the back of the marquee and inhaled the scent of bruised grass, wet umbrellas and new books. It was by no means one of the biggest or oldest of the literary festivals of the summer, but it still had a lot of prestige. She'd had lunch with some of the committee, a right honourable, two merchant bankers and a sculptor who had known her mother in the dim and distant past and wanted to hear all about what her parents were doing now.

And her agent had been there as well.

She still hadn't got used to the sound of those words. Maybe she never would. When she'd asked, rather hesitantly, if someone could get her tickets to the festival, a three-day pass had appeared, within forty-eight hours, along with the invitation to lunch and to the reception tonight for new and aspiring authors. Everyone had seemed amazingly gratified when she accepted. She already had a booking to speak at *next* year's festival.

Surreptitiously she put her hand on the canvas of the tent behind her, spreading her fingers to feel the texture of the fabric. She'd been doing that a lot lately. Grounding herself. Making sure that everything was real. That *she* was real.

It had all happened so fast, so incredibly. She'd hoped for a publishing deal, maybe with a small independent press. She hadn't expected a whirlwind. Dan and Nevada had supported her from the sidelines. Without their help, and the tie with Misty, to keep her feet on the ground, she wasn't sure how she would have coped. Of course, Griff remained totally unimpressed by any of it.

The afternoon of the auction, when each of the bids was more outrageous than the last, she'd nearly broken Nevada's fingers, hanging on to her hand. Now at last she was Mallory Francis and there was no going back.

The knowledge was terrifying.

Almost as terrifying as the thought of seeing Drew again. Her heart lurched, making her feel sick.

The crowd in the tent was clapping, all eyes focused on the stage. One of the committee members – the Rt Hon – was introducing the three speakers as they filed on to the platform to take their places. Lori slid quickly into an empty seat, afraid her knees would give way if she remained standing. *Debut author faints at festival.*

The committee member introduced Drew last. Lori drank in the sight of him and the sound of his voice. The beard was gone, so the planes and angles of his face were more pronounced. *He looks tired.* No one else would notice it, from the banter that was going on between the three panellists, but the slight stoop of his shoulders sent a spasm of concern into her already churning stomach. *Oh, behave yourself. He's a grown man. He doesn't need you mooning over him.*

The talk was going down well. The audience was laughing. Drew was talking about his latest book. Lori focused on his mouth. That mouth …

Alarmingly, a flood of heat washed over her. Oh God, she wanted … She wanted … *We all know what you want, girl.* The voice in her head was a filthy low-pitched whisper. *Going to go up there and rip his clothes off, are we?*

Horrified, Lori swallowed the wrong way, choked, and smothered the cough with her hands, earning her a reproachful look from the woman sitting next to her.

'Sorry,' she wheezed, getting control of her breathing. Andrew Vitruvius brought out the absolute worst in her. It was shaming and exciting and she couldn't tell which was which.

They were answering questions now, deftly dealing with a forest of hands. Most were directed at Drew, leaving the other man and the middle-aged woman who were with him on the platform, looking slightly out of it. The woman wrote historical romances that Lori had read and enjoyed. The other man, Lori thought his name was Phipps, looked unwell, but maybe that was the effect of the greenish light in the tent? When he wasn't speaking, but just following the discussion, his faced looked … haunted.

Lori shook off the idea. *Writer's imagination.*

Although she tried not to focus too much on Drew – this was a *panel* discussion – her eyes kept sliding back to him as he batted questions to the others, seeking support, opinions, argument, bringing them back into the conversation.

He's good.

Not just a pretty face and a hot body.

'Oh, do go away.' Lori put her hands to her reddening face as the woman sitting next to her shot her an alarmed look.

I'm a writer. Writers often talk to themselves.

The burst of applause signalled the hour was over. The rest of the row was reaching under chairs for festival tote bags and producing books to be signed. Lori didn't know whether to be amused or horrified to see one of the women had brought a massive pile of dusty second-hand paperbacks for signing.

'You're going up there?' A woman sitting in front of her, dressed to the nines, in what looked like her best wedding outfit, with matching shoes and handbag, brandished Drew's latest book.

'Er ... no. I don't think so.'

'Ah, never mind love.' The woman looked sympathetically at Lori's simple beige sweater and white jeans. 'Expensive things, these hardbacks.' She wagged her head, knowingly. 'You want to wait until the paperback comes out, love – maybe you'll get the chance to have him sign it then.'

Lori suppressed the laughter that had just the tiniest edge of hysteria in it, as the woman waddled off to join the signing queue, which was being directed to a side annex of the main marquee. Marshals were retrieving litter and forgotten umbrellas, and gently clearing lingerers from the seats, in preparation for the next session.

Lori hesitated a moment. What would it be like, if she joined the queue? If Drew looked up, and into her eyes? Her heart was beating in overdrive, just at the thought of it.

She stood up slowly. She wasn't going to do it. She'd seen Drew again. She had what she came for. Unfortunately she hadn't achieved her objective. Quite the opposite. Her stomach sank with the knowledge of what she'd just effortlessly proved to herself. Andrew Vitruvius's power to turn her inside out hadn't diminished at all.

In fact, it seemed to be getting a whole lot worse.

Chapter Forty-One

17 August, 7.15 p.m.

Drew lurked close to the wall of the tent, sipping a dry white wine that wasn't as bad as he'd feared it might be, and watched the show. The small side tent, where the official signings took place, was thronged with the newly and very nearly published, and those who wanted to be. He was indulging in a mildly malicious guessing game of separating the sheep from the goats. Was the smug air of the hipster with the amazing beard because he was published, or because he knew it was only a matter of time, as he was self evidently a much better writer than anyone else in the tent, published or unpublished? The girl in the white frock looked too young to be drinking. She had to be aspiring, surely?

Brandon Phipps was holding forth in the centre of an attentive crowd and a few of the other panellists in the afternoon sessions had also gathered small groups around them, dispensing words of wisdom. Drew had snagged a glass and sidled for cover before he'd been recognised and buttonholed. In a moment, when he needed another drink, he'd make a move and mingle, but now he was content to watch.

Actually he wasn't sure he was up to chatting intelligently to a lot of strangers. He rubbed the back of his neck. Maybe he *was* tired. Or maybe it was just the contrast of weeks of self-imposed solitary confinement, with the press of people at the reception. He'd poured every emotion he'd ever had into Stren's story.

It hadn't stopped him thinking about Lori.

He'd even imagined he'd seen her, for a second, this afternoon, at the very back of the audience. By the time he'd been free to investigate, the woman, whoever she was, was gone. *Which proved it wasn't Lori, or she would have come forward to speak to you.*

There was some sort of announcement being made at the other side of the tent. People turned to listen. Drew sidled towards a break in the crowd, where he could see, even if he couldn't hear. One of the festival committee – the sculptor Jessmayne, who lived in one of the houses on the square, was standing in front of the long trestle table that held the drinks. He seemed to be introducing someone to the audience. Drew knew the guy slightly. He'd bought one of the sculptor's smaller pieces for his flat, once his royalty cheques had become large enough to support art *and* gas bills. Jessmayne had been instrumental in Drew's invitation to speak, so at some point he really did need to go and say hello, and thanks. Now the guy was ushering forward the person the fuss was about. The crowd surged and Drew got a partial glimpse of a young woman with fair curly hair, in a sleek dress of pale blue linen, before the crowd shifted again and blocked his view completely.

'Who is it?' A loud stage whisper came from an elderly woman in front of him. He caught the tell-tale pink stub of a hearing aid as she turned her head to her companion.

'That new author. Mallory Francis. She's going to speak here next year.' Drew took a few steps forward, curious. This was the woman Brandon Phipps had been talking about. He edged around the clump of people, realising with half an eye that a man at the edge of the group had spotted him and was nudging the person next to him.

Well you did intend to mingle. Eventually.

There was a smattering of applause, signalling that the introduction was over. Relieved from the need to be polite, the volume of chatter immediately rose again. Unable to get a glimpse of the debut author, Drew put his head down and aimed for the bar. If he was going to do the right thing, then he was going to do it with a fresh glass of wine in his hand. With luck he'd catch Jessmayne too, before he was swallowed back into the crowd.

Jessmayne was still standing beside the improvised bar. He looked up as Drew emerged from the press, smiling and waving him over.

'Andrew, good to see you. Great session this afternoon.' The woman in the blue dress was standing beside him. 'Come and meet Mallory.'

It happened so fast he barely had time to take it in.

Someone on the other side claimed Jessmayne's attention, at the very moment that the woman turned towards Drew.

Drew really thought the marquee swirled over his head as he looked into the face that had stalked his dreams for months. Everything else seemed to fade away.

All he could see was Lori.

She was looking up at him. He couldn't read her expression, but what he saw in her eyes looked like dismay. *Fuck, fuck, fuck.* 'Um – Mallory?'

'Mallory Francis.' She held out her hand. He took it. It was warm and familiar.

So, that's the way it is. This is the first time we've met. Well, you did agree never to talk about Christmas.

He let her go, instead of taking the firm hold on her that his body was suddenly demanding, so he could carry her out of the tent.

For God's sake, to do what?

The breath he took was shaky, but the tiny hint of challenge he could see in her eyes fired something. 'Andrew Vitruvius. Pleased to meet you,' he said demurely.

He could be part of the game.

'Oh, good.' Jessmayne had turned his attention back to them. 'You've introduced yourselves.'

'We have.' Lori looked at the sculptor with a dazzling smile.

Look at me like that, dammit.

They didn't get any further. The two men who had spotted him in the crowd made their move, and a woman with startling pink hair pounced on Lori, and they had to turn away from each other to make conversation.

But I've got you back.

His brain and his heart and all his senses were skittering about like newborn lambs, seeing grass for the first time. He inhaled, trying to catch her perfume. Nothing. Just damp canvas, too many people and warm wine.

He really didn't want to make conversation about the technical intricacies of writing believable fantasy. *Just bloody do it and leave me alone, so I can focus on enticing this woman into joining me in a quiet corner somewhere.*

He rocked on his heels. *For God's sake, get a grip!*

With a conscious effort he relaxed, from the shoulders down. He could afford to be generous to these people, who were really interested and interesting, he discovered. And they bought his books. He'd found Lori – Mallory – and what the hell did anything else matter?

The crowd was thinning. The evening programme of talks would be beginning in a few moments in the main tent. People were drifting away to claim seats or find places to eat dinner. Arrangements were being traded and confirmed around and across the tent.

Dinner. He could take Lori to dinner.

When his last interrogator departed and he was blissfully free, he turned and touched her arm, holding his place in her attention while she finished talking to Strawberry Hair and a cheerful looking girl with a round face and a sweater with a corgi on the front.

At last they were alone.

'Have dinner with me,' he blurted it out before anyone else could grab either of them. Thank heaven Jessmayne had disappeared too.

'I can't. Jess and his wife have invited me to supper at their house.' Her face wasn't telling him anything.

He took a deep breath. 'But if you could, would you?'

She nodded, and the tension in his chest went away so suddenly he almost fell over. 'Then let me take you home, afterwards.'

'But ...' Now she was smiling, no, she was laughing. At him. It felt wonderful. '... you have no idea where I'm staying.'

'Hampstead? Notting Hill? Inverness? Wherever you want to go.' *The further the better.*

Something flickered in her eyes. *God, I think she would go to Inverness with me.*

'Gerard's Cross.'

'I can do Gerard's Cross. It's closer than Inverness.' Over her shoulder he could see Jessmayne and his wife approaching to claim their prize and take her away. 'I'll wait outside their house.'

'But you don't know what time—'

'However long it takes,' he said firmly.

She was still laughing, and shaking her head. 'You're crazy.'

Yes, about you. He put out a hand, she put hers into it. *As natural as that.*

'I'll wait for you, Lori. In the words of that famous cliché, we need to talk.'

Bad choice of phrase. He hoped that the hollow ring of the words wasn't an omen. 'I'll wait …'

Chapter Forty-Two

17 August, 8.30 p.m.

Excitement was spluttering in Lori's throat. She swallowed, trying to concentrate on the food in front of her, but the splutter was hard to control.

He wants to see me. He wanted to take me to dinner. He's taking me home. He'll be waiting.

The thrilling litany was speeding up and up – sending waves of heat through her body.

It hit the ground again when another thought intruded.

What if he just wants to see you to remind you to keep your mouth shut?

Being found chained in a farm hut, by a woman and a child, would hardly be a high spot for a man who made his living writing action-packed adventure books. Who *lived* his action-packed adventure books.

He'd said they had to talk – and that usually meant …

Lori's heart, which had been showing a tendency to burst out of her ribs and sing, plummeted again, curling into a small protective ball. *Don't give anything away.* If he is warning you off, at least you have your self-respect.

Somehow she plodded through the food on her plate. She was sure it was completely delicious, but the ping-pong games going on in her head wiped everything else from her consciousness. No one looked at her in a strange way, so she must have kept up some semblance of conversation. She had very little idea what. At last it was over. Fending off the offers to call her a taxi, she took her jacket and walked out into the street.

Drew was skulking on the corner, like an assassin. Reaching him, she had the impression that he might actually have been pacing the pavement, like a caricature of an expectant father. He reached out and pulled her close, and everything inside her flew towards him, like a magnet. She wanted to plaster herself against him and drag his head down for a kiss. It took everything she had to hold herself back.

He was looking down at her, his face shadowy, only partly illuminated by the light from the street-lamps. Then he moved his hand. She felt his thumb run across the edge of her lip. The shiver went down to the very balls of her feet and possibly through her stupidly expensive shoes and into the pavement.

'May I?' His voice had a distinct tremor in it. *He's asking to kiss you.* Before she could respond a burst of noise – applause and voices – came from behind them with a sudden glare of light as tent flaps were pulled back to let people spill into the square. The event in the marquee had ended.

Drew muttered something she could couldn't quite catch but she suspected was a curse, and let her go, grabbing her hand again to pull her towards a big black car parked by the kerb. 'Let's go, before we get caught.'

Belted in and settling into the luxurious leather of the seat – she didn't know what make or model this was, but it was a lot higher up the food chain than her Fiesta – she kept quiet as he piloted them out of the maze of residential streets around the square. She'd never seen him drive. His hands on the wheel looked sure and confident.

'I looked for you.' His voice in the dark was soft and husky. 'You don't have any of the usual stuff – Facebook, Twitter …'

'I do.' She was processing the fact that he had looked. 'It's in the name of Mallory Francis – PR for when I got my big break,' she said shakily. *He looked for you.*

'I sent cards. I went to the barn. There were strangers there. They said it was a holiday let.'

'Oh, Drew.' She didn't know what to say, other than his name

'I couldn't find you. Why the hell, Lori? You just vanished.' The car veered fractionally as he looked over at her. He corrected it immediately, eyes on the road again. 'I even got a friend to hire a bloody detective. Then ... I wondered if you didn't want to be found.'

Anguish shot through her. All she could manage was a half-strangled whisper. 'Ahhh.' She swallowed and tried again. 'I think it might be better if we talk when we can look at each other.'

'Probably.' There was warmth in his voice now. The turmoil inside her started to settle. 'But you will have to give me a hint about where we're going – or do I just head for the motorway?'

'Inverness?'

'If that's what you want.'

She navigated them competently through the quickest route out of town.

At last they reached the gates of the house that Dan had rented for the summer. She dealt with the mechanics of the gates and then they were rolling up the drive, coming to a stop on the wide gravel sweep as the moon emerged from behind a cloud, spilling cool light on a perfect Georgian manor house.

'Bloody hell!' Drew was leaning forward to stare at the house, arm lax on the steering wheel. 'Who the hell are you, Lori?'

Chapter Forty-Three

Drew had to take a deep breath. The moon was washing the front of the house and the raked gravel they were parked on, with clear light. Lori released her seat belt and the noise was loud in the quiet night.

'My name is Mallory France. My friends call me Lori, but my pen name is Mallory Francis. When we met at Christmas I was an office manager who wanted to be a writer. Now I am a writer.' Her voice wobbled. 'Like you.'

He began to have maybe a tiny inkling of what had been going on. Pride and independence came into it, but Lori was still talking. 'My mother and father run a holistic retreat in Santorini, with my younger brother. I have a younger sister and a four-year-old niece, Misty, whom you've met. The rest of the family – well, you'll see.' She was looking at the house. 'Soon, I think.'

Lights had come on in the windows, presumably at the sound of the car. The front door opened. 'I think we should go inside.'

Two minutes later Drew found himself in a square, high-ceilinged foyer, with a black and white chequerboard floor and a magnificent staircase, shaking hands with Dan Howe.

'Dan Howe. My ex-brother-in-law. Misty's dad,' Lori introduced them.

Shit! The guy was as big and physically impressive off-screen as he was on. *And looking* you *over as if you're a pimply teen who wants to take his kid sister to the Prom.*

Realisation was hitting him like falling bricks. 'Mallory France. Your sister is Skylark France.'

'Misty's mother.' Lori nodded.

He could see it now; a resemblance between the sisters, but where Lark France was delicate, ethereal and fey, Lori was warm and earthy, like the woman standing on the other side of Dan Howe.

Nevada Shaw, glowing with expectant motherhood, was giggling the throaty giggle that had launched a string of box office rom-coms straight at the awards ceremonies, like heat-seeking missiles. She was looking from him to Lori. 'Andrew and would that also be ... Drew?' She gave Lori a sparklingly wicked look.

Lori was blushing. It looked glorious. 'Take no notice.' Lori gave her not quite sister-in-law a narrow-eyed glare. 'She knows nothing.'

Nevada lifted her head in a provocative gesture and gave him her hand. *I'm holding the hand of Nevada Shaw.* 'I'm Misty's step-mum. I think you've met her.'

Drew was doing some very fast thinking. As Misty had been mentioned when Lori introduced him, 'yes' was an obvious answer, but something else was clearly expected. And he was *still* holding Nevada Shaw's hand. 'If I admit that I have, will that serve to incriminate me?'

Nevada shot Lori a delighted look. 'I like this one – you can keep him.'

'Thank you,' Lori replied dryly.

Dan was looking from one to the other of them, unimpressed at the byplay. 'There's something cryptic going on here that I'm missing.'

'Yes, darling.' Nevada let go of Drew and cuddled herself

under her husband's arm. 'And you can go on missing it,' she told him kindly. 'We're going to leave these two together now.' A distinct prod in her husband's ribs.

'We are?'

'Definitely.' Nevada shepherded her husband towards an open door at the rear of the hall. 'Don't keep each other up too late.' She was laughing as she closed the door.

Drew wasn't entirely sure what that last remark meant. He suspected that it might be Nevada giving her blessing to … At this point his overloaded mind gave up the struggle. He simply stepped forward, into Lori's space. She put up a hand to touch his cheekbone. 'Nevada doesn't really know anything. Misty chattered about Christmas. She mentioned your name. Nevada was winding us all up. I think you passed.'

'Thank God for that.' The relief was genuine. 'Um …' He couldn't help himself. 'Did she just mean what I think she meant?'

'I think maybe she did.' Lori was laughing. 'God, that was convoluted.'

Easily, as if it was the most natural thing in the world, Lori leaned into him. He was more than ready to hold her. He stood still, inhaling the scent of her hair. No cinnamon now, just lemons and Lori. 'We don't have to … I didn't expect … Oh hell, can I just kiss you?'

'I thought you'd changed your mind.' She reached up on her toes and pressed her mouth to his. He took five thorough minutes to show her exactly how much he had *not* changed his mind. They came up for air, briefly, then he showed her again. It was exquisite. Breathing heavily he held her away from him. 'Does it sound daft to say I missed you?'

She shook her head slowly. 'No-o, not daft exactly.' She stepped out of his arms, to pull him towards a doorway at the front of the house. 'I'm not sure I understand everything though.' There was a darkness in her eyes. 'We do need that talk.'

Drew followed Lori. As the door opened a familiar white and orange head popped up from behind the arm of a chair. After a short stare, it popped down again. Griff obviously didn't consider him interesting enough to lose sleeping time.

Suitably chastened, Drew looked around the room. It would probably have been referred to as a small salon, when the house was built. Where the lady of the house conducted her correspondence and read scandalous novels under cover of doing fine needle-point. Now it had good quality reproduction wallpaper and a mix of old and new furniture that worked surprisingly well.

Drew took a moment to ease the darkness of uncertainty out of Lori's eyes. She tasted better each time he kissed her, and her body pressed against him. The fabric of his suit trousers was uncomfortably tight, but this unfortunately was not the time. Maybe there was cause for that darkness.

They settled on a sofa, side by side. Drew put out a hand and Lori took it. He trailed a finger over the top of hers. She shivered in a way that gave his heart a little kick.

Drew cleared his throat. 'When Devlin, that's the friend in the helicopter, dropped me off, I just holed up in my flat. I was afraid to contact *anyone* – we'd worked out that whoever snatched me had to be someone who knew the arrangements for the kidnap, but I didn't know exactly who, or if they were working for someone else. I was afraid they might be watching, hacking into my mail … anything. I couldn't be sure who I could trust and I definitely didn't want anything to come near you and Misty. The police think I got free myself and called Devlin. I'm not exactly comfortable with that and I don't imagine they would be very happy if they find out it's not true, but I hope they never will.'

He could see from the way her eyes shifted that she knew *just* how unhappy the police might be. 'It was a conscious decision and I'd do it again. Even more, now I know who Misty is. Who you are. The press would have a field day.' He shut his eyes, briefly. He could imagine the headlines. 'It didn't take long for Devlin to work out who was responsible. He set up a sting, which confirmed what he suspected. You know about the arrests and the trial?' Silently Lori nodded. Drew couldn't help the sigh. 'I thought, once someone had been arrested, and I could come out of hiding, that I'd be able to get in touch. But I had to leave for America almost immediately and then when I got back, you were gone ...' His heart scrunched with the memory. 'I could have dug deeper – the P.I. might have found you, I think. But ... I wasn't sure. I didn't know whether that was what you wanted. To disappear. I thought you might have been squatting at the barn, illegally,' he confessed. 'Another reason for not involving the police. And ... I just didn't know whether ...' He shrugged. 'It was just a few days with a stranger.'

'Drew!' He saw the hurt in her face. 'I didn't intend to disappear. Misty and I were at the barn by accident.' As she explained, an icy finger inched its way down his spine. If Lark France hadn't dumped her daughter for the Christmas holidays ...

How long would it have taken them to find your ... body?

He shook himself mentally. The past could be a bad enough place, without constructing alternative realities in it. *And you would know all about that.*

Lori was studying his face. 'When you didn't contact me.

I didn't think that you *couldn't*. That was *so* stupid. I told myself that it was just … well a bit of a thing. Ships in the night, and all that. I still … I still kind of wondered if it was all a stunt that had gone wrong,' she confessed, softly.

'And I wondered if there would be an exposé in the papers, if you'd tell your story for money.' He gave a shaky laugh. 'Maybe we both have work to do in trusting each other.'

'We need to *learn* about each other,' she corrected, quietly. 'I didn't tell you about the writing. That was pride,' she said bluntly. 'The same reason I don't usually talk about Lark and Dan and Nevada. That will probably come out eventually.' She made a small deflecting gesture, that made Drew want to gather her in and kiss her until they both passed out from lack of air. But that wasn't the right thing now. 'I wanted to make it on my own,' she continued softly. 'To be chosen, if I *was* chosen, because of *me*. Of what I wrote, not because someone might be influenced by the family I happen to belong to. Does that make sense?'

'Perfect sense.' Gallant, crazy, adorable, perfect sense. 'So …' He let go of Lori's hand to lean forward, pressing his fingertips together and letting his hands lie loosely between his knees. He hadn't intended the gesture, but as he moved he saw her eyes widen. He looked down. His shirt sleeve had ridden up. The scar of the cuff was fading, but still visible.

'Drew.' The pain in her voice when she said his name made what he was about to say even harder, but he had to say it. It was tangled up with what they both were.

The knowledge had been building in his head. Now it had risen, inextricably, to a point where he had to voice it. 'I …' He looked over his shoulder at her. Her face was concerned, puzzled. 'I don't want to say this, but I think you will understand. I hope that you've got an idea of how I feel, and where I'd like this to go. Where I'd like *us* to go.' He managed a smile. Probably lop-sided and clearly not as reassuring as he wanted, seeing that the darkness was back in her eyes. Grey, such a clear pure grey. *Get on with it, Vitruvius.* 'I don't think we should see each other until after the trial.'

'Oh.' It was less an exclamation, more a long exhale.

'Do you understand?' He turned fully towards her, searching her face, saw the moment when she did. 'I can't talk much about it, and I'm praying it will be over quickly, but whatever happens in court, it's going to be messy and there will be stuff in the media and some of that probably won't be pleasant. And if we're known to be together, some of it will come your way, not because of Christmas, but simply because you're involved with me.' He clenched his fist. 'I know the kidnapping brought us together.' He tried a wobbly smile. It felt like crap. It probably looked worse. 'I don't want us, or the start of your career to be tainted by it. I think we need to stay apart, until it's over.'

He couldn't read her expression, but she hadn't burst into tears, or thumped him, or yelled for her brother-in-law. *Yet.* 'After that …' he said tentatively. 'Well, people saw us meeting today, when Jessmayne introduced us. Maybe we can meet again at some other event, and take it from there?'

The silence was long and thoughtful. Not because she was trying to torment him, but because she was working things through. He could see it in her face. At last she nodded. 'If that's how you want it.' Her eyes were intent, holding his. 'I'd like to be there for you, and I'm not afraid of standing beside you, but I get that you would feel better if I didn't, and that you want to be free and clear before we …' There was a deliciously delicate flush slowly working up from her collar. '… take this any further.' He watched the colour climb, enchanted and *really* turned on. *Hell!*

She gave him a tremulous smile. 'If you hadn't been kidnapped and we really had met for the first time today, we might still have liked the look of each other.'

'If I'd had a grain of sense.' Relief eased the tension in a dozen muscles. 'Although I have to warn you that there is a commonly held belief that I don't. You know that I do dangerous stuff.' *Might as well get the whole thing on the table.* 'It's part of who I am.'

'Cross that bridge when we come to it.' She reached out and brushed his hair from his face. He wanted to turn his face into her palm and purr like Griff and then hold on to her and never let her go. 'Just take care, Drew, please. And I'll see you on the other side.'

'Oh.' Nevada emerged from the back of the house, as Lori shut the front door. 'He's gone?'

Lori paused, until she heard the car. 'Yes.' Nevada looked disappointed. *Not half as disappointed as I am.* 'It's complicated.'

'Oh, sweetie.' Nevada gathered her into a hug. 'You know what I say – the good ones always are.' Her face had turned inwards and Lori knew she was thinking back to when Dan had been trying hard to stand by his newborn daughter and a wife who'd decided she no longer loved him. 'Is it the trial thing?' *Smart cookie.*

'Yes.' Lori inhaled Nevada's expensive perfume and felt comforted. 'He doesn't want me to be involved.'

'Then he's a gentleman,' Nevada decided. 'Old school, but still sweet when you can find one. You don't need to say any more now. You can tell us all about it when it's finished.' She stepped away. 'Now come and reassure Dan that he doesn't have to play the heavy brother-in-law.' Nevada turned her mouth down in a comical grimace. 'I think he was rather looking forward to it.'

The parcel arrived the next day, by special delivery. Puzzled, Lori opened the packing box. Inside was another box, the kind that held printer paper. It was heavy and there was a card. 'But it's still not everything.'

There was no signature, but Lori didn't really need one. She lifted the lid.

His name was on the cover page, under the title.

Stren's Story

Chapter Forty-Four

3 September

Drew was emerging from Green Park Station when his phone began to ring. He ducked on to a convenient bench inside the park gates to answer it. The espresso shot he'd just drunk seethed queasily in his stomach as he recognised the lawyer's number.

'Andrew. Good news.' The seething got worse. *What constitutes good news from a lawyer?*

'You've got final confirmation of the trial date.' Drew was afraid he was going to disgrace himself by heaving his heart up in a public place.

'No, far from it. Just got the word. All three of them have changed their plea to guilty.'

There had been more, about legal formalities and sentencing, but Drew wasn't listening. Once the lawyer had rung off he sat for a while, staring at the phone.

It's over. Just like that, it's over.

'You all right, luv?' An elderly woman in a checked coat and dark green fluffy hat sat down on the other end of the bench. She was clutching a packet of bird seed. 'Only you look a bit out of it, like. Not on any of those drugs are you?'

'No.' He shook his head, starting to laugh. 'I'm fine and I'm not taking any drugs.'

The woman gave him a wide grin. 'Pity, I was going to ask for a share.'

Cackling, she opened the packet of seed and began to scatter it. There was a whirling and a flurry of wings. Drew got out, before he was engulfed. He was going to be late for the meeting at his publishers.

'The new book. It's different.' Alyssa, his editor, wasn't giving anything away. Drew sat in her comfortable visitor's chair, trying to look relaxed.

'Too different?' he tried, tentatively.

'No.' Suddenly Alyssa's face broke into a wide smile. 'It's wonderful, Andrew.' She leaned forward, dropping her voice. 'I cried.' *Wow, if you can make Alyssa Jones cry. And admit to it!* 'The readers are going to love it. It's the story they've been waiting years for. I wasn't sure you were ever going to write it.' She stood up, looking at her watch. 'Is it too early for lunch? No.' She walked him towards her office door. 'Let's go and celebrate.'

They went to a hotel on the South Bank that had just re-opened after some costly renovations. Before the work, the restaurant had been modelled on the dining room of an old style country house. It had been one of Drew's favourite places to eat lunch in restful surroundings. Last time he'd been here he'd run into up-and-coming agent Tanya Trevelyan, he remembered. She'd been saying goodbye to a client in the foyer. She'd followed him into the dining room and they'd shared a lunch table and professional gossip. Now the place was sleek and high-tech, all shiny surfaces and stark black and white décor. Looking round, Drew decided he preferred the old look, but Alyssa was clearly thrilled with the updating. 'Isn't this awesome? And I'm told the food's *amazing*.' She settled into her black leather chair, nodding to the waiter. 'Champagne, please.'

Drew managed to keep to two small glasses of champagne. The food *had* been amazing, and he'd got used to the décor. Luckily, after they'd eaten, some friends joined Alyssa, to help finish the bottle, and he was able to slip away. He was later than he'd expected to be, crossing London to his agent's office. In the back of the taxi, stop-starting along the Embankment, he checked his watch, then felt for his phone. He'd tried Geri a couple of times, only to get her answering service. This time she picked up. 'Sorry darling, lots of stuff going on here. Piles of paper for you to sign, plus the draft contract for the new book.'

'Already?' Alyssa's assistant had been busy when they were at lunch.

'Not sure I'm happy with it. We'll talk. Get here when you can. Oh, and congratulations on the trial folding.'

'You heard about that?'

'News travels, darling. You must be feeling pleased with yourself. See you soon.' Geri disconnected.

Drew leaned forward to look out the window of the taxi. There was a hold-up ahead, what appeared to be some sort of march was winding its way across the road. He subsided back into the seat. The journey was going to take a while. He stared unseeing at the traffic, inching forward alongside them, and the pedestrians clogging the pavements.

For the first time in a crowded day he was alone, with time to process. The weight he'd been carrying, and only been half aware of, was gone. He tasted the sensation of finally being free of it, after all these months. It felt …

He wasn't quite sure yet how it felt. The congratulations on the guilty pleas, and Geri's last remark, sat uneasily in his mind. He hadn't wanted to go through the trial. The thought still made him nauseous. But he'd done nothing to deserve congratulations.

Just got lucky.

He shut his eyes as the taxi jerked forward a few feet.

Now he could shake off the memory and the weight. It was a new start. A new start … and Lori.

He'd get the paperwork done with Geri as fast as possible and then, to hell with it, he was going out to Gerard's Cross. He'd howl at the gate, if he had to, until someone let him in.

Lori pushed her way through the swing doors into the hospital corridor. Dan was standing at the other end, with Misty on his hip.

'Hello, pet.' Lori held out her arms. Misty climbed into them and clung like a monkey. Her lower lip was trembling a little. 'Nevada is poorly.'

'Not poorly.' Lori hitched her into a more comfortable position. 'The baby is coming, that's all.' Over her niece's head she met Dan's eyes.

He grimaced. 'When Misty got out of school we came into town. Nevada wanted a new pair of shoes – like she doesn't have a wardrobe full of them already. They have their own cupboards!' He paused for minute to marvel. 'We were going to the Hard Rock for hamburgers. Her waters broke in the shoe department of Harvey Nichols.'

Lori had an irresistible urge to laugh, and maybe that was no bad thing if it would reassure Misty. 'This baby already has style.' She jiggled Misty up and down, smiling. 'It's nothing to worry about, sweetie. By the morning you'll have a baby brother.' *Please God*. She shot Dan a questioning glance.

'Everything is fine. The doctor says that everything is as it should be.'

'There you go.' Lori dropped a kiss on Misty's hair, cuddling her in. 'Now we must let Daddy go back to help Nevada have the baby. You and I will go home and see Griff and Polly, and we can come back tomorrow and visit. Okay?'

After a moment's thought, Misty nodded and wriggled to be let down. With a hurried kiss for both of them Dan disappeared back into the maternity suite.

Lori negotiated their way out of the building, remembering that she'd seen an ice cream parlour on the corner as she came in. Over two scoops of vanilla with raspberry sauce, Misty cheered up considerably. Lori sucked her own rum and raisin off the spoon and flipped casually through a copy of the *Evening Standard* that someone had left in the booth.

Her teeth bit hard on the metal as she came face-to-face with a picture of Drew.

Kidnap trial plans halted. Defendants change plea.

Her heart started to thump and for a moment she felt dizzy. Automatically she reached for her phone to ring Drew, stopping with her hand halfway to her bag. *You don't have his number and he doesn't have yours.*

For a moment her stomach, and the rum and raisin, did a nosedive. *But he knows where you're staying.* Blessing Nevada's insistence that she remain with them until the birth of the baby, Lori looked at her watch. Dan's driver would be bringing the car any time now, to take them back to Gerard's Cross.

Then she would simply wait.

Chapter Forty-Five

He'd been in the office for hours, signing things.

Well, at least one *hour.*

The sound of voices, door slamming and feet on the stairs had died away some time ago. Geraldine had gone into the next room to take a call from another client, raising perfectly arched brows at the slightly hysterical-sounding male voice, audible on the other end of the line. He'd finished skimming the paperwork she'd insisted he read. He got up and wandered over to his favourite place in the office, the old-fashioned multi-pane window. It was getting dark, long shadows creeping across the courtyard below. He traced a shape on the pane of glass – a heart, he realised – September already, and soon it would be Christmas again.

And this year …

He turned at the sound of a door closing in the corridor, hoping it was Geraldine coming back, but the door to the office remained shut. He leaned on the window ledge, looking into the courtyard. There were pigeons roosting on one of the window-sills on the adjacent building, which reminded him of the old lady with the bird seed. This morning. It seemed longer.

He really wanted to get out of here. He still had to pick up the car before he could get on the road, or perhaps a taxi would be better considering the champagne? Could he just leave Geri a note and go? He rejected the thought immediately. He wasn't scared of Geraldine, even in her best Bette Davis mode – *well, not much* – but he did owe her gratitude and good manners. She'd always done well by him.

With a sigh he went back to the desk and flopped into the visitor's chair as the door opened.

For this relief …

'Sorry about that.' Geraldine crossed to the desk. 'You've been very patient.' She scooped up another wad of papers and pushed them towards him. 'Now that the trial has resolved itself – have you thought about that tour of Australia? The publishers are keen. I can get someone on to it straight away – not someone who wants your heart, this time.'

It was a tiny slip, an unguarded reference that he might not even have noticed.

It was her sudden stillness that gave it away.

A dark cloud chased across his vision.

'Oh, God. You knew.' He looked up at his agent's face, which had suddenly frozen like a mask, everything inside him turning sickeningly to ice. 'You knew what Aveline was going to do.'

Barely realising that he was moving, he got to his feet. They faced each other across the desk

'Of course I knew.' Animation was coming back to Geraldine's face and with it a flash of disdain. 'You think there is anything going on in this office that I *don't* know about?'

'But …' Drew tried to focus. 'Why?'

'You were seen.'

'Seen?' Drew echoed, blankly. *Doing what, for God's sake?*

'Having lunch with Tanya Trevelyan,' she flicked the words at him like drops of acid.

Drew put his hand to his head. 'You were willing to see

me dead because I had lunch with another agent! It was a coincidence, we were in the same restaurant and we shared a table.' *And you know that maybe it wasn't such a coincidence on Trevelyan's part, but in the event she never made a move and nothing happened.*

Except it almost got you killed.

He shook his head, unable to find words.

Geraldine leaned forward, bracing her hands on the desk. 'You were just a snot-nosed kid with a scrappy manuscript and a dream when I took you on. I *made* you. And you were having lunch with *Trevelyan*.' Geraldine's face sparked back to full bitter life. 'If I was losing my star client – but maybe not so star …' She tilted her head. 'The books aren't so good now, are they, Andrew? Just a little tired? Same old, same old. I don't have to bother to read them these days. I know what will be in them. And how much longer are you going to be able to keep up all that schoolboy daredevil stuff?' Her eyes raked over him. 'If I was losing you anyway, maybe it wasn't such a bad thing to let that girl make it permanent, knowing you'd already passed your best?'

Drew just stared, still unable to speak. *Madness …*

'And of course there was that life insurance policy you took out three years ago, naming me as beneficiary.' Her tone was almost meditative. 'Never anticipated collecting on it in *quite* those circumstances, but what the hell …' She flashed him a grin where the eyes didn't match the mouth. 'An unexpected bonus. Every little helps, as they say.'

'But …' Drew was struggling to keep up. 'I remember we talked about insurance …'

Three years ago – after the fall in Switzerland and before the trip to Indonesia. Geraldine had been uncharacteristically prickly about the risks he was taking.

Which might have been influenced by the plaster casts on your wrist and ankle?

He shook his head. 'We talked, but we never took it any further.' The conversation had raised a superstitious aversion that he hadn't known he possessed. He hadn't wanted to think about it.

'Oh, but we did, darling. A modest nest egg, just in case one of your stunts finally did end in terminal damage. You never noticed the policy in amongst all those forms and contracts you sign so impatiently, without really reading them.' Her chest heaved as she drew in a deep breath. 'Bit of advice, Andrew. Always read the paperwork.'

Abruptly something snapped inside his head. The ice in his chest travelled upwards, leaving his thoughts cold and clear. 'I'll take it, you can be sure of that. But whatever and wherever I sign next, it won't be in *this* office.'

Somehow he got to the door. He wondered if she'd come after him, try to block his passage on the stairs, call him back to her. *When she comes to her senses.*

To his bone-melting relief, nothing happened. His footsteps sounded hollow on the narrow wooden treads and that was all.

One set of stairs.

And out of the door.

He had to struggle to get it open. For a moment panic flared, then his stiff fingers closed on top and bottom locks and the door swung towards him.

The shallow portico outside was blotted with shadows, although the sky, high above the buildings, still showed a vestige of pale grey. As Drew stepped out, a motion sensor activated a light beside the door. It wasn't very powerful and it didn't reach very far, but it was enough for him to see his way down the shallow steps.

He'd moved away from the entrance when there was a muffled curse and a figure walked out of the darkness at the edge of the light.

Adrenaline fizzed through Drew's system, screaming *run*.

But the figure was between him and the only way out.

Drew took a pace back. The figure took a pace forward. Tall, male, dressed in black, with a wicked looking commando knife glinting in his hand.

Drew barely recognised the ravaged face as Brandon Phipps.

'Do you know what you've done?' Phipps' voice was hoarse, but something in the timbre clicked. *The man that Geri spoke to on the phone, who'd sounded near hysteria.*

'What—' Drew coughed and tried again. 'What have I done?'

'Aveline. She k … killed herself. This afternoon. You were drinking champagne at a fancy hotel and she *killed* herself!' It came out almost as a sob. 'Her stupid parents persuaded her to plead guilty, to protect the family name.' Phipps' voice rose. 'So that it wouldn't be dragged through the court in a trial. Then, when she realised she would be in prison for *years*—' Phipps' head dropped to his chest. Drew wasn't sure if he was weeping.

'Look, I'm sorry.' *A bloody inadequate word.* Drew spread his hands in a placatory gesture. 'I didn't want that …'

Phipps' head came up with a jerk. 'Who cares what you want … It's always about *you*. I *loved* her. She did it for *me*.'

Phipps took a step forward. He was holding the knife in a surprisingly business-like way. Drew had a brief mental flash of those violent war sagas. *Oh shit.* His body was tense, teeth clenched, eyes darting around the small, enclosed space in front of the doorway.

Walls all around and only one way out.

There *was* no way out.

Only through Brandon Phipps.

Brandon Phipps and his knife.

If that's all there is, get on with it—

With a sigh and almost without conscious thought, his body relaxed into the stance that Chris and Ray had drilled into him in all those painful self-defence classes. He was no knife fighter, but if the alternative was getting his throat cut ...

When Phipps lunged he counter-moved with a jerk to one side. He saw the surprise on Phipps' face as the man stumbled. He dragged in a breath, already starting to sweat. He had to stay on his feet. If he went down ...

Phipps swung towards him and thrust the knife. Drew feinted again.

One more move and he'd be out of the circle of light and running for the alley that led to the main road. *Where there are people, traffic.*

Drew kicked out, making his opponent jump back in surprise. It bought him just enough time. He took off, flying, feet skidding dangerously as he hurled himself into the alley, activating another light as he stormed past.

Phipps caught up with him halfway down the passageway, spinning him and slamming him against the wall. The knife rattled against brick, an inch from Drew's head. Drew used his arm and his knee, the way he'd been taught. Gasping, Phipps fell away from him. *But he still has the knife.*

'Andrew?' A woman's voice. Geraldine was standing under the light at the top of the alley, peering into the darkness. 'Oh my God.' She'd seen that there were two of them, seen the knife. 'Brandon, this is crazy. Stop.'

At the sound of his name Phipps turned, still bent over

and half staggering. Drew didn't wait; he took off again in the direction of the street, dimly aware of a noise, a hard metallic voice. 'This vehicle is reversing. This vehicle is reversing.'

The flash of the tail-lights spilled across his eyes as the reversing lorry kept on coming and the voice kept on repeating. 'This vehicle is reversing.'

With a massive effort, that pushed the muscles of his legs to what seemed like tearing point, Drew threw himself across the alley and into the narrow shelter of a bricked up doorway, bracing himself against the frame as the side of the vehicle ground past, inches from his face.

Over the roar of the engine he heard the screams.

Two voices.

One female, one male.

Chapter Forty-Six

3 September, Late Evening

The chaos took a long time to abate. Ambulances, police, snarled traffic. Brandon Phipps had died on impact with the vehicle. Geraldine was still breathing when the first responders arrived, then she too was gone. The traumatised lorry driver had been taken away. The police had found the knife.

Drew had given a statement. The attack, the chase, the tragic consequences. Yes, he and Mr Phipps had previously been on good terms, they'd shared a platform at literary events. Yes, Mr Phipps had appeared to be very distressed and talking wildly. No, Ms Ennis had not witnessed the scuffle but had come across the scene and called out to Phipps. No, he had not been aware of the lorry backing into the turning, until it was almost on top of him, despite the warning announcements. No, he had not seen what happened at the point of impact.

He'd shown them the niche in the wall where he'd jumped to avoid the lorry. He could only assume that Ms Ennis was trying to persuade Mr Phipps to give up the knife and both had been unaware of the danger.

At last it was over. Drew collapsed into the back of a taxi, head in his hands. The events of the day jerked back and forth in his head, like a badly edited film.

He paid the driver and scrambled out at the top of the street. A couple of people were loitering on the steps in front of his block.

Reporters?

He looked up at the dark windows of his flat. He could run the gauntlet, go up there and try to sleep.

Or not.

Abruptly he turned, heading for the garage block.

Like a homing pigeon, he was going to Lori.

Lori smoothed a strand of hair away from Misty's face. Her niece snuffled in her sleep and curled up, clutching Bunny and sucking her thumb. Lori had found and cooked beef burgers from the freezer, to make up for missing the trip to the Hard Rock. Lucy, Misty's nanny, had come back from an afternoon off and listened carefully to the story of the baby, and then they'd both tucked Misty up in bed. Lucy was in her small suite at the end of the corridor. Lori could hear the muffled sound of the TV.

She'd tidied up the kitchen, fed Griff, taken Polly for a walk in the grounds and watched a re-run of an old comedy show on TV, before going up to check on Misty.

It was gone midnight.

Hope and expectation had thinned to nothing.

Drew wouldn't come now.

After a moment's hesitation at the top of the stairs, Lori went to her room, took the manuscript Drew had sent her out of the drawer and carried it down to the small salon. She smoothed her hands over the pages. She'd read it now.

Three times.

The writing was awesome. Better than Drew had ever done, and with that wild edge that had appealed to her from his first book. There were the characteristic Andrew Vitruvius action scenes, the ascent of a mountain in the Alps and an underwater scene around an uninhabited island with a wrecked submarine on the sea bed. The final chase, across the rooftops of Paris, time jumping between the

French Revolution and the present, had her forgetting how to breathe, it was so vivid.

But at the core of it was the story of a man – and two women – one haunting the past, the other lighting the way to the future. And the guilt, betrayal and love that lay between. She knew that Stren *wasn't* Drew, but the journey he made through the book, becoming a man who might be able to love, might allow himself … The resonance chimed with something deep inside her. Drew could *write* that … The thought made her dizzy. But he'd said it wasn't everything. She needed to see him.

She needed to *know*.

The gates were shut, which wasn't surprising as it was approaching three in the morning. He'd given up on the idea of howling. It wasn't civilised behaviour, and in any case he didn't think he had the energy. He tucked the car neatly on the grass verge, beside the gate, and killed the engine. He wasn't going in, but he could wait. And, God help him, think. He was swimming again in waters he'd left behind him years ago. It was by turns exhilarating and terrifying. At the moment, in his depleted state, terror was winning. In the morning … later *this* morning, when those gates opened, what was he going to say to Lori?

'I don't know if I'm capable of love. I sure as hell don't know if I deserve it, but with you I'm on the verge of … something.'

She'd have read the book; would she understand it? That it's me and not me?

And the worst isn't there.

The hard, damning kernel of knowledge that he'd carried so long and never shared? He had to give her that. Then, if she walked away … karma … coming back through the passage of time. *It isn't in Lori's gift to forgive you. It isn't her you've wronged all these years.*

He coughed, putting his hand down between the seats for the remnants of a bottle of water, drinking, then splashing some on his face and wiping it off with his sleeve. Three a.m. blues.

Will you listen to yourself, asshole? You're here making up deep and gloomy scenarios and it could be that Lori has already decided she doesn't fancy you after all. Simple as that.

A million romances probably began and ended every minute of every day and not all of them were Romeo and Juliet. *And didn't that one end well?*

Maybe he and Lori would date for a few weeks, a few months, and then drift apart? Maybe even now Dan Howe was waiting to punch out his lights and tell him to stay away from his sister-in-law? Despite himself, Drew could feel a laugh bubbling.

The bruises from his encounter with the wall in the alley were making themselves felt, so what was one more?

Abruptly he sobered. The scene in the alley ... and what went before. *How twisted people can be.* People you thought you knew and could trust, hiding behind a mask. *Sound familiar?* He wanted to start again. To *try* a new start. With Lori as part of it, if she'd have him. If she'd give him a chance.

But it's not always about you.

The rapping on the glass startled him awake. He flailed, disorientated. It was still dark and someone was shining a torch through the car window. Blinking, Drew put up his hand to shield his eyes.

In the muted illumination from the lights on the gateposts

222

he could see the outline of an SUV and two uniformed silhouettes. Of course Dan Howe would have a security patrol.

Yawning, he sat up straight, rubbing his eyes. The security guard was still peering at him. 'You can't park here ... sir.' The tagged on 'sir', surprised a bark of laughter from Drew. They'd clocked the car. *How many paparazzi or celebrity stalkers turn up in a Ferrari?*

He opened the door and nearly closed it again. God, it was *cold* out there. 'Sorry.' He stifled another yawn. 'I drove down on impulse to see Miss France – then realised what time it was. I thought I'd better wait until a more civilised hour.' He looked around, figuring out how best to reverse into the road. 'I'll find somewhere else, more suitable—'

'Oh – wait.' The man had got a good look at him now, in the light of the car interior. 'It's Mr Vitruvius isn't it? Andrew Vitruvius?' Drew admitted that it was. 'Well that's all right then – at least ...' He conferred briefly with his colleague. 'If we open the gates, would you like to take the car inside to wait? This is a quiet lane, but even so.'

He was looking over the points of the Ferrari, clearly weighing up the possibility of a carjacking on his boss's doorstep, should any passing villain fancy their chance.

'That would be very kind.' Drew put up his hand to rub his eyes, which felt as if he had half the Sahara in them. Then there was the kink in his spine. How many idiots spend the night sleeping in their Ferrari? There was clearly a knack to it. One he'd yet to acquire.

The colleague had slipped off to make the necessary arrangements for the gates. The first man stayed. 'Got all your books, I have. Get them as soon as they're out. Hardback, like. Bloody good read.'

'Thank you,' Drew said quietly. 'What did you think of the latest one?'

The man's expression flickered a little 'It was good. They're all good, but maybe not my favourite, like.' *Just a little tired. Same old, same old.* The cool acid *dead* voice whispered in Drew's head.

'I hope the next one will be a real winner. It's going to be Stren's story.'

The man's face brightened. 'Ah, now that'll be a good'un. And here we are.' Behind him the gates were opening slowly. Drew started the car, bumped off the verge and drove through.

Lori hadn't bothered to go to bed. She was too on edge. It was probably the drama with the baby, but somehow it felt like more.

Nothing to do with Drew Vitruvius. He'll be here when he can.

The text from Dan came in at five-forty. 'Orlando Maximilian Alexander Howe debuted, screaming, 4.30 a.m. 8lb. 2oz. Red hair!!!! Milkman? M&B doing well. Pics soon. Xxx.'

Grinning, Lori responded with congratulations and a 'relieved' emoji. Orlando Maximilian Alexander – the kid had to grow up to be an actor. Faint hints of daylight were appearing at the edge of the curtains. She went to the window to drag them back and look out at the approach to the house.

And did a double-take.

It wasn't a tank parked on the lawn, but there did appear to be a Ferrari parked on the drive.

He'd slept again. There was a vicious crick in his neck and it was getting light. How soon could he approach the house?

He hitched himself up in the seat, relieving his neck and rolling his shoulders. Reaction to the night before was setting in. Nausea washed over him in waves. He opened the car door, dry heaving over the gravel. Thank God he hadn't eaten for hours.

He was shaking, the memory of screams echoing in his head. He pulled the door shut and leaned back in his seat, scrubbing his hands into his eyes. He was a mess and he felt like shit. Maybe he shouldn't go near the house at all? Maybe he should just turn and leave?

He held up his arm, checking his armpit. He didn't smell too bad, but God knew what he looked like. He rubbed his chin. Nearly twenty-four hours of beard. *But she* has *seen you like this before.*

He tipped his head back against the seat, starting to laugh and wondering if he was going to be able to stop. He'd hardly won Lori over with his suave good looks. He was still laughing a little, hiccupping gently, when someone opened the car door.

'Drew?'

She was there.

Clumsily, shaking again, he almost fell out of the car and into her arms. He dragged her close to him, as naturally as breathing. She simply held him and they stood, swaying slightly, as the sun came up. At last, when the shaking stopped, she moved away from him, taking in the car. 'This isn't what you brought me home in that time. Did you steal it?'

'No, it's mine,' he admitted, ducking his head. 'Boys and their toys.'

'Mmm.' She put her hand up to cup his cheek. 'What happened, Drew? I know about the trial. I thought …' Her voice tailed off, and he heard the hurt. 'But this is something else?'

'I came as soon as I could. At about three o'clock. The security people let me in. I didn't want to disturb you, so I just waited.

Something in her eyes flickered. 'I was awake. Nevada went into labour – I couldn't settle. The baby arrived, it's a boy. Misty doesn't know yet.'

'Misty is here?' He looked at the house. 'Of course she is. I'm not thinking straight.' Another deep shudder took him. 'The lawyer rang me about the trial yesterday morning. I had to see my publisher and my agent and then I was coming here but—' He jerked in a breath. In terse, bald sentences he told her the rest.

'Oh, Drew.' She pulled him close again. He dropped his chin to rest on her hair. 'I seem to be a bit accident-prone lately. But I think this is the end of it.' The attempt at lightness failed miserably. His voice was still too uneven. With an effort, drawing on reserves that were buried somewhere very deep, he pulled himself together. There were still things that needed to be said. 'Did you read the book?'

'I did.' She moved back, to look at him. 'But you're exhausted, we don't need to talk about that now.'

'We do.' He tightened his hold on her. 'I need to know where I stand, before I leave here. Whether … whether we have any kind of future. If you want to try to … to be normal. Date and stuff. I …' He lifted a hand to trace a finger down her cheek to the corner of her mouth. She was heavy-eyed with lack of sleep. She looked beautiful to him. 'I … care … about you. I think maybe I more than care.' He dropped his hand. 'I'm not very good at this, in fact, I suck at it, and I have absolutely no idea now what you think about me.'

This time he managed a smile. His face was stiff. He probably looked like an axe murderer. 'As you haven't called the security people to have me removed, I guess I might be in with a chance.' He took a deep breath. 'At Christmas we only had a few days together, very intense days, and now ...' He was *not* going to start to shake again. 'It sounds a bit crazy, thinking of building a future on that, but ... I really hope you might want to try. And if you do, there are other things that I need to tell you. Things I've never told anyone.'

At that she slipped out of his arms. Alarm flared, but she was pulling him towards the house. 'Come inside then, and tell me.'

Chapter Forty-Seven

4 September, 6.30 a.m.

Lori took him to the small salon. The manuscript was lying on the coffee table. Drew stood in front of the sofa, looking at the box of printed pages. Lori reached up and pulled him down to sit beside her.

'My editor says it's the best thing I've ever written.'

'It is.'

'You've read the others?'

Rumbled. 'I may have glanced through one or two.' She faked nonchalance. The surprise and pleasure in his face set a warm glow in her chest. They were sitting side by side but not touching. She put out a hand and ran a finger over the box. 'There were things I get ... in the story. Stren's struggle towards ... love.' Just the vibration of the word in her head made it hard to breathe. Drew had documented Stren's attempts to understand the emotion, his struggle, his *need* to fight towards it. An aim still not quite realised by the end of the book, but with an ending full of hope. Words that seemed to be written in heart's blood. Now she could see every one of them in Drew's face.

But the ghost love, calling Stren back to the past, chaining him with guilt at causing her death? It was romantic, dramatic, lending emotional punch to the story and heart-rending pathos in the final act of release and forgiveness.

There was something buried there, she knew that instinctively, but the facts didn't fit. In no way was Drew responsible for his wife's death. Lori had read the story in the papers. Kimberly had been returning, with their baby, from the seaside town where they'd spent the day flat hunting. Instead of travelling with them, Drew had stayed on to catch the next train, because he had an interview for a job. The crash had simply been a terrible accident.

So why?

Survivor guilt, because he should have been with them? The helpless feeling that he might have been able to do something to save them – or at least been there at the end? Had they maybe argued, before she left? Was it somehow tied up with the successes he'd achieved? His life had moved on in unimaginable ways and theirs had been impossibly brief.

He was looking at the box, not meeting her eyes. 'A part of me …' He stopped. 'I felt … I felt … As if I had been set free.' His voice was flat, harsh and unfamiliar. His body jerked as he turned on the admission to look at her, eyes dark and bleak. 'I didn't want to be married, with a baby, stuck in some crappy flat in a crappy job, struggling to make ends meet, proving that I started life unwanted and worthless and that was how it was always going to be.' The words came out in a rush. 'I knew the way the world looked at me, that I wasn't worth anything, that I didn't *deserve* anything. I wanted to write. I had these stories, people in my head, demanding to be let out. I wanted to let them out more than I wanted to be a husband and a father.' His voice broke as he ground to a stop.

Lori folded her hands on her lap. Much as she ached to touch him, it wasn't the time. Not until they'd got beyond this.

'You were eighteen,' she offered carefully. Not a justification, but maybe a reason.

'Young and stupid.'

'Maybe.'

Now that he'd made the confession some of the bleakness had gone from his eyes, but the pain was still there. The pain of self-loathing? She hadn't expected this, but perhaps she should have? 'Did Kimberly know?'

'No.' He shook his head, vehemently. 'I'm sure of that. She wanted a fresh start, by the sea. She was full of plans for the baby, for our own home.'

'So she died believing in it. Does that make it worse or better?'

He shoved his hand into his hair in a familiar gesture. 'I really don't know. I defrauded her of her dreams, in order to have mine.'

'You weren't responsible for what happened to that train. You didn't want her dead.'

'No, but, I might have wanted her *gone*.' He was digging his fingers into his scalp. Gently she pulled his arm away, then let go. 'I loved her. And the baby, but it was a needy love. On both our parts. Both brought up in care. We clung to each other. The baby, of course, was an accident. We were kids, too stupid to manage the precautions properly. But Kimberly *wanted* that baby. She was so happy and I felt about ten feet tall because I'd given her that. And I wanted to stand by her, to provide for them, which is why we got married.' His voice was softening now, with recollection. 'We didn't have the proverbial pot to piss in, but love was going to conquer all. Then, that day, trailing round dark damp rooms and chasing after dead-end jobs, with dozens of others with a better chance of getting them, it felt like the prison was closing in. And panic. Kimberly was talking about Christmas, about the stuff she wanted for the baby. I didn't have money to give her any of it. I wasn't even sure where we were going to get a deposit on a flat.' He'd folded his arms across his stomach, holding in old pain. 'And then, all that was lifted off me.'

And from there the guilt grew. Lori could feel a lump in her throat.

'I got one of those dead-end jobs in the end, and threw myself into the writing. And today I have it all and Kimberly and Tyler have been dead nearly twenty years.'

Now she did touch him, just a hand on his knee, warmth and contact. 'You loved them.' She'd seen the sad little dedication in his first book. 'Cliché time. Would Kimberly have wanted you to be unhappy?'

'I don't know. Maybe.' His voice was rueful. 'She had a temper. And the baby. He'd be a young man.' His face creased with the lost possibilities.

'Around the same age that you were when you fathered him.'

'God, yes. Maybe he would have been the writer, instead of me.'

'And perhaps he would have preferred computer games or taking motorcycles to bits. It's over, Drew, and you can't change it by beating yourself up. And no one else can forgive you. You have to forgive yourself, or learn to live with it. Which you have done, all these years.'

'Until I put some of it down on paper. And now I've told you.'

'A step towards resolution?'

'I don't know.' He looked thoughtful and in her eyes his expression was lighter. 'A step towards *something*. Thank you for listening.'

'Thank you for telling me.' She twisted her fingers into his. 'I really mean that. I am honoured by your confidence, and I will keep it.' It was an oddly formal speech, but it felt right to say it. 'You're human, Drew. Not one of your super beings with magical powers. Human, with all the rag-bag of messy stuff that comes with it. You suffered a violent, traumatic bereavement that, thank God, few people experience in their lives. Hopes, fears, regrets – all sorts of emotions that you might have been able to resolve were left without an ending. You don't know what might have happened. You might have made a success of the writing *and* being a husband and father. People do.'

'And it's not always about me.' The words were soft and she sensed a meaning behind them, but he didn't say any more. He yawned suddenly. 'God, I'm knackered.' His shoulders sagged. 'Do I leave now and take that—' He nodded at the manuscript. '—with me? Or can you take a chance on a messy human?'

'I think I can risk giving it a go.' Something she recognised as a kind of happiness rippled through her. She pulled him down, for a soft sweet kiss. He rested his head against her shoulder.

Which is how a delighted Misty found her aunt and Drew when she came downstairs with Lucy, looking for Griff and Polly; fast asleep on the sofa, with the morning sun spilling golden light over the small salon.

Chapter Forty-Eight

Late November

What were the odds? Two publishers' Christmas parties in the same hotel on the same night?

Drew caught Lori on the stairs going down to hers, while he was going up to the suite he'd hired, carrying his bag. He shuffled her into a side landing and using the bag as a barricade, trapped her against a convenient wall. She dared him to kiss her and get lipstick all over her face and his. A luscious deep red, that went straight to his groin and was *so* going to come off over *everything* later tonight.

Balked of her mouth, he put his hands on her instead. The dress was close-fitting dark red velvet and felt like heaven under his fingers. The bodice had some sort of stiffening in it and the contrast of the plush stiffness with the warm softness of the woman inside it had him hard and needy in seconds. Warm, soft, *wriggling* woman. She squirmed to get away from him, laughing, and he moved even closer. He'd been forbidden her mouth – but he got his revenge, kissing every inch of the curve of her breasts, exposed by the heart-shaped neckline of the dress and offered up by the moulded bodice. She got her own back too, with her hands on *him*, before she finally managed to squeeze out, pink, ruffled and still laughing, from under his arm, to escape down the stairs. He was still grinning when he reached the suite.

Now he was standing in front of the mirror, meant to be concentrating on getting the bow-tie just right. He looked down. Remembering the encounter on the stairs had hardened everything again, under his tuxedo trousers, and a king-size bed visible behind him in the mirror was firing his imagination about what they might be doing there, once the parties were over.

He set his teeth and focused on the tie.

Right over left.

There!

He let out a soft whistle. He'd succumbed to vanity tonight, and gone for broke. Lori had twice picked him up off the floor, a broken mess. *Tonight* he was going to look the part, even if she wouldn't get to see it until later.

He was looking forward to *later*.

There was champagne and a late dinner on order from room service and roses and scented candles and everything else the hotel had to offer that was romantic.

Tonight, he hoped, would be magic.

He had a ring, diamonds and sapphires, in a drawer in his flat, but he hadn't brought it with him. It was too soon. He knew that, but having the ring was a kind of promise. A whisper of sadness hung in the air at the thought of Kimberly, and the tiny diamond chip on the narrow gold band, that he'd bought for her. He'd scraped together every penny he had. She'd been so proud of it.

Remember that pride, and let the rest go.

He was seeing a counsellor, finally, who was helping him deal with events nearly two decades old. Other scars were closer to the surface. He shook his head, dislodging the sound of screams in a dark ally. The post-mortems on Phipps and Geraldine had thrown up one surprise – Phipps had succumbed to massive injuries from the collision, but Geri had died of a stab wound to the neck. The police had speculated that a struggle over possession of the knife would explain their failure to appreciate the approaching danger.

The thought that in an instant of terrible clarity, after

Geraldine fell, Phipps might have turned *towards* the lorry, rather than away from it, hovered in Drew's mind.

Writer's imagination. And you'll never know for sure.

He was glad of the impulse that had stopped him mentioning those last few minutes in Geri's office.

She was good to a snot-nosed kid. Back in the day.

He was learning how to put all those memories behind him.

He turned away from the mirror to look for his shoes, sitting on the bed to put them on.

His life was moving into new places. He was deep in edits for Stren's story, but the next book was on the horizon and he knew it had to be different – more of a quest and less of a rollercoaster. There would still be the adrenaline-fuelled set pieces but they weren't going to be *all* the book. He hoped he could take the readers with him on that.

If not …

Maybe he'd try something completely different? Maybe when he got a new agent, there would be new ideas on the table? He'd had some approaches, but he'd not yet signed with anyone. It would be a new relationship. He needed to come to it as an adult, not the kid he'd been, touting a manuscript that was badly typed and fifty thousand words too long.

Time to join the grown ups.

That, and to stop running, and calling it research.

Hard to think about guilt and blame, and grief, when you're halfway up a mountain and the only reality is where the next hand and foothold might be. And if you miss that foothold … atonement?

He finished tying his shoes and stood up. Lori was the constant star in his life now, and he was starting to hope.

He looked over the softly lit room. It wouldn't be the first night they'd spent together. But he wanted it to be special.

Thank you, Lori, for saving my life.

The party was winding down. Lori drained the last few drops of her elderflower and lemonade and looked around the ravaged room. Balloons and streamers drooped and empty glasses filled most of the available surfaces.

For a moment her stomach wobbled. Advance copies of the first of her trilogy would be going out in the New Year. *Then* she would know if she really was an author.

There was a slight commotion going on at the door. Some good-humoured jeering about a gatecrasher. Curious, she moved forward. The crowd at the door parted and Drew was standing there, looking amazing, his dark hair and eyes emphasised by the stark black and white of the designer tux.

And the man beneath it …

She swallowed, over a dry mouth.

She'd seen him at his lowest, but this …

Suddenly shy, she took a step back. And then he smiled. His whole face lit up. Looking at *her*.

'I only came to collect Cinderella, before you lot turn her into a pumpkin.'

He held out his hand, head tilted in invitation. She closed the gap between them with a rush, losing her breath entirely as Drew swung her up into his arms, amidst more jeers mixed with catcalls of encouragement. She buried her burning face in his neck, embarrassed and loving it in equal measure.

He didn't set her on her feet, even when they got to the lift. 'Top pocket.'

'Huh?' she lifted her head.

'The key to the room is in my top pocket.'

'Oh!' She felt about and found it. 'I thought we were having dinner?'

'We are.' When the doors opened he still didn't let her down. Worried about the weight, she squirmed against his chest. 'Stop that, I like it.' He nuzzled her neck.

'I'm too heavy,' she protested, breathless, as he nibbled and nipped his way along her throat. Mercifully the lift was empty and fast and they reached what appeared to be the right door without sprawling on the thick carpet of the corridor. With a deft movement of the key, Drew got the door open, still holding her.

When they were inside, with the door shut, he finally let her down, to stand in front of him, facing the room, his arms around her.

'Oh!' She let out a long sigh.

It wasn't just a room, it was a suite. Over by the window, with a view out over city lights, a table was laid for two. There was a trolley with covered dishes and an ice bucket, with champagne, on a stand beside it. There were two huge sofas, original art-works and an enormous flat-screen TV that took up half a wall. Through an open door she could see the bedroom, and the corner of what looked like a king-size bed. There were flowers and candles and the air was scented with something complex, subtle and exotic. She turned in his arms. 'Oh Drew ...' There were tears prickling at the back of her throat.

'You like?'

'I like.' She laid her head against his chest. 'When you said you'd get a room, I never expected anything like this.'

'Thought I'd brought you up here to eat pizza and watch dirty movies?' He leered so convincingly she thumped him.

'Mood wrecker!'

Alarm flared in his face. 'I didn't mean ...'

'Neither did I.' She framed his face with her hands. 'It's beautiful. Although pizza would have been fine,' she added generously.

'I'll bear that in mind.' He took her hand and pressed a kiss into the palm. That never failed to send shivery spikes up her arm, in a way that was almost painful.

'Let's eat. I'm starving.'

The meal was a fluffy risotto with fennel and prawns and a crisp salad, followed by a chocolate and raspberry mousse that melted on her tongue, with an alcoholic kick in the aftertaste. They gossiped about their respective parties, who they'd seen and what had been said.

After three flutes of champagne, Lori had bubbles in her head and her bloodstream, and something warm and strong bubbling around her heart.

One of the sofas was placed in front of the window. When they'd finished eating Drew led her across to it and they sat, wrapped together, watching the lights from the buildings and the traffic far below.

'You can't see the stars.'

'But you know they're there.' Drew nuzzled under her ear, kissing in a slow arc down her neck. She turned in his arms, so that she could reach his mouth, but he held her back. 'What about the lipstick?'

'I think I've eaten most of it.'

'In that case, go and put some more on. I've been fantasising about that lipstick all evening.'

'Oh … kinky.'

'Yes please.' He slid his hand down her body as she stood up, making her shiver. She reached down and pulled at his tie, hanging loose now under his collar.

'Come and watch me.'

The bathroom had huge mirrors, two sinks, a lot of

marble and a *very* large shower. Lori giggled at the way Drew was eyeing it. 'I can hear you thinking.'

'Thought is free.'

She leaned over and kissed his cheek. 'I'm putty in the hands of a man who can quote Shakespeare.'

'Good. Now … lipstick.'

She rummaged in her bag, found the bullet and applied it, lavishly, studying herself, wide-eyed in the mirror. She looked a complete hoyden. Being with Drew made her a different person, a sexy confident woman. Drew was a shadow behind her, eyes on her face.

She turned, pushing him against the vanity unit with deliberation, watching his pupils dilate as she worked her way down his shirt, unbuttoning it and pushing it aside. She heard the hitch in his breath as she followed the path her fingers had taken with her mouth, branding him with her lips and feeling the muscles of his abdomen vibrate as she printed kisses on his skin, circling lower and lower.

'Now I think you're mine, Andrew Vitruvius.'

'Always.' His voice was raw and husky. It shimmered over her skin, raising goose-bumps.

They made it, eventually, to the bedroom and the bed, a tangle of limbs and deep hot kisses, collapsing onto cool slippery sheets. Drew eased down the zipper of her dress. She shivered as air hit her skin, although the room was warm. She'd had the sense to wipe off the lipstick before it transferred itself all over the bed, as well as the white shirt, overcoming Drew's complaints with kisses and whispered promises, as she dragged the shirt down his arms and tossed it into a corner. The sight of the red lace that was *under* her dress successfully distracted him.

That, and the pencil-heeled red shoes.

His hands and mouth travelled over her, caressing and

demanding, making her moan low in her throat. He toyed and coaxed, until her skin and the lace were damp and her nerve endings were stretched and trembling, her breath shuddering in her chest.

And then they were naked and together on the bed, entwined. And it was long and slow and easy, want and need and demand and promise building, in a soft slow glide. She loved his body, the planes and hardness, the way he responded to her touch, the darkness in his eyes as she kissed and stroked. She quivered as he touched her, as his mouth found every sensitive place on her body, licking and caressing.

At last it was time. 'Now Drew.' She was breathing hard, her breasts heavy and taut with kisses, damp between her legs and wanting. *So wanting.*

This was the point ... the ... connection. Her chest constricted as he found her and slid inside, watching her face as he filled her, brushing back her hair so he could see her eyes. 'I love you, Lori.'

Then he began to move and she moved with him, as they looked into each other's eyes. And he kissed the hollow of her throat and made her cry out, and took her flying into the darkness with him.

Chapter Forty-Nine

17 December

It was a stiff, printed card.

'You are invited to a Christmas Kidnapping. (Is that in horribly bad taste?)

Well. Yes, it is, but how can I resist?

Dress code: travelling attire of choice, an evening ensemble, or two, boots, warm sweaters.

Passport required.

If you are minded to respond to this invitation, a car will be waiting at 0900 hours tomorrow.

It was signed with three kisses.

So far, so James Bond.

She tapped the card against her teeth. The clues were in the choice of words. *Somewhere at a distance. And cold. And you need evening clothes. Hmm.*

What wasn't there made her grin. It must have taken heroic effort not to mention underwear. She had some ideas on that score. Also shoes. The red pencil heels she'd worn to the party had been a big hit, she recalled.

She took herself off to rummage in her wardrobe; grateful for the overhaul Nevada's stylist had conducted, supervised by Nevada, with contributions from Misty and Orlando. The red dress from the Christmas party was one of Misty's choices. *And that had worked out rather well.*

Confident that the contents of her wardrobe was up to the task, Lori flung open the doors.

18 December, Morning

Drew sat in the coffee shop, listening to the muffled announcements over the station tannoy.

Would she come?

It didn't matter if she didn't, except that it did. He needed ... this, to wipe out the memories of last year. They hadn't talked about arrangement for the holiday. She'd mentioned casually that she'd be spending it with Dan, Nevada, Misty and Orlando – and, of course, Griff and Polly – and that he was welcome to join them, and left it at that ... He stared at the cup of coffee in front of him, too wired to drink it and catapult himself into caffeine overload.

Nearly a year ago you were trapped in that hut, thinking about dying.

He shifted his arm, looking down at his wrist. The mark of the metal cuff had almost faded. He looked at his watch. It was time. He got up, leaving the coffee behind.

The driver delivered Lori to St Pancras, taking charge of both her cases and directing her to the platform she needed. She was beginning to get an idea ...

She threaded her way through the crowds, feeling like a complete VIP, with her driver and her luggage following behind her. Drew was standing by the entrance to the Eurostar platform, dressed in a smart dark overcoat, his leather gloves in his hand, looking like the hero of every romantic black-and-white film she'd ever watched.

You're amazing. And I love you.

Deserting the driver, she ran towards him. The look on his face when he saw her told her everything she needed to know, as he pulled her into his arms.

24 December

Lori stood at the window of the chalet, looking out over snow-covered peaks. The overnight stay and last-minute Christmas shopping in Paris, followed by the train journey across Switzerland, had been sheer magic. Now they were high in the mountains. They might be alone in the world.

The room was warm, fragrant with the scent of the enormous and heavily decorated pine tree that stood in the corner. The only sound was the occasional crackle from the fire in the hearth and the whisper as a log collapsed in on itself.

Drew came up behind her, putting his arms around her and pulling her against his chest. They stood together, looking out. 'I wanted to go back to where it started, but different. Does that make sense?' She felt his laugh. 'I'm a writer. So good with words.'

'Perfect sense.' She tipped her head back against his shoulder, to look at him. 'And you can't expect snow in the Brecon Beacons every Christmas.' She snuggled a little closer. The sky was darkening. 'You can see the stars.' She turned in his arms to brush a kiss over his mouth. 'We've come a long way.'

'You rescued me. All along the line.' He rested his forehead on hers. 'I'm different now, and I want to keep changing. This is …' He gestured to the snowy landscape. 'It's a circle, but … it's new. A different beginning.'

He was drawing something out of his pocket. 'I didn't know …'

It was a box. A small box. Lori's heartbeat picked up.

'I was going to wait until tomorrow to give you this, but tonight seems right.' He put it into her palm.

Her fingers shook a little as she opened the lid.

The ring glittered like the snow behind the glass.

Drew put his hand around hers, enfolding her and the ring box. 'I've lived most of my life with risk. Somehow this seems the biggest risk of all. And the biggest prize. Can you take a chance with me, Lori? I love you. Will you marry me?'

Lori looked down at the ring. If she'd ever imagined a proposal, it would never have been like this. With a man like this. *But just because you couldn't imagine it doesn't mean it isn't real.*

She knew what it meant for Drew to give her this. To ask that question, to put himself back in another place, another time. *With another woman.* But that *was* the past. It would always be part of him, and she didn't want to change that. But they could have something else. *Something new.*

She swallowed and raised her head. Drew's beloved and anxious face swam over her. She was *not* going to cry. *Well, maybe just a little.* 'I love you, Andrew Vitruvius. And yes. I'll marry you.'

The light in his eyes as he lifted her off her feet, in a breath-stealing hug, flew straight to her heart. She clung on and lifted her face for his kiss.

'Happy Christmas.'

Thank You

I hope you enjoyed reading *What Happens at Christmas*, and exploring a slightly darker side to the festive season. I really loved telling Lori and Drew's story, which was largely written over the Christmas holiday. Some chapters were actually written on Christmas day, but I can't remember which ones. It was fun too to give my Mr Cool, Devlin, the chance of a cameo appearance and provide a little glimpse of family life with Kaz. (If you haven't encountered Kaz and Devlin before, their story is told in *Never Coming Home*).

Christmas is a busy time, but I hope *What Happens at Christmas* has given you some moments to put your feet up, with a mug of something indulgent, and escape to the snowy Brecon Beacons. Now that you have finished the book, if you could spare another moment to write and post a review online, this would be very welcome. Reviews are vital feedback, when the author gets to find out what you, the reader, thought about the book, and the time spent in posting is much appreciated.

Thank you for reading *What Happens at Christmas*, and letting me be part of your holiday.

Evonne

About the Author

Evonne Wareham was born in South Wales and spent her childhood there. After university she migrated to London, where she worked in local government, scribbled novels in her spare time and went to the theatre a lot. Now she's back in Wales, living by the sea, writing and studying for a PhD in history. She still loves the theatre, likes staying in hotels and enjoys the company of other authors through her membership of both the Romantic Novelists' Association and the Crime Writers' Association

Evonne's debut novel, *Never Coming Home* won the 2012 Joan Hessayon New Writers' Award, the 2013 Colorado Romance Writers' Award for Romantic Suspense, the Oklahoma National Readers' Choice Award for Romantic Suspense plus was a nominee for a Reviewers' Choice Award from RT Book Reviews. Her second romantic suspense novel *Out of Sight Out of Mind*, was a finalist for the Maggie Award for Excellence, presented by the Georgia Romance Writers' chapter of the Romance Writers' of America.

See all of Evonne's novels next ...

www.twitter.com/evonnewareham
www.evonneonwednesday.blogspot.com

More Choc Lit

From Evonne Wareham

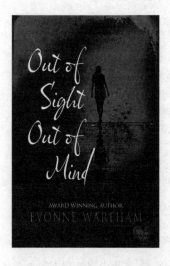

Out of Sight Out of Mind

Finalist for the Maggie Award of Excellence

Everyone has secrets. Some are stranger than others.

Madison Albi is a scientist with a very special talent – for reading minds. When she stumbles across a homeless man with whom she feels an inexplicable connection, she can't resist the dangerous impulse to use her skills to help him.

J is a non-person – a vagrant who can't even remember his own name. He's got no hope, until he meets Madison. Is she the one woman who can restore his past?

Madison agrees to help J recover his memory, but as she delves deeper into his mind, it soon becomes clear that some secrets are better off staying hidden.

Is J really the man Madison believes him to be?

Available in paperback from all good bookshops and online stores. Visit www.choc-lit.com for details.

Never Coming Home

*Winner of the 2012 New Writers'
Joan Hessayon Award*

All she has left is hope.

When Kaz Elmore is told her
five-year-old daughter Jamie
has died in a car crash, she
struggles to accept that she'll
never see her little girl again.
Then a stranger comes into her
life offering the most dangerous
substance in the world: hope.

Devlin, a security consultant and witness to the terrible
accident scene, inadvertently reveals that Kaz's daughter
might not have been the girl in the car after all.

What if Jamie is still alive? With no evidence, the police
aren't interested, so Devlin and Kaz have little choice but to
investigate themselves.

Devlin never gets involved with a client. Never. But the more
time he spends with Kaz, the more he desires her – and the
more his carefully constructed ice-man persona starts to unravel.

The desperate search for Jamie leads down dangerous paths
– to a murderous acquaintance from Devlin's dark past, and
all across Europe, to Italy, where deadly secrets await. But as
long as Kaz has hope, she can't stop looking …

Available in paperback from all good
bookshops and online stores. Visit
www.choc-lit.com for details.

Summer in San Remo

Anything could happen when you spend summer in San Remo …

Running her busy concierge service usually keeps Cassie Travers fully occupied. But when a new client offers her the strangest commission she's ever handled she suddenly finds herself on the cusp of an Italian adventure, with a man she thought she would never see again.

McQuire has returned from the States to his family-run ctive agency. When old flame Cassie appears in need lp with her mysterious client, who better than Jake to in?

Events take the pair across Europe to a luxurious villa on the Italian Riviera. There, Cassie finds that the mystery she pursues pales into insignificance, when compared to another discovery made along the way …

Available in paperback from all good bookshops and online stores. Visit www.choc-lit.com for details.

Introducing Choc Lit

We're an independent publisher creating
a delicious selection of fiction.
Where heroes are like chocolate — irresistible!
Quality stories with a romance at the heart.

See our selection here:
www.choc-lit.com

We'd love to hear how you enjoyed *What Happens at Christmas*. Please visit **www.choc-lit.com** and give your feedback or leave a review where you purchased this novel.

Choc Lit novels are selected by genuine readers like yourself. We only publish stories our Choc Lit Tasting Panel want to see in print. Our reviews and awards speak for themselves.

Could you be a Star Selector and join our Tasting P Would you like to play a role in choosing which nove decide to publish? Do you enjoy reading women's fiction Then you could be perfect for our Choc Lit Tasting Panel.

Visit here for more details…
www.choc-lit.com/join-the-choc-lit-tasting-panel

Keep in touch:
Sign up for our monthly newsletter Spread for all the latest news and offers: www.spread.choc-lit.com. Follow us on Twitter: @ChocLituk and Facebook: Choc Lit.

Where heroes are like chocolate – irresistible!